OVERWORLD

THE REVELATION

Overworld

The Revelation

Philip Narsingh

This is a work of fiction.
All the characters, organizations, and events portrayed in this novel either are products of the author's imagination or are used fictitiously.

Overworld © 2021 by Philip Narsingh. All rights reserved.

Published by Author Academy Elite
PO Box 43, Powell, OH 43065
www.AuthorAcademyElite.com

All rights reserved. This book contains material protected under International and Federal Copyright Laws and Treaties. Any unauthorized reprint or use of this material is prohibited. No part of this book may be reproduced or transmitted in any form or by any means, electronic or mechanical, including photocopying, recording, or by any information storage and retrieval system, without express written permission from the author.

Identifiers:
LCCN: 2018956939
ISBN: 978-1-64085-433-8 (paperback)
ISBN: 978-1-64085-434-5 (hardback)
ISBN: 978-1-64085-435-2 (ebook)

Available in paperback, hardback, e-book, and audiobook

All Scripture quotations, unless otherwise indicated, are taken from the New King James Version®. Copyright © 1982 by Thomas Nelson. Used by permission. All rights reserved.

Some names and identifying details have been changed to protect the privacy of individuals.

TABLE OF CONTENTS

Dedication vii
Endorsements ix
Foreword xiii
Preface xv
Verse xvii

Chapter 1: Reality 1
Chapter 2: Roxy 4
Chapter 3: Beginning of the Circle 13
Chapter 4: Julie 21
Chapter 5: The Beach 27
Chapter 6: Full Circle 36
Chapter 7: Jump-Point Alpha 42
Chapter 8: Overworld 57
Chapter 9: Phantom 70
Chapter 10: Red 80
Chapter 11: Damien's Circle 90

Chapter 12:	The Return of Sullivan	108
Chapter 13:	The Wilderness	111
Chapter 14:	Dark Dream	122
Chapter 15:	Scarlet	129
Chapter 16:	Pressing Forward	141
Chapter 17:	Fire	145
Chapter 18:	The Destroyer	157
Chapter 19:	Walk with Fire	163
Chapter 20:	The Others	174
Chapter 21:	The Tournament	184
Chapter 22:	The Creator	187
Chapter 23:	A Battle to Fight	193
Chapter 24:	Round One	201
Chapter 25:	Round Two	230
Chapter 26:	Round Three	245
Chapter 27:	Battle for the Circle	255
Chapter 28:	A New Dawn	278
Chapter 29:	A New Perspective	284

Acknowledgements	289
About the Author	291
The Journey Continues	293

DEDICATION

To my Lord and Savior Jesus Christ, who chose me for this. He had a plan all along.

To my wife Sharon, who has supported and partnered with me on this journey.

To all my family and friends, who were with me through many parts leading up to this.

To current and future readers. Get ready.

ENDORSEMENTS

Philip Narsingh has an unusual insight into a future where people connect, not just through words but, also, through an anointed, spiritual connection. In his book, Overworld — the Revelation, Philip takes his readers on a journey of discovery where life itself depends on these connections. Who can be trusted? Who will betray? As you begin this journey, you may find that you are being drawn deeper and deeper into the story, as though you are becoming one of its characters. This is a story of good and evil and it is also a story of identity — strengths, gifting, purpose — and how the characters come to understand that they are meant to collaborate in order to succeed. A gifted author and Life Coach, Philip Narsingh's compelling story may challenge you to examine your own life's journey.
~ John Edwards, author of Despite Me | Founder of Life Quest Seminars & Convergency Leadership Systems | www.lifequestseminars.com | www.convergencysystems.com

Just when Philip's everyday world became too much for him, it collided with another. With new friend Roxy as his guide, Philip gets caught up in a cosmic battle of good versus evil.

"Overworld" explores a dimension that is both beyond human reach and strangely familiar. In it, we all find a part of ourselves and discover we have a role to play.

April Jurgensen
Author

There are those unique people who cross your path in life that you are drawn to because of their joy and genuineness. That is Philip. I met this great man nearly a decade ago and witnessed his passion for life, commitment to growth, and pursuit of what he loved. His creativity abounds in a variety of ways, his gift of writing being one. He has a most incredible way of ushering you into another world through his creativity and detail. Overworld is a wonderful example of this exquisite talent. I am so excited for you to go on this journey into the creative mind of Philip and get a glimpse of who he is and the story he has to share. It will be a truly remarkable experience.

Centa Terry
Mindset Coach and Trainer
Centaterry.com

I love a story that has the ability to transport you to a new place and time, yet is totally here and now. That's what author, Philip Narsingh, has done in the novel, Overworld. We all have a story within us, a story where we wrestle between the light and the dark. Throughout Overworld,

Philip has given language to many of the questions we face as the hero of our own stories. This is a book you can get lost in. You get to experience all that comes with life's most difficult questions from the eyes of the main character. I often found myself asking, "If I were in Phil's shoes, what would I have done?" I highly recommend Overworld and am excited to see what Philip puts out next.

Mary Valloni
Author, Coach and Speaker
maryvalloni.com

FOREWORD

What if an evil power could set up its dominion, its kingdom on top of you, overlapping your existing world? Would you run, would you surrender and accept your new way of life, or would you mount a resistance? If you did choose to fight, where would you get your weapons, let alone your team.

Overworld takes you on a journey both deep inside the characters and then far beyond each of their breaking points. Throughout the book, we follow Phil and the team as they learn about the imminent crisis, the role they could play in preventing this. Along the way, we are introduced to a variety of creatures and characters that may offer greater strength to this fledgling team; yet could also be the source through which everything the team holds sacred is not merely stripped away but destroyed. Decisions will be made, alliances forged, and lives sacrificed.

They will face trials that will challenge and potentially rip apart everything they know about themselves, their faith, their lives, all the while learning how to function as a team, along with the challenge of adapting to and honing the special abilities they each have been given. If this wasn't enough pressure, there is a life and death tournament they and other groups are going to duel in which may or may not give the winner the upper hand in the upcoming looming catastrophe.

Choosing to engage and commence this journey and discover this both beautiful and dangerous new world may change you. As you interact with the various characters, you may see glimpses of yourself staring back at you.

Philip purposely leaves questions unanswered that serve as perfect bridges to the subsequent novels.

We all have a hero inside of us, or we would like to think we do. For Phil and his team, they learn a true hero doesn't always come out victorious. It is in the times of greatest loss; can they keep going or do they even want to?

In Overworld as in the Bible, the gift of free will and the choices or consequences of each choice is continuously woven throughout the pages.

Do the ends truly justify the means? Even if that means by crossing the line you resemble your enemy. Is there ever a time when murder is acceptable?

Ephesians 6:12 "we wrestle not against flesh and blood but powers and principalities in the heavenly realms." This verse mentions realms as in more than one. Overworld is the exploration of just one of these realms and the ramifications that can take place as seen and unseen realms are on a trajectory towards collision, in which nothing will ever be the same. The first in the series of novels debut AAE author Philip Narsingh presents Overworld.

Martyn Wood
speaker, coach, trainer

PREFACE

Overworld has been on my mind as far back as I can remember. I believe God has given me this idea to share with the world. It is one of the things I need to accomplish before I go to heaven. God created us to share his light and show how amazing He is. Drink in this story deeply and see what God is speaking to you through it.

Thank you and God bless,

Philip Narsingh

VERSE

Matthew 11:12 New King James Version (NKJV)
¹² And from the days of John the Baptist until now the kingdom of heaven suffers violence, and the violent take it by force.
New King James Version (NKJV)

1
REALITY

Phil opened his eyes, took the gun away from his temple, and looked to see who was following him. The dream he had last night was still fresh in his mind, *but why would he remember it now?* He looked around the alley. It was hard to see anything in the darkness, but someone was there. A woman spoke.

"Don't do it. This is not your end. You do have a purpose," she declared in a hopeful voice. "Please put the gun away."

Phil turned toward the voice.

"Who's there?"

It was a black, tempestuous night. The rain had picked up. Someone approached in the darkness. She had long black hair. There was something familiar about her, though he didn't recognize her voice. It was a soft, sweet voice. She was calm, though Phil had a loaded gun. She came closer.

"You don't know me. I've been looking for you for quite a while now," she explained.

She paused and came into the light. He could now see her dark brown eyes as she focused on him.

"I saw your band play earlier. You guys were great. Good show."

She was referring to the concert Phil had performed earlier that evening. The show he felt was a failure.

"Well, then. You weren't paying attention. That show was bad. Our band is done. I'm done," Phil snapped.

His anger was not subsiding. He couldn't believe those words were coming out of his mouth. She moved toward him despite his response. She wanted to reach him—to get through to him. He knew this. It was reassuring, but he remained guarded. *Why did she care?* She was persistent.

"My name is Roxy. Would you like to talk? I can help. Is there somewhere we could go?"

Phil did not respond. He was angry and confused. Roxy gave him a second, but then insisted.

"Would you like something to eat? We're getting soaked. You must be hungry. The rain isn't letting up. What do you think?"

She seemed sincere. Phil decided to take her up on her offer. She was right—the weather was only getting worse. He knew several places that would still be open but didn't trust her.

"I'm broke. It wasn't a good night. Everything went wrong," Phil muttered.

"It's okay. I understand. I'll buy," Roxy replied.

"Okay, sure," Phil responded in a quiet voice.

"By the way, do I look familiar to you? Have you ever seen me before?" Roxy asked with a hint of encouragement.

"No, not really," Phil lied.

REALITY

He didn't want to admit he recognized her, but he did. It was too weird. He was unsure of her motives. She looked exactly like the woman from his most recent dream. He was sure of it but wondered how this was possible. Phil remained guarded. *What was he afraid of? Could she tell he wasn't honest with her?* Phil unloaded the gun and put it away.

"Well, you do look a little familiar. Maybe I did see you while I was performing. It was a small crowd," Phil replied.

Phil had seen her during the show. He had been distracted by her, to the point that his whole band noticed. She was the one Phil saw in the dream. That fact he had no doubt.

"Let's go. And get out of this awful weather. You could use the company, and I'm a good listener," Roxy assured Phil.

"Okay," Phil answered. "I guess so. "

They started to walk. Phil wondered why Roxy would be looking for a complete stranger.

"Why were you looking for me?" Phil asked.

"I'll explain," Roxy replied with a smile. "Come on."

2
ROXY

They decided to head to a late-night diner called Antonio's. It was decent and still open. It was a bistro with a wide range of wines to choose from. Phil liked their house wine. The food was good and reasonably priced. Phil's mind was off the day's events. He was curious about Roxy. She had sparked his interest.

They got a booth away from the bar. The restaurant was quiet with very few staff. They had the place pretty much to themselves. Phil and Roxy sat down at the table. He noticed that Roxy was careful not to touch him. Not a handshake. Not a tap on the shoulder. Nothing. He found it a little odd but didn't think anything of it. Any time their hands got close; she pulled away. Phil watched her closely. The waitress came over.

"What would you like?" the waitress asked.

"The house red would be fine," Phil replied.

Phil was less on edge. He wanted to find out more about Roxy. He was getting intrigued.

"I'll have the bruschetta and some red wine as well," Roxy replied.

She looked at Phil and smiled. She seemed more relaxed now. This made Phil more comfortable. Roxy was beautiful, even after being soaked in the rain. She was in her mid to late twenties and in excellent shape. Her hair was the deepest black Phil had ever seen, and it was shimmering, even in the dull light of the restaurant. Her hair looked like a model's hair in one of those shampoo commercials. It caught Phil's eye. It had also caught his attention in his dream when he first saw her. Phil had many questions running through his head.

"You'll have to explain to me what you were talking about when you said you were looking for me. Why?"

Roxy smiled at him. "I'm not sure where to start."

"We have never met before tonight. Do we have a mutual friend?" Phil asked.

Roxy looked down at her hands. She seemed nervous again.

"I don't think so."

"Well, I'm wondering why you were looking for me," Phil pressed.

"I know this sounds weird, but I had seen you in a dream I had recently."

"Really?" Phil was shocked but not completely surprised.

"You are familiar. Are you sure you don't recognize me?" she probed.

Phil hesitated. It was like she knew he had a dream about her and was trying to get him to admit it. The dream he had the other night where he was running through a desert towards a cliff flashed through his mind. He'd seen Roxy guiding him to jump off the edge. Phil ran to the cliff and leaped without a second thought. He started to fall, and everything around him was exploding and on fire. He continued to fall with no bottom in sight, and then, he awoke. This dream had stuck with him for quite a while though he didn't comprehend it's meaning. He remembered it as clear as day.

"Please don't think I'm crazy and hear me out. I know how this must sound," Roxy exclaimed.

Did she know what Phil was thinking? Or good at reading his body language? Was she psychic? Could she have gone through Phil's mail beforehand, or his trash? He wasn't sure, but his guard was up again. This was all sounding fishy. *Could she be trying to trick him? How could any of this be true? How could she know this?*

"Well, I may have had a dream about someone that looks like you. It's not that unusual. But I don't go around looking for the people I see in my dreams." Phil explained covering up his curiosity. "It does sound a bit weird."

Phil had almost done the same thing when he saw Roxy at his show earlier that night. He almost laughed out loud. *Could she tell he wasn't telling her the whole story?* She looked at Phil intently and then cracked a smile. He wasn't ready to admit he was looking for her during the show or that he was wondering the same thing about his dream.

The waitress came back with their order. Roxy prayed and gave thanks to God for the food. Phil started to sip his wine. He stared at her and then started to eat.

Phil thought for a second. *Did he ever thank God for anything?* He should have been thankful, but nothing ever worked out the way he planned. *Why would he be thankful, especially now?* He was *mad* at God, if anything. *Didn't Phil have a right to be upset?* Everything was going wrong, and not just today. From working at a music store for next to nothing to working at his dream to be a performer but never even getting close. Things just never seemed to work out. Phil was getting upset but held it in. He put his focus back on Roxy. He calmed down and took another sip of the wine. It helped him relax.

Roxy drank her wine slowly, but never touched the bruschetta. Phil hadn't planned on eating, but he was hungry. He wondered why she didn't eat it. He hoped she didn't hear his stomach growl.

"You're not eating?" Phil asked.

"I don't really like bruschetta, and I already ate," she replied with a grin.

Why did she order it, then? Phil wondered. He gave her an odd look and kept on eating. *How could she know he liked bruschetta and had wanted some?* Roxy focused on him.

"Listen," Roxy said intently. "I know you think I'm nuts. In fact, nothing I say or do will convince you. You'll just have to trust me. A step of faith. Maybe more like a leap of faith." She smiled again and seemed nervous.

"Okay. Trust you with what?" Phil asked. "What do you want?"

Phil's hand was on the table. She reached over and lightly touched his hand. Immediately, he felt a flood of information and experiences enter his mind, things he had never thought of before. It was intense and uncomfortable at first. It was an information overload. It was all her thoughts, feelings, memories, past, dreams, knowledge. *What was she doing to him?* Part of Phil was shocked, and part of him was intrigued by what he was seeing. He saw her in New York at her apartment deciding whether to come to Toronto to find Phil or to dismiss it as an afterthought. Though it all happened in a split second, it felt like hours. So many images and experiences. It was like he was living her entire life in a moment.

Phil jerked his hand back. It wasn't painful as much as startling and unexpected. He was unclear about what had happened. He was a little dizzy but fine. He took a moment to pause and get his bearings back. He looked at her and around the bar. He looked at his drink and food. What an odd experience. Phil still needed a moment. All these thoughts were rushing through his head. He tried to make sense of it all.

Roxy watched patiently. After a few moments, she spoke up again. "Are you okay?" she finally asked. She was getting concerned.

She could see that Phil was still recovering and trying to understand what had happened. Roxy looked at him with compassion. She would give him as much time as he needed. Phil looked at her with a confused look.

"What did you just do to me?" Phil asked. "Did you put something in my drink?"

Roxy gave him a shocked look.

"No," she laughed. "You are so defensive."

Phil glanced at his drink. Phil was defensive, to the point of being paranoid. He was getting ready to get up from the table and leave but stopped. He was trying to make heads or tails of all the information he got when Roxy touched him. He suddenly knew everything about her. Her history, where she lived, all her hurts, all her pain, all her dreams, all her disappointments. Everything. She had freely shared all of herself with him. He saw her travelling to Toronto by bus and still second-guessing herself, trying to convince herself that she wasn't crazy. All these details were now a part of his memory.

Phil looked at her, and it was like he was looking at a totally different person. She looked different to him but not on the outside. He knew everything about her on a much deeper level. Right to her core. Right to her spirit. Phil looked at her and could see little flashbacks of every moment of her life. She had laid it all on the table like an open book for him to read. Nothing was held back. Nothing was censored. She was willing to be that open and honest.

He knew her on the inside but at the same time still didn't trust her, but it was something inside of him. It was not her. Phil didn't believe someone could be that open and honest. *Was it because of what he had gone through? Was it something deeper?* He knew that she was sincere. Phil had no reason to doubt her now. All these thoughts ran through Phil's mind in an instant.

Phil got up from the booth they were sitting at and almost fell over. He was dizzy and overwhelmed by the whole experience. The waitress thought he was drunk, even though he only had a little wine. Roxy got concerned but could tell Phil was okay. She thought it was funny for a moment. Phil didn't see any humour in the situation at all. Roxy spoke up with a more serious tone to try to clear some of his confusion.

"I would never put anything in your drink. You should know that now. You know me a little better now, don't you? You sure you're okay? Take a moment and pull yourself together."

Roxy didn't want to bombard Phil, but she was excited that their connection was real. She began to think of the possibilities. Phil took his time. He was getting his bearings back.

"I know we have a special connection just by your reaction when we touched," Roxy explained. "Isn't this great?"

She smiled again and had Phil's full attention, and she was right. He knew that she wasn't that type of person. Phil was trying to give her a chance. He could see and appreciate people for who they were. No more surface level interaction but a genuine relationship. He needed more of those in his life. He had shallow relationships but what he had experienced with Roxy was totally unique. It was as if he knew her all his life. It was amazing. With each second that passed, Phil was remembering more and more details of her life—a lifetime of memories in a split second. Phil still did not speak. So many thoughts were running through his mind. He was still trying to put all the pieces of her life together in a way he could understand, but it would take time. Roxy again spoke up.

"I believe there are more of us with similar connections out there," Roxy explained. "More that have this ability, to be close, this deep, heart-level, open connection. There is one person I can talk to telepathically. I have been able to for a long time. I know this sounds weird, but I think you understand now. At first, I thought she was in my imagination, but she is real. I am sure of it. Sounds crazy, doesn't it? There was no way I could have explained any of this. You had to experience it. You had to feel it. I felt a sense of urgency, so I had to do it this way."

She looked at Phil with an accepting, loving look. Roxy had seen Phil's thoughts and life experience as well. At least the ones he wasn't afraid to share. She had beautiful eyes, and he could sense her innocence. She was open and vulnerable to him. She was taking a chance being this honest with him. She did this to save his life. She knew that if she hadn't, Phil might have killed himself. He knew this now.

"Yes, it does sound crazy," he replied and paused for a moment to think. He knew that person Roxy spoke of. He could see her in his thoughts.

"Her name is Julie. The one you are connected to," Phil explained with confidence.

Phil took another moment. He could sense Julie too. Sensing her was getting easier. He focused more on what he had learned about Roxy from this connection. The details of Roxy's life were still going through his head. Phil knew Julie as well. *Possibly from a dream?* Connecting with Roxy helped clarify this relationship. *How many more connections like this were there?* He tried to make sense of all the information he now knew.

"You were studying business?" Phil asked. "And were taking several courses on leadership?"

Phil got these details from the connection with Roxy but was still trying to understand what was going on in his head. It didn't make sense. *How was this possible?* He never thought people could connect through thought and touch alone. He was still not sure he believed it, yet he had experienced it. He continued to ponder all his thoughts.

"Yes, I did," she responded with joy. "Business management and leadership."

"You don't live in Toronto. You came here searching for someone," Phil reasoned, still understanding everything he sensed.

"And I found you," she replied with excitement. "What a step of faith to find you. I saw your dream when I touched you. You were expecting and looking for me too. It was me in your dream."

She laughed. She came looking for Phil on nothing more than a dream— something she sensed in her heart. Wow. Phil had never stepped out like that. He was too afraid. He was getting to know Roxy's heart and was glad she found him.

"I had to find you now," explained Roxy. "You were hitting a low, and I couldn't wait to meet you. Glad I wasn't too late."

She was right. Phil was hitting a low and might not have been alive if she hadn't found him. Too many things were weighing him down, and he couldn't take anymore. Roxy found him at the perfect moment.

3

BEGINNING OF THE CIRCLE

"Julie is looking for you," Phil advised. "She isn't too far from here. I was sensing her through you. She shares the same connection we have. I believe I have dreamt of her before."

Phil's awareness increased. His sense of Julie was getting clearer and clearer. He was connected to her and now remembered a long-forgotten dream he had of her as well. It was becoming clear like he had dreamt it yesterday. He remembered seeing her face in a dream where she saved him from destruction.

Phil was unsure of his newfound ability. He was gaining some confidence, still learning, but it was developing fast and getting stronger within him. He was still processing all the details. He now knew about Roxy, and the connection with Julie was getting stronger. The connections to them both were strengthening his insight.

"Yes," replied Roxy. "You're right. You're getting the hang of this. I'm not sure why I can't communicate telepathically with you, but maybe it just takes a little time. I have communicated with her all my life. This other person

I'm looking for, Julie: She's close. At first, I thought of her as an imaginary friend, but she is real. She is beautiful inside and out. I've already told her telepathically that I've found you. She's excited that there are more of us with this type of power. She knows you, by the way. I can sense her more clearly now that we have connected, Phil. The connection with you makes my connection with her more powerful. I'm still trying to understand for myself what is going on."

Roxy and Phil both sensed Julie. Every so often a thought or a daydream of what she was seeing would pop up in their minds. They could feel her reaction when she sensed them as well. Being connected gave Julie a sense of what was going on.

"Okay, this doesn't make sense," Phil reasoned. "Do you understand how this sounds? Are we both out of our minds? Who do we tell about this? No one will believe us."

"I know it's crazy. I'm just kind of going with it. Following my heart and seeing where it leads. Just the fact that I found you is encouraging to me. This is not by accident. I believe this is all leading somewhere, but I'm not sure where yet."

"So, what do you want from me?" Phil asked. "You must want something—or are you here just to make new friends?"

She couldn't have come this far just say to hi and buy him dinner. No one does that. He wasn't that naive. There is always a catch, always fine print. Phil was skeptical. He didn't deny the experience, but there must be some strings attached. Even with her self-revelation through touch, he didn't sense any ulterior motives. She did seem genuine, but Phil wanted to be sure.

BEGINNING OF THE CIRCLE

"No," she responded. "I just wanted to meet. I felt I was being led here, so I stepped out and went for it. It was a gut feeling—a woman's intuition, I guess."

She laughed joyfully. A part of Phil thought she was out of her mind, yet she had gotten this far on gut instinct. Phil could never have done something as bold as this. He was in awe. He felt special that someone had gone so far out of their way for him.

Phil continued to ponder the situation. He still thought this whole experience was way out there, but he couldn't deny his dreams. He couldn't deny this experience. It was too amazing to be a coincidence or chance. Her actions made him feel special. He knew that she did this to save his life. Phil wasn't special. He was only seconds away from shooting a bullet through his head, and this stranger came along to stop him.

Was it fate? Phil wasn't sure he believed in fate, in things that happened unavoidably, that he had no say in and had to simply accept. It didn't sit well with him or feel right. Surely, he had more control of his life than this.

As they sat and talked, Phil was getting more comfortable with this new ability. This connection was getting stronger and clearer. Roxy and Phil exchanged the most intimate of details with each other. She was wide open and honest. She held nothing back from him. Phil could read her like an open book, and she didn't mind. She read Phil's mind and knew him so much deeper.

However, he wasn't as open as she was. Phil held some things back. He didn't want her to know he was scared. He had trouble trusting people, and she sensed it, but she was working with him where he was at. She saw all Phil's recent dreams. Roxy knew all his fears as well. She knew some details of Phil's life before they met, but when they touched, she got so much more insight. She wasn't judgmental or critical, but rather loving, caring, and encouraging. They knew each other on a heart-to-heart level now. Phil knew her motives were pure. He knew she was honest, caring, and sweet. Roxy brought something to Phil's attention that intrigued him.

"I saw that you had a dream about a woman who saved you from drowning. That woman looked the same as the one I talk to telepathically. Julie is the one from your dream, and we will meet her soon. She is excited about meeting you. She's not too far now. She's close."

Okay, this can't be an accident, Phil thought. Roxy was right. That was the dream, and he couldn't make sense of it. He remembered the dream vividly now. If he met this woman, and she looked like the girl from his dream, he would have no reason to doubt. He wouldn't know what to think after that. He had sensed Julie before, but he had no idea who she was.

This can't be happening. This is unheard of. Phil thought it might be the same woman but ignored the notion. He was not sure what to make of all of this. All this was difficult to believe, yet it was happening.

Phil could tell Roxy was herself looking for answers as to what this all meant. *Why they were drawn together?* It could not be chance. Phil didn't believe in chance either. He didn't believe in luck. He was still processing this new knowledge. Things were getting clearer, but it would take time. It would be a process, but Phil wanted to know more. He wanted to go deeper. The desire was too strong. He couldn't stop now. Phil was too intrigued.

Nothing else mattered. This new quest, on the other hand, gave him purpose.

"Wow," Phil exclaimed. "To meet another person whom, I had only known in a dream. This is freaky."

Roxy laughed at Phil's enthusiasm. She was more joyful at his excitement. Phil had been negative and depressed. Part of him was skeptical and filled with doubt; another part was excited and curious about the possibilities. Phil's expectations were rising higher. He had new hope. Phil continued to dream. Roxy was amused by his pondering and deep thoughts.

Roxy and Phil held hands again at the table. They went even deeper. Phil was more trusting this time. The connection was getting stronger. They both knew that to take full control of this ability, they would need to be more vulnerable and honest. Phil, especially. He needed to be a lot more open, but he was afraid. *What if he revealed something that would scare her off?*

This all must be leading somewhere, Phil wondered. This new knowledge and ability were changing everything. He wasn't thinking of suicide anymore. He sensed Roxy's relief. Phil wanted to experience more. It was developing a hunger within him.

They had a strong connection now. It was more solid and powerful than Phil had thought possible. It was deeper and more real than anything he had ever experienced, yet it barely scratched the surface. Phil could sense the depth of this power. He wanted to dive deeper, but it wasn't that simple. He was yearning for more. There's much he didn't understand. It was a process. He held her hand tight a second longer.

They released hands, and there was new contentment and excitement building to find the others. There were more of them. Phil knew that for sure now. He was different on the inside after this experience. He was getting a real sense of Roxy's heart and why she came after him. She really did care about him.

The waitress came back with the bill. Phil didn't feel right with Roxy covering the bill, but she'd already offered to do it, and he had accepted, so she paid. Roxy wanted to cover it and bless Phil any way she could. She also left a huge tip.

A fifty-dollar tip on a fifteen-dollar bill? Phil was surprised. *Isn't that a bit too much?* On second thought, he had never seen a generous person who lacked anything; still, fifty bucks was a lot of money. She was investing in this waitress as well as Phil. The waitress was overjoyed and thanked Roxy. Phil knew Roxy wasn't rich and that it was a stretch for her, but she did it with faith. She had a faith that Phil had never seen.

They left the restaurant. It was late, and they were both getting tired. It was close to one in the morning by this time. Phil was running on empty, but meeting and connecting with Roxy was exciting. He couldn't remember the last time he had felt such passion and excitement.

Roxy was excited. Julie was getting closer, and Roxy was looking forward to meeting her. They both noticed their connection continuing to grow stronger. Roxy's excitement was rubbing off on Phil as well. He was just as excited as her.

They headed down the street. It was dark and quiet. A peaceful Toronto evening—or early morning, as it were. The rain had subsided to merely a drizzle. The only light came from the moon and a few streetlights. A typical night, but nothing was typical about anything that had happened that night. It'd been the strangest night he'd ever experienced. Phil would never be the same. Everything was changing; things were different now.

As they walked, Phil suddenly sensed someone else with the same ability, like the connection he had established with Roxy. It hit him like a daydream or vision. The connection with her appeared to make it easier to sense others with this ability. It was Julie, and she was now close. It was unmistakable. Phil was hesitant but knew he sensed Julie. Roxy noticed Phil's preoccupation.

"I'm still new at this," Phil said, "but I do sense something."

Roxy laughed.

"Go with your heart. Use your gut instinct and intuition. Use your spirit. Don't be afraid. Never, ever fear. Your senses are very accurate."

Phil took her advice. He needed to listen to his gut, to use his instinct.

"I'm sensing Julie is even closer, the woman from your dream. I've never seen her so clearly until I saw your dream. You have a strong connection with her."

It had been a vivid dream, and it presented itself as vividly now as it did before. It was like the dream had happened seconds ago. It gave Phil an idea of what Julie looked like. Though Roxy had a deeper connection with her, Phil could see her now. She was beautiful with blonde hair and blue eyes. In his dream, she had a sword and was wearing armor. Phil looked forward to meeting her. Roxy and Phil had no doubt they would encounter her soon. It was exciting.

Roxy and Phil continued to talk, joke, and laugh about all the things they knew about each other. All the foolish things they did when they were younger. Other silly things they did not too long ago. She had some real embarrassing moments, as did Phil. She now knew that he had followed a woman earlier in the day he thought was her, but then realized it wasn't Roxy. Not even close. Roxy found it hilarious; Phil now knew that Roxy came looking for him without even knowing his name. She only knew what he looked like, that he was in trouble, and where he would be. That was enough for her to travel from New York to find him.

They continued down the road when something made them both stop to look ahead. Someone was walking toward them. It was Julie.

4
JULIE

Julie approached and saw Roxy and Phil together. She stopped with a look of surprise. It was her. It was the other woman Phil had dreamt about. There was no mistaking her. Julie was stunning. She had the most beautiful blue eyes. She was overjoyed and shocked that she had found others with these abilities, but at the same time excited and wanted to know more. Julie was the woman in his dream, the one who had saved him from drowning. He knew it was her. There was absolutely no doubt. Perhaps she could explain what the dream meant. Phil had no idea what that dream was about. He had forgotten the dream until meeting Roxy. It was fresh in his mind now though.

Phil had met two women he had never seen before, except through dreams. It made him think more about his dreams. Phil wondered what this meant. *What were these dreams trying to tell him?*

Julie took a long look at Roxy and broke into the widest smile. They had been communicating telepathically for a long time and had never met face to face until now. Roxy was overjoyed to meet her.

"It's an honour to meet you," Roxy said.

"It's about time we met in person. The honour is mine," Julie replied.

They embraced and began to talk and share their lives. Phil could sense the flow of information when they touched. They communicated telepathically and verbally. It was amazing to witness this connection between them. This was the power they all shared. They were intimately connected.

Julie closed her eyes when she embraced Roxy. She opened her eyes and looked at Phil. Julie looked at him with a big smile at first. Then, she had a concerned look. *How well did she know him? Did she know about the dream he had, and did she dream about him?* By the look in her eyes, she recognized him. She was so sweet and innocent from what Phil sensed of her. It was amazing to look at her. He was still wondering what all this meant. He thought more about the dreams.

Julie continued to hold Roxy with a long embrace. They held each other close. They hugged as if they had known each other since childhood.

"We should have done this sooner," Julie advised.

"Yes, we should have," Roxy agreed.

It was beautiful to see them so close. Sharing a connection that was deep and true. Phil could feel their connection getting stronger. They would speak at times, and at other times communicate telepathically. Their connection was deep and intense.

"I knew what your voice sounded like, but it's good to actually hear it," Roxy explained.

JULIE

    Phil had some doubts about communicating this way, but with his dreams and connection to Roxy, he was more open to it. Julie and Roxy had proven how close two people can get. They already had a deep connection telepathically, and it only strengthened when they met. They both found it odd that Phil couldn't communicate telepathically the way they did. They were not sure why. Julie and Roxy both agreed to communicate verbally around Phil for the time being.

    Phil communicated best in dreams it seemed. Most of his experience with Roxy and Julie were from dreams. This was the only way he knew who they were until he met them. Julie turned to Phil with much interest.

    "Pleased to finally meet you face to face," she said with a smile.

    "Nice to meet you," Phil replied.

    Julie reached out to shake Phil's hand. They both knew where this was going. They knew that when they touched, they would know each other on a much deeper level. She may have learned a lot about Phil from her connection with Roxy, but she was ready to open herself to him with a direct connection, to be completely open. Phil was not quite as ready, but he was willing to try, to be more vulnerable and trusting. He went with it.

    Establishing these connections with Roxy and Julie showed Phil he wasn't as open as they were, that he was shallow. It was becoming clear he had been given an opportunity to get out of the closed-off mindset, and he was resolved to go for it. Part of him was afraid, but he didn't let his fear hold him back. Phil looked into Julie's eyes, then at her hand, then back to her eyes. She smiled at him again.

Julie and Phil clasped hands tightly in what started out as a handshake. They held each other's hands firmly yet gently. Her hands were soft and smooth. Phil felt that rush of information and knowledge, and it was easier this time. It didn't feel so weird. It felt more natural. He was more open.

Phil was comprehending the power of this connection. It moved like a circle. Power was flowing in and out. He could feel the energy flowing between himself and Julie. He believed this was what the connection was called: The Circle.

All of Julie's experiences flooded Phil's mind. It flowed even easier and more natural then it had with Roxy. He could tell that Julie had seen his dream. He could tell what she felt about it. She was excited. She never looked at herself as powerful or wielding a sword. Her personality was gentle and kind. She had an unconditional love that seemed to cover anything and everything negative. Love was her ultimate weapon. She was always encouraging and compassionate. He could sense all of this from that brief touch. From this one touch, Phil knew Julie intimately. She was even more open than Roxy. She had some gut-wrenching moments in her life. She also had many embarrassing moments and joyful moments, and Phil now knew them all. He felt the same feelings she felt in several moments of her life. Every emotion and feeling. Julie could sense Phil knew all these things, and still, she never held back. Not even once. He knew about one of her brothers who had died when she was young. He knew about another brother she had never really known who disappeared. He knew about a sister she had lost contact with and really wanted to reconnect with.

JULIE

Julie also knew many details about Phil. How he was evicted from his apartment and couldn't go back. That his relationship with a woman named Victoria ended recently ruining his future of a life together with her. Julie's heart broke for him when she received these memories. She kept them and Phil close to her heart.

Phil was stepping further outside his comfort zone. His connection with Julie was strong. Maybe stronger than the connection he had with Roxy. He was intrigued by Julie now that he knew more about her. He wanted to know more.

Julie and Phil released each other's hands, then she embraced him close and kissed him on the cheek. She surprised him by getting too close, but he knew she was affectionate and loving. She hugged Phil as tight as she could. They were now intricately connected. Roxy watched and smiled.

Now when Phil looked at Julie, he saw her quite a bit differently, as if he had known her all his life—even deeper than he knew Roxy. It was an unusual feeling to be this close to someone. To know all their deepest desires. To allow someone in that close. Phil wasn't close to anyone, not even Victoria, his ex-girlfriend, before their relationship ended. That was his longest relationship when it ended shortly before his show.

"That was an interesting dream," Julie said smiling.

"Yes, it was," Phil replied. "I never thought I would actually meet you. I can't believe all of this is happening."

"I knew we would, and that's why I came here. To find both of you. I'm so happy I found you. I had my doubts. I thought I was going insane all the way here, but you proved I'm not out of my mind." Julie's enthusiasm bubbled over. She laughed, and Phil smiled at her.

It was a leap of faith for her, as it had been for Roxy. She had come all the way from California on the faith that the Circle was real and to find Roxy and Phil. He had never stepped out in faith like that. It was too big of a step for him to take. He felt envious of the steps they had taken to bring them all together. It was beautiful. It was awesome.

"What do we do now?" Phil asked. "It's getting late."

Phil was ever the practical one. They were still enjoying the moment. They didn't want it to end. Phil didn't want it to end, either, but it was almost 2 a.m., and they didn't know what they would do next or where they would stay.

"Let's get a hotel," Julie replied. "I think we all need sleep."

"Agreed," Roxy replied.

"I would've loved to get here earlier to see your show," Julie said to Phil.

"You didn't miss much," Phil responded.

"Okay," replied Roxy. "There is a hotel close by. And the show was better than Phil thought."

He appreciated the encouragement. Phil needed it.

5
THE BEACH

They went to a hotel close by. Julie and Roxy both knew Phil had no money, but they had no problem covering the cost. They had more than enough cash and wanted to bless Phil. He appreciated it and was thankful.

"We got you," Julie said joyfully. She knew the challenging time Phil had that day.

"Thanks. I owe you both now," Phil lamented.

"You don't owe us anything," they both responded at once. They paid for the hotel room, a simple room with two queen beds. It was time for sleep, but they were all too excited. They knew they would be connecting with others like them in the morning. Now that the three of them shared this connection, they all had a broader view of what was happening. Their Circle was growing.

They were also noticing they could share each other's abilities. For instance, Julie was focused, and it rubbed off on Phil. Roxy was decisive while Phil was not, but with her in the Circle, he was more decisive. These abilities they shared made them all better. They relied on each other more for this reason. Phil was stronger than both Julie and Roxy, and his strength affected them. Being connected to each other increased their strength. They were noticing these different skills that each could share with the other.

Their ability was indeed called the Circle which allowed them to be connected. They were sure of it now. A group of people brought together for a purpose. Not by accident or chance. They were designed to be together. A higher calling. Not by fate, and not by coincidence. This connection was for a specific reason. Phil could sense all this with Julie and Roxy. His perspective was changing and expanding. It was what he was looking for. A reason to live. Something greater than merely getting by each day.

Phil thought about why they were being brought together. *Things don't just happen, do they?* He was asking even deeper questions now than he ever had before. He thought it was because Julie and Roxy were asking the same questions. This connection gave them similar thoughts and motivations. They were of a like mind. This was all a part of the connection they had established. Their relationship wasn't surface level. It ran much deeper. Their Circle was close and intertwined in ways they couldn't even imagine or understand. Phil sensed they were only scratching the surface of this circle. Questions like these continued to abound in their hearts.

They reached the room of the hotel. It had all the basics but was overpriced since it was downtown. There were two queen beds, a mini-fridge, and a small desk. From the window, they could see the street and not much else. At least it was quiet tonight. They were all ready to turn in after an eventful evening.

THE BEACH

Roxy and Julie shared one of the queen beds, and Phil had the other one to himself. He lay down as he was tired but was restless. Roxy was fast asleep already. She wasn't usually up this late and was out. Normally, Phil would fall asleep in seconds but not tonight. He was excited about the events of the day but was also concerned about his future. *What was he doing?* He thought he would be dead by now. He hadn't looked past this day. All these thoughts clouded his mind, and it was hard to sleep with all that weight on his shoulders. He twisted and turned some more. He could not sleep. He was having trouble laying still. Julie had gotten up to get a glass of water. She saw that Phil couldn't wind down. She came over. She was concerned about him.

"Can't sleep?" Julie whispered. "You look restless."

Phil sat up. He was irritated.

"No, I can't," he replied with frustration. "There is still a lot in my mind."

"Lie back down," Julie replied quietly.

Phil looked at her, puzzled. He could not relax.

"Trust me," she assured him.

Phil did as Julie said. She put her hand on his shoulder to get him to relax and gave him a reassuring smile. She massaged his neck and shoulders. He was stressed from the day. Julie could feel that when she touched him. He was tense all over.

"Okay, that works," Phil responded.

He started to relax. Her massage was helping. Julie smiled. Phil got more comfortable. Julie continued to rub his back. He was typically tense at night. He would normally take hours to wind down before he was able to fall asleep, unless he was dog tired, which was most of the time, and he would be out quickly, but not tonight.

"You really need to relax," she whispered, making sure she didn't wake Roxy.

"Yes, I do. So much to think about."

"Clear your mind, Phil."

"I don't know how," Phil protested as he tried to get back up.

Julie put her hand on his back to calm him down.

"Close your eyes and relax. Slow your breathing. Lie still."

Phil gave her another chance and got comfortable. She stayed with him, massaging his back. Her touch was soothing and relaxing. It made him calm down and fall gently asleep. The stress Phil felt faded away. Julie kissed him on the cheek as he drifted off to sleep. She went to bed and fell asleep herself almost immediately.

Suddenly, Phil was at a beach. It was a beautiful sunny day without a cloud in the sky. The white sands were clean and shimmering under a radiant sun and a soft breeze. It was a perfect day. Phil must have been dreaming, and he was. Phil knew he was. Waves of water washed up on the shore. Then, out of the blue, someone hugged him from behind. It was Julie. She knew he loved going to the beach.

"How do you like this?" She grinned. "This should help you sleep and clear your head."

She was right. Phil was relaxed, without a care in the world. She knew him well, thanks to their connection through the circle. It appeared he was in a dream with Julie.

"This is a dream, right?" Phil asked her.

THE BEACH

"Yes. It's my dream, and I drew you in. We are together in this dream and aware that we are dreaming. This is a shared dream."

"Wow," Phil replied. "It's so real."

"As real as you want it to be."

Phil took some of the sand in his hand. He felt the breeze and inhaled the fresh air. Everything was so vibrant and vivid. He looked at Julie, who was now in a swimsuit. He noticed how attractive and curvy she was. She pulled him toward the water.

"Come on. There are more interesting things than sand here."

"I'm okay here. I don't know how to swim anyway."

She laughed and looked at him.

"You can't drown here," she explained. "If you drown, you will just wake up. It's a dream."

She went to the water and dove in. Phil watched her for a bit then he sat down in the sand. He was getting sand all over himself. He imagined having a beach towel, and it appeared under him. His thoughts had become tangible here.

Julie fell in the water, got back up, and looked at Phil. He smiled back. She was having so much fun. Julie was enjoying every moment. She loved the beach and the water. She was trying to lighten the mood. Phil watched her as he relaxed in the sun. His cares all melted away. Everything on his mind was forgotten.

Phil looked around the area. There was another island not too far away. The sky was beautiful and clear as far as he could see. It was a perfect setting. Perfect in every way. He didn't want this dream to end. He had no anxiety now. Julie's plan had worked. She had wanted him to lighten up.

Julie appeared beside Phil in a jogging suit and was completely dry.

"This is a dream, but how did you get dry so quickly?"

"Anything is possible here. There are no limits, except our imagination. We control the whole world here. It is a dream. This is one of the abilities we have. I'm not sure why we have it, or how we got it, but I know how to use it. At least I think I do."

"Our bodies are asleep right now?" Phil asked.

"Yes," Julie replied. "All of us are sleeping peacefully in the hotel. We'll be well refreshed in the morning."

They walked along the shore. Julie paid a great deal of attention to Phil. She drew him close every so often and kissed him on the cheek. They took their time. There was no need to rush. Time was non-existent. They had all the time in the world.

It was a beautiful experience. Phil couldn't think of a better way to relax and unwind. It was only a dream, but he was thinking about how amazing it was. He wanted to go deeper. He wanted more dreams like this. It was a vivid dream, and he would never forget it.

From what they could tell, this was another part of the Circle's ability. It was another level that connected them. Phil seemed to have a deeper connection when he dreamed. Dreams seemed to be to the most impacting way for him to connect with the Circle. Not like Roxy, who used telepathy the best. Julie seemed to be able to do both effectively. Using dreams and telepathy made their connections to each other stronger.

THE BEACH

They made their way to the edge of the water. They could see another island in the distance. It was as beautiful an island as the one they were on. From far away, it glowed and shimmered. They were being drawn to it, but they had no way of getting there. Since it was too far. They didn't have a boat or any other transportation. Phil wanted to go to the island.

"I have a challenge for you," Julie said. "A race. Let's see who can get to that other island first."

Phil had no idea how to get there. The other island must have been fifty miles away.

"How do I get there? I don't have a way. I can't swim." Phil protested.

"You don't have to know how to swim here. It's a dream. You're completely safe and couldn't drown. If you did, you would wake up."

She waited to see how he would respond. She was challenging him. by taking him out of his comfort zone. She wanted to see him grow and go to a new level, and he needed it. Phil needed to be awakened. He needed to think bigger. Phil knew something was holding him back and decided to push forward, break through to a new level.

Julie watched Phil. *How would he get across the water to the other island? Was this a trick?* She gave him another one of her beautiful smiles. By her look, he could see she believed in him. Julie continued to encourage him.

Phil closed his eyes for a second. Julie saw what he was doing and got more interested in what he would come up with. Phil opened his eyes and looked to the shore. She turned around and looked to the shore as well, and a metal boat appeared. It was a small fishing boat with two oars. It would do the job. He imagined and manifested it into the dream. It was the best he could come up with.

"It would probably take you an hour to get to that island," Julie responded as she laughed.

Phil didn't think that was funny. She wanted him to come up with a way to get to the other island, and that is exactly what he did. It would work. It wasn't the best way, but it would work.

"It's a race," she exclaimed. "You would lose for sure against me."

"Well, how do you plan to get across?" Phil asked.

"I'm not going to tell you. You have an imagination. Use it," she replied. "There are no limits here to imagine and finding a way to that island"

Phil thought of a speedboat, and it appeared, replacing the fishing boat. This boat would surely win him the race.

"Still not fast enough," Julie replied. "You can do better than that. Come on."

She was right, he could do better than that he thought to himself. He decided to forget water transportation options and looked up into the clear blue sky. It was beautiful. He saw a dove fly by as swift as the wind. *What if he could fly there?* Phil imagined himself flying. Immediately, light and energy surrounded him, and he began to float off the ground. Julie watched what he was doing. He flew towards the other island, going faster and faster. This was a hundred times faster than using a boat. Julie watched for a moment as Phil flew. He headed towards the island at full speed. Right before Phil got to the island, Julie disappeared and reappeared on the island right before Phil touched the ground. Phil landed, and she was there smiling as always. She had won the race. She had outsmarted him.

"I win," she proclaimed, doing a dance.

"Hey, that's not fair!" Phil protested. "I never thought of that."

"You could have done the same thing, and you would have beaten me," Julie replied. "I win. Our next dinner is on you."

She gave Phil a hug and kissed him on the cheek. He didn't like losing, but he got her point. She made the point clear. Phil could see that Julie operated with a different spirit. Her attitude and free spirit were something he desired.

"Never limit yourself. You are capable of so much. Don't let anyone tell you otherwise. You are so special," Julie told Phil with the most loving eyes. She spoke with boldness and intensity. Phil listened with an open heart. Part of him didn't trust what she said but connecting to Julie and Roxy on this level would require trust. *What was holding him back?* He took Julie's point to heart. It would take Phil some time to trust like they did, even with a connection as deep as the Circle. He was willing to try. Being part of this Circle was opening him up to new possibilities.

They continued walking along the shore together. It was a beautiful dream. It showed Phil that there was more he wanted out of life. He had never quite seen things this way. It gave him a new perspective. Julie held his hand and continued to encourage him.

6
FULL CIRCLE

Phil awoke. It was all a dream. He remembered it so clearly and vividly. This dream would remain with him forever. Phil would never forget that beach and the feeling of flying. He did something he didn't think was possible, even though it was a dream. It changed him on the inside. Phil was getting a grasp on what had happened. This dream felt like a landmark he would always remember.

Roxy was awake and getting ready. It was 9 a.m. Phil sat up, and Julie came over and gave him a hug yet again. She had awoken right before him.

"Good morning," Julie said with tons of energy, like she was awake for hours. "Wasn't that a fun dream?"

"So, it *was* you in the dream and not just my imagination. Yes, it was a fun dream," Phil responded in awe.

"It sure was. Imagine the possibilities." Julie replied with a laugh.

What an incredible dream. She had pulled Phil into her dream. He could remember it as clear as day. He could remember every detail. It was so vivid, the smells, the sights, the sounds, and the feelings. That made the dream even more impactful. The connection through dreams was fulfilling. They had a deep connection, and it was opening Phil up more and more. He had never been this transparent until now. Roxy and Julie knew him better than any of his past relationships. The amazing part was that they wanted to know him even better. They knew all his embarrassing moments and his flaws, but they still chose to love him, and it was love. Julie especially was loving. Phil could feel it from her. It was that tangible. She made him feel special every chance she got. She also made Roxy feel loved as well. She had such a beautiful heart. Phil loved everything about her.

Phil got up and got ready. He was still wearing the same clothes as last night, but no one seemed to care. He was a mess, which didn't seem to matter either. Phil had cologne, but that was it. He didn't even have a toothbrush. They were a rag-tag bunch, but they all knew something greater was happening in all of them, something special. As a result, no one was concerned. At least Phil wouldn't *smell* bad.

None of them understood what was happening or why. It was a step of faith for them all. They got breakfast and were planning their next steps. They knew there were others, and they would meet them today. They had little knowledge of these others. Nowhere near as close as the connection Roxy, Julie, and Phil had, but there was another woman who was part of their Circle that was strong in guidance and direction. Once they found her, a lot of questions would be answered. Their next steps weren't clear yet, but they sensed once everyone was together, they would be revealed. Things were getting clearer as they spent more time together. It was another revelation they had about this Circle they were all a part of.

Once they finished eating, they checked out of the hotel. Julie covered the entire tab. She was as generous as Roxy had been with the tip. It was awesome how the hotel staff responded to her when she gave the tip. She really blessed them. They were all appreciative. She made all the staff smile with her love and personality. She hugged as many of the staff as she could. They would never forget meeting her.

They could sense there were several others with the same connection close by. Very close. They were getting better at understanding their senses. They could feel their presence. Phil was getting a better sense of the other members. Roxy locked arms with him on his left side, and their senses and vision increased tenfold. Julie locked arms with Phil on his right side, and again there was an increase in their senses and connection. This connection was beyond words; the power of being drawn together left them in awe.

Their own senses were increasing in sensitivity. Smells became stronger and easier to distinguish. Colours were more vibrant as if the three of them had never seen them before. It was as if they had opened their eyes for the first time. All their senses were renewed and more intense. Their clarity continued to increase.

"There are three of them," Julie advised.

"And Tina is the one guiding them," Roxy added, finishing Julie's statement.

This level of sensitivity was new to Phil. He could only tell that there were others like them close. He was still learning to use this ability. It seemed like this was only the beginning of a powerful journey. Phil could tell Tina was as powerful as Julie or Roxy and that she could sense them as well. He continued to learn and grow.

Phil noticed he was becoming protective of Julie and Roxy. It was an instinctual thing; he was concerned for their safety. Phil felt as if he were meant to be their guardian. He watched them and their surroundings to make sure they were safe by instinct now. Phil kept a close eye. He wanted to meet the others, but a part of him was guarded as well.

Julie and Roxy stopped walking. Phil stopped and looked at them. They turned around and noticed a woman with blonde hair, and she had two men with her. One of the guys was slim with long, dark brown hair. He looked the athletic type, like he could run a marathon without breaking a sweat. The other had long, curly, black hair, and he looked like a bodybuilder. Phil wouldn't want to mess with him. He continued to make sure Julie and Roxy were safe but also wanted to meet these new members. They approached, and Phil was curious about them.

"I'm Tina," the blonde-haired girl announced. "This is Daniel, and this is Jon."

Daniel was the skinnier of the two. He was of a medium build but smaller than Phil. Jon was the biggest of the three of them. He looked like a powerlifter and the strongest. Tina had golden blonde hair. She was slimmer than Julie and Roxy and in excellent shape. She looked athletic and strong.

Jon and Phil shook hands, and once again, Phil received a flood of information and knowledge. He knew that Jon loved the band Megadeth and was heavily into powerlifting. It was like he'd known him all his life now. Phil shook hands with Daniel, and as they touched, the Circle became even stronger. Phil now knew how closely Daniel worked with animals and preferred nature over the city. Tina came over and gave Phil a hug, and again, he got a knowledge transfer. Now they all knew each other intimately. They were all deeply connected. Tina was a free spirit that loved getting away from civilization and being out in the wilderness. The power of their Circle had increased one-hundred-fold. Their awareness and perception increased and saw everything clearly. All of them. Together.

They were all now connected, and it was an even more powerful connection than Phil had experienced with Roxy and Julie. To know someone that intimately. They weren't strangers anymore. They had only known each other for a short time, yet now it was like it had been a lifetime. Tina, Julie, and Roxy hit it off together right off the bat. They were asking and questioning each other on how they all found each other and were laughing. They all knew all the details because of the connection of the Circle, but they discussed it anyway. It increased everyone's faith as they learned how accurate these connections were. They had all stepped out in faith to bring everyone together. None of them were sure each other even existed until this moment.

Tina communicated with them telepathically. This ability seemed to come easily to the women of their Circle. Phil wondered why that was. He thought, perhaps, that men weren't as open as women are—but that was a guess. Daniel appeared to have the most open connection. He seemed to communicate the best telepathically of the guys.

Jon and Phil didn't seem to have this ability beyond sensing. Neither of them could communicate telepathically.

Now that everyone was together, their sensitivity was even greater. Tina sensed that there would be a seventh person in the Circle. A woman, but they could not sense her at all. It was like she wasn't on the planet even though the connection was quite strong. They found that odd. They could not get a location on her at all. The other members of the Circle had found Phil, but not this person. It was odd and confusing, given their current understanding of how this all worked. Tina and Roxy seemed to be the best at locating people with connections, but neither could find this person. Julie was a close third in this ability, but she couldn't locate the other member either. They had no way to locate this person. They weren't sure what to do.

In fact, this was unusual because Julie had come all the way from California to find Roxy and Phil. The connections worked well, even over long distances. Julie had communicated closely with Roxy to bring all the Circle members together. They could all tell they were only scratching the surface of all of this. There were more realizations to come. They were all excited at the possibilities that lay ahead. They continued to ponder about the missing member and what to do next. They followed Tina's lead.

7
JUMP-POINT ALPHA

Tina led them to the outskirts of Toronto. They needed to leave the city and get to a quieter, more secluded place. They needed the stillness and quietness the city could not provide. They were being called away and all sensed this leading. Tina was following her gut feeling. Everyone agreed to follow her. No one was sure of where this journey would take them. They had been brought this far for a reason, though. It wasn't by accident. None of it made any sense to Phil, but he couldn't stop now. He couldn't turn back. If he did, he would be spending the rest of his life wondering what could have happened. They left the city. Tina had a minivan that would comfortably fit all of them. She knew she was going to have some additional passengers, so she had chosen a larger vehicle before they all met.

They all sensed they were being led, *but by whom?* This thought hadn't crossed Phil's mind before, but Tina talked about being guided to bring everyone together. Julie had talked about being led before. *Who was this mysterious guide?* They continued to follow Tina's lead.

Was God leading them? Did God even exist? Phil thought there was a God up there somewhere, but not someone who would lead them and bring them together. Phil couldn't explain how they all found each other, *but did God have something to do with it? How could Phil be sure? How could any of them be sure? Was there a way to prove it?* Phil couldn't think of any, but he couldn't explain their journey either. It defied explanation.

Phil continued to ponder these things. He knew that something was at work in all of them. He was sure of that. He wanted to go deeper. He wanted to learn more. Phil had to. There was no turning back now. He was at his wit's end and couldn't continue the way he had been going. He knew the way he'd been heading before he met Roxy was a dark place from which he would have never returned.

They were well outside the city following Tina's guidance. She sat in the front passenger seat guiding Jon, who was driving. Roxy and Dan were sitting in the middle, and Julie and Phil were in the back. They had a good time all the way out of the city. They discussed more moments of their lives and made sense of all the experiences they had exchanged when they had touched.

Phil chose not to think about his band failing or any other challenges. Julie could sense it and was happy Phil chose not to worry.

They all got along well and shared stories with each other. Everyone knew each other's stories, of course, but some still required explanation. They would know *what* had happened without always knowing why. Every second they spent together was like knowing each other for years.

Phil now knew how Tina sought out Daniel and Jon and brought them together to find Roxy, Julie, and him.

They reached a park about forty-five minutes outside the city. It was quiet and peaceful—exactly what they were looking for. There were a lot of trees and a beautiful clearing they could walk to. It was late morning by this time, close to 11 a.m. The day was sunny with a few clouds but no rain—a much calmer day than yesterday. They made their way to the clearing.

They were all comfortable and at peace. Their excitement built with the connection between them getting even stronger. They felt the energy around them build as they got quiet and still themselves. Their minds were clear and open with their senses heightened. They borrowed each other's abilities and strengths. They leveraged each other to focus on a common goal. There was no fear, no worry, no sorrow. Everyone knew each other's issues and weaknesses. Everyone knew each other's lives, the ups and the downs alike, but none of that mattered. They were connected, and Phil could feel the love developing in all of them, even though they had only known each other for a short time. Their Circle was drawing them closer and bringing them to an even deeper level of connection. The closer they got to each other, the stronger they became as a group. Their individual strengths made the Circle more powerful.

Every moment their connection grew and went deeper. They were not sure what it was about the place that was peaceful and quiet, but it only fed the power of their Circle. Something was happening to the Circle they had formed. It was like there was energy all around them, and they were absorbing all of it. It was increasing in all of them. Especially when they got quiet and still. They felt almost unstoppable.

"You guys all trust me, right?" Tina asked politely.

"Of course," Julie replied.

This gave Tina some reassurance. Tina was going by faith and following a hunch. It seemed to be working.

They all gathered closer together and made a small circle and huddled. They joked and laughed with each other. This was the first time they all came in contact at the same time, and it was even more powerful. Their awareness continued to increase, and they were absorbing all the energy around them even more than before. They all felt stronger and more aware. Phil had been tired earlier this morning, but now he was awake, alert, and fully oriented. They were aware of the rest of the Circle and the whole area around them.

"Everyone close your eyes," Tina advised.

Tina closed her eyes and took a deep breath. They all closed their eyes as well. Everyone held each other's hands tightly. They began to feel a soft breeze swirling in circles around them. They felt hot, then cold. It was as if the ground shook. It also felt as though everything around them was changing, even though they hadn't moved.

"What's happening?" Phil asked.

"Keep your eyes closed," Roxy responded playfully.

He did as she said. It felt like everything was moving all around them, but Phil could still feel his feet firmly on the ground. Power and energy were all around them and flowing through them. They continued to keep their eyes closed and hold onto each other. The power of the Circle was being exerted. Some of the power was coming from within each of them. Phil could feel his feet starting to lift off the ground. They held onto each other more tightly. Their feet were completely off the ground now, but none of them were scared. No fear whatsoever. They all continued to hold onto each other.

Then, with a huge thud, they all landed, lost grip of each other, and fell back. They were again in a forest clearing, but everything was different. They were somewhere else. *Were they dreaming?* It wasn't the same forest where they had been.

"This is Jump-point Alpha," Tina proclaimed.

"What does that mean?" Phil asked.

"I have no idea," Tina replied, "but I know that is the name of this place."

They were relying on Tina for answers, but she had few this time. They all looked around in awe and wonder. This place was somehow familiar to them. They felt they knew this place. There is no way they could have been here before. *Why was it familiar?*

"Jump-point Alpha?" Phil repeated.

"Yes," Tina replied.

There were mountains and fields in one direction. It led off in the distance to a cliff. The sky was bright blue, and the sun shone with a soft breeze in the air. The odd part was that in each direction, there was a different atmosphere. One was sunny and dry like a desert. Another was snow and ice. The third was green and flourishing. The fourth was a seashore with water with no other land in sight. Four different atmospheres at the same time. All co-existing, without affecting each other.

The different seasons didn't interfere with or interrupt each other in any way. It was quite a sight to see. The snow and the sunny desert were co-existing together.

The seashore was also unaffected by the snow. There was snow, yet the beach had tides and waves coming in. No ice. *How was this possible?*

The atmosphere that had the cliff looked familiar to Phil. It reminded him of the cliff in his dream—the one in which he had seen Roxy and from which he had leapt. *Did he dream of this place?* He wondered if he had been here before. He would surely remember this place.

There was a structure not too far off. It was a large, modern building, made of shiny silver metal. It was durable and well built with many doors and windows. This futuristic building looked like it belonged in a major city, yet it also had the feel of a castle. It shone a silvery white colour in the sun. They made their way toward it.

Phil knew they were at Jump-Point Alpha, *but where was that? Was it another planet?* This combination of weather was impossible. Of course, the last day or so had been impossible according to Phil's former beliefs. He was trying to figure it all out, but it wasn't working. It was illogical. This wasn't the type of experience he could put into words.

The members of the Circle noticed they were stronger than normal. Julie had long suffered from a slight limp, and her leg would get sore when she walked or ran too much. Yet now, her pain was gone, and she was running, jumping, and laughing. She was overjoyed. It was beautiful to see her free and healed. She was a positive person in general, and now, her joy radiated even more genuinely.

Phil felt stronger and more agile. He felt at least ten years younger. His energy was greatly increased. *Was there less gravity? Was this part of the Circle's power?* It felt like he had a million watts of power running through his veins.

He felt powerful and unstoppable. He noticed his back and shoulders, normally tight and sore, were completely pain-free and loose. He had no fear or anxiety. He was free in every sense.

Daniel was extremely quick. He was the smallest but had the best physique of all the guys in the Circle. He was agile as well. He was testing out this new-found energy with much enthusiasm. He could move swiftly and turn on a dime.

Phil noticed their awareness had again increased. They all noticed they had all their memories and everything they learned at their fingertips. Their mental capacity had increased. They needed it here because they had known nothing of this place before now. It was all new to them. Everyone in the Circle had grown smarter, and they were using each other's skills and knowledge to move forward. They were working together.

From what Phil could tell, they were in a world between Earth as they knew it and another world, they knew little about. The place seemed able to open a gateway to yet another new world. This place appeared to be their destination. They were being drawn there with power and a sense of urgency. They could all feel it; there was no turning back. They had no idea how to get back, anyway. They had to explore this place. This desire burned in all of them.

They approached the shimmering silver building. It looked a little like a castle but more modern. It had devices and systems they had never seen before. All the technology they could see was advanced.

They were greeted by an older man, somewhere north of fifty years old. He had a medium build and seemed to be in a hurry. There were others working with him, but he appeared to be their leader. He came out to greet them.

"I was expecting you," he announced.

"You were?" Julie asked.

"Yes. I am Sullivan. Come here quickly."

They were all surprised. *How could he have been expecting them?* With everything that had happened to them, though, it didn't shock them too much.

"What took you so long?" Sullivan asked. "No time to waste! So much to do."

"Is this place called Jump-Point Alpha?" Roxy asked.

"Yes, it is, but you already knew that." Sullivan replied.

He was right. They did already know that. It was more of a confirmation. They wanted to be sure, but they had so many more questions.

"You have to learn to trust that voice that speaks softly to you on the inside. You don't trust it yet? You must start sometime. You will soon. Why not now? If I were you, I would start now," Sullivan mumbled with excitement.

He spoke all this with a smile and haste. He spoke a mile a minute. *Was he right?* Phil wasn't sure, but he sounded like he was onto something. He seemed crazy, but he spoke words of wisdom. Sullivan seemed to speak without any thought whatsoever. They continued to listen to his words. Roxy and Phil gave each other a look. *Is this guy for real?*

"That voice that speaks softly on the inside?" Phil asked. "I'm not sure I understand."

"You will come to understand," Sullivan reassured him. "Oh, boy, you will. You will soon know exactly what I mean. You are meant for more. There is so much more.

Be ready. Get ready if you are not. You want more? Well, it's coming. Ready or not. More of everything."

This guy is nuts; some were thinking. *But who knows?* Some of his words were off-the-wall weird, but some of his words really hit Phil and got him thinking. It activated something in his heart, but still, he had to ask himself: *What was Sullivan talking about?*

The door slid open, and Sullivan led them into the building. There were a few people in white lab coats. There were many computers displays and screens. Jump-Point Alpha was an advanced outpost. It had more devices and objects they never knew existed. Holograms and scanners were humming and glowing. The castle-like building had hundreds of rooms and corridors. It would be easy to get lost here.

"What is Jump-Point Alpha?" Julie asked.

Julie always spoke with a sweet, innocent smile. She was so sincere. Phil wasn't sure why it stood out to him, but it did. Sullivan turned to her.

"A place to gather everyone to send you to Overworld, of course. That's the place you are going. Not everyone is allowed into Overworld, but you all are invited. You must go there—and soon. No time to waste. Times are urgent. Better get moving. You all are already late."

He looked at Phil. "You are a guardian. Your job is to protect everyone in your Circle. Keep them safe. Do not lose any of them or any of the others who will join you. Many will fight against you, but you will not fail unless you quit." Sullivan spoke gravely, but then his countenance lightened up, and he smiled.

"I thought you would be a bigger guy, you know—taller and more intimidating. With your abilities, you'll be fine, though. You'll face a few challenges, but you can overcome. The Cobra's reign will begin. Your power to strike is unmatched. Become the leader you were meant to be. Step into your power. Never fear. Become fearless. And don't cry. I hate it when men cry. Although, it's okay to cry sometimes."

He stepped closer to Phil and got serious. "They attack you because they are afraid of you. Stand your ground. Stand firm, and you will overcome. You are an overcomer. Who can stand against you? No one. Not with what you possess. Am I making sense? Of course, I am. I always make sense."

Phil was confused. Sullivan talked to him as if he knew everything, but his answers only led to more questions. Phil, on the other hand, had no idea what he was talking about. *Wasn't Phil intimidating?* He could take Sullivan if he wanted to. He was tougher than that old man. He was powerful. And dangerous.

Sullivan continued to show them around. He led them to a courtyard in the back of the building. It was an incredible view of a cliff from Phil's dream. It again reminded him of that dream. *Why did it keep standing out to Phil?* It had been such a vivid dream that Phil knew he had been here before. He continued to think about that dream while he looked at the cliff. Sullivan then looked at Roxy.

"You are the divider. You determine where the power lies. You are the leader. Your decisions will affect many. You have many gifts that will be realized. All power flows from you and to you. You have unmatched power. You decrease so that others can increase, but you will increase beyond measure. You make others better."

Roxy was in awe of his words. She kept these words in her heart. She believed these words, and so did Phil. When he connected with Roxy, he could see how amazing she was, inside and outside. She had something powerful within her that would come forth in the proper time. Sullivan's words reinforced what Phil had sensed in Roxy.

Sullivan walked over to Julie. He spoke some powerful words to her. "You cannot be killed. You are a healer. You give life. You will bring many to life. You will restore. You are a restorer. You are not weak." He said all this with a serious tone, and then he went to his goofy mode. "Is *restorer* a word? Sounds good to me. It's got to be a word."

Phil looked at Roxy, and she smiled. *What is this guy on? Cheap drugs? Too much coffee?* He babbled and made no sense sometimes. He was odd and unusual, but his words were powerful, and he spoke with authority. He had some hidden wisdom, but sometimes it seemed too well hidden. Phil gave him the benefit of the doubt and listened to his words.

Julie received the words from Sullivan with excitement. She was stronger than anyone in the circle thought. She was strong and independent. She pondered these words in her heart. The words seemed to light a spark within her. Phil saw the power within her beyond everything he learned about her when they touched. There was something special about her.

Sullivan kept going. He spoke next to Jon. "You are powerful. Some may underestimate your strength, but there are few as strong as you, physically or otherwise. Your strength will save many. You will fight when others give up. You are a source of strength for the weak. Your strength will increase when others draw back in fear. Many will look to you."

Jon was also amazed. These were the most encouraging words he had heard in a long time. He had faced many challenges and discouragement. He grasped hold of those words. He chose to forget his past and moved forward with these words.

Sullivan looked toward Daniel. "You have the vision. You are quick. You look ahead and move forward. Few see farther than your gaze. You have the wisdom and revelation. Your connection with animals is unmatched. You are a trailblazer. Few will follow where you will lead."

Dan was a insightful guy. These words held deep meaning for him. He did have a special connection with animals. He loved to be around animals, and they loved to be around him. His power seemed to lie in this fact.

Sullivan became more serious as he looked at Tina. "You are the guide, the seer. You have been shown the way. You know the way. You are trusted with much knowledge. Few are wiser than you. You will show many the way. You shall lead them who cannot see. You will make them see. You are a leader, by word and by action."

Sullivan said these words with confidence and boldness. He meant what he said and did not doubt a single word. His words were so powerful that it cut right to their hearts. He seemed to know exactly what they needed to hear and said it. They all received his words with joy.

Tina believed these words. What was amazing: she had these doubts about herself since Phil first met her, but she chose to step out despite that and led them there. She overcame much of her fear as well. Phil admired her for that. They all did.

Sullivan focused. "Okay. Time to send you to Overworld. You are needed there, trust me. You must go quickly and go soon. Do not delay."

"But we have so many more questions," Roxy protested.

"No time for questions. All the answers are within you. Listen to that voice inside of you. Use your instinct. Your gut feeling. Trust it. You'll find out exactly what I mean. Before you go, I have to give you something."

His staff came out and gave them all navy-blue coloured clothing. It felt comfortable, sturdy, and of the highest quality any of them had ever seen. The clothing was personalized to each of them. The outfits were as comfortable as a jogging suit yet fit and sturdy enough for martial arts. Phil went aside to put the clothing on, and it fit him perfectly. It felt tailor-made. Everyone else had the same experience. They were the best pieces of clothing they ever wore. They felt comfortable and strong. The material of the tops and bottoms seemed to change and adjust automatically as they moved with it.

"Thank you, Sullivan," Julie said.

"You are very welcome. Now say goodbye to Jump-Point Alpha and come with me," Sullivan replied.

They took a last look at Jump-Point Alpha and its surroundings. Phil could have spent weeks exploring. He got a good look at the area and the cliff. He wished they could have stayed longer. They followed Sullivan further into this journey. They had so many more questions, but Sullivan moved quickly. He was visibly concerned about something and moved them along fast.

He led them to a room: the solitude room. This room was white with no discernible edges or markings. It was a solid white wall around and above. All they could see was white. The light was even and without a shadow. There was a soft hum, and they could feel power and energy moving around the room and through them, like what they felt when they huddled in the park.

"Thanks again, Sullivan," Tina said.

She embraced him. They all took turns hugging him. The women got a little emotional in the short time they had with Sullivan. They all wished they could spend more time exploring Jump-Point Alpha and with Sullivan.

"Oh, stop," Sullivan replied. "You're making me blush!" His eyes were a little misty as well. He was getting emotional, and they could see it. Under the crazy exterior, he was a tender, loving person. "Be who you were meant to be. Go to the Creator. Beware of imposters and people with fake Circles. Stand tough. Stand firm. Do not be shaken. Ariel will help and guide you as well. Stay together and trust each other."

With that last statement, he was gone. He left the room, and the door sealed. The edges of the door were no longer visible. It was like the door disappeared. The room was a solid white now. The slight hum was gone. It was silent except for their voices.

There were still so many unanswered questions, but they would have to wait. They were on their way to a new world, "Overworld," as Sullivan called it. *But what was Overworld? Who was Ariel?* They had more questions than answers. They listened to Sullivan's advice. They wouldn't forget the words he spoke. Hopefully, they would see him again soon. They continued to ponder his words.

"Any sense of what Overworld is or why we are being sent there?" Phil asked.

"I'm not sure," Tina replied. "I have no clue."

She was right. It seemed like they were the only ones who didn't know. It was exciting and intriguing but nerve-wracking, all at the same time. They had absolutely no idea what to expect. The unknown was a little bit unnerving, but the mystery and curiosity were hard to resist.

"What do we do now?" Roxy asked.

"Do we huddle again?" Julie pondered.

"I'm not sure," Tina replied.

They started to feel a sudden burst of energy. Power was increasing all around them. They all huddled together and held each other close. This time, the released energy was even stronger. They could feel shaking and vibrations all around them. The energy was flowing through them all. It was exhilarating. They were being lifted off the ground and began to spin. They were phasing between Jump-Point Alpha, Earth, and Overworld. They were not sure where these worlds were located, but they looked forward to going there.

8
OVERWORLD

They were now all off the ground. It felt like the room was shaking and moving, although they were not in direct contact with it. They were in mid-air. They could sense the power around them and in them. They kept moving and turning. *Was this a wormhole or some type of teleportation?*

They all shook and then landed. They were now in Overworld. They had landed on their feet without falling over this time. They were standing in a field covered with green grass. The sun was out in full force. A soft breeze blew all around them. Every direction was quiet and peaceful. Gentle meadows of lush vegetation. A few clouds were in the sky, and it was bright and beautiful.

This is Overworld? It seemed a bit plain, but it was a beautiful and peaceful place. It seemed normal, at least on the surface. It was serene and tranquil. They also detected something big coming. This felt like the quiet before the storm. They all sensed something, but on initial inspection, all was quiet. It was calm. There was no noise but the wind. It seemed a lot like Earth, but it was different. There was something in the air.

Was this the place they had been guided to with such urgency? Was this the place Sullivan said they needed to get to immediately? It doesn't seem out of the ordinary, Phil thought. It seemed almost heavenly how peaceful it was. It was comfortable and tranquil. *It's almost too quiet.* They kept their eyes open and stayed alert.

"Let's all come together," Tina advised.

They all huddled together again. They could feel the Circle getting stronger within them all. They fed off the energy within them and around them. It was making things clearer, and they were gaining insight. They took a moment to gather it all in. They were getting acclimatized to Overworld.

"Overworld is like Earth. It is familiar so that we wouldn't be left disoriented. It's less of a shock this way, but things are changing fast here. This will happen here, then to our Earth. Everything is being made new," Tina declared. She spoke with confidence and boldness.

"Everything seems so normal here so far," Phil explained. It looked so much like Earth; he couldn't see a difference. This fact made Phil look at everything more closely because they all knew they were not on Earth anymore. They tried to look below the surface, deeper into everything.

"So far it does," Julie replied, "but there is much more to explore."

She was right. They hadn't seen anything yet, and they weren't here by accident. They knew too little. Phil still wondered why they were here. They all had that question in the back of their minds.

As power increased in the Circle, Tina began to glow. She was healthier than normal, as was everyone in the Circle, but she was the only one glowing. Everyone moved back, and she continued to glow. She was filled with power. Light was shining from her being. The glow was emanating from her center.

"Our Circle has been activated," Tina announced. "All of us will walk in our proper callings. It is time. We are needed. We have no time to waste. Now or never."

Tina spoke with passion. She was powerful, and it was showing through. Any self-doubt she had was completely gone. Her words hit them all hard. Words seemed to have more power here. Phil could feel her strength and belief behind the words she spoke. Her words shook them to their innermost being. The words were more powerful than when Sullivan had spoken.

"Are you all ready?" Tina asked.

"I think so," Roxy replied. "Ready for what?" Roxy looked at Tina with expectation. Phil had no idea what was coming. Roxy was now getting stronger.

Tina laid hands on Roxy and spoke words over her. "You are Roxanne. The divider. You will determine who has the power and who does not. You will lead us, but you are not above us. We will support you as you lead."

Roxy stepped back and absorbed these powerful words. They were true. She knew they were true. She laid hold of them and believed what Tina had spoken. Roxy needed a moment but was fine. Power moved from Tina to her.

Tina looked a little drained from the experience. She needed a moment. She had tears in her eyes. It was an emotional moment for them both. Roxy then turned to Tina and was glowing like her now.

"You are Tina. You are Stinger. You are the guide, the counsellor. You are a teleporter. You have strength few have or understand, an enforcer of this Circle. You will guide many and show them the way. Your wisdom will save many."

Roxy spoke these words with even more boldness than Tina had spoken earlier. Tina fell over and lay on the grass. She was deeply touched by the experience and was okay. Roxy turned to the rest of the Circle. She was glowing brighter now. She turned her focus to Phil.

"You are Phil. You are the Cobra. Few can survive your strike. You are the guardian. You are the protector. You will save many and protect many more. You will become one of the greatest guardians. This is your Circle: Cobra's Circle. You will touch many. You are a warrior. You were born to fight, born to lead, born to defend."

Phil was speechless. He didn't have words to describe what he was feeling. It was like every word she spoke had power and energy and infused him with all that strength. She was barely touching him, but it was like a surge of power. It was stronger than when they had exchanged thoughts and memories. Phil drew back and went down to his knees. He needed a moment to recover, to clear his head and get his strength back. The touch drained him and slowly revived him with more power and strength. Roxy went to Julie.

"You are Julie. You are the healer. You are the love of God. You cannot be killed. You are rooted and grounded in love. You love the unlovable. You make cold hearts grow warm. You restore and revive."

With those words, tears came to Julie's eyes. She was deeply touched, as were all of them. Roxy again spoke those words with boldness and faith. Julie received them with joy. Her eyes teared up. Julie was cut to the heart. She needed a few minutes and stepped back. Tina was back on her feet by this point. Roxy and Tina went to Daniel.

"You are Daniel. You are the spirit. You move like the wind. You move with God's speed. You look ahead and watch at the towers. You are a watchman. You have eagle eyes and the power of the wolf. Spirit is within you," Tina proclaimed.

Daniel was taken back. Some of their words didn't make sense. Some were right on. Daniel took the words to heart. He chose to believe them. Phil could sense a change in him even shortly after these words were spoken over him.

Roxy continued to talk with Daniel. Tina turned her attention to Jon. Phil joined her as she spoke to him.

"You are Jon. You are the breaker. You are the strength. None are stronger. You are raw power. You walk with strength and might," Tina proclaimed.

Phil stood aside as Tina spoke, but then some words rose inside of him, and he had to let them out. They were words for Jon. Phil decided to speak in faith and trust his gut feeling. It was a fire inside of him that had to be released. He couldn't hold it in even if he wanted to.

"Jon, you are the power. You will save many, and you have the power to strengthen those who can't fight for themselves. Your role is to help the weak. Many will rely on you. You have the strength of God. You fight when others won't. You defeat enemies' others run from. You overcome where others fail."

Phil spoke, and although he didn't feel all that bold, his words came from his lips with power. Phil sounded like he knew what he was talking about. What a powerful experience! *But where did these words come from?* He had no idea but continued to ponder it.

Jon was blessed by these words and touched deeply. He took a moment to let the words sink in. He believed the words.

They all had powerful experiences. They all needed a few more moments to understand what had happened. It was an amazing feeling, potent for all of them.

The power of the Circle continued to increase in them all. It now didn't matter if they made physical contact or not. They drew power from somewhere that seemed almost limitless. They gained strength with no sign of slowing down. They were going to a new level, a higher calling.

Everyone was getting healthier by the moment. They were all stronger and more focused. Daniel noticed they could borrow each other's ability, to greater and lesser degrees. Roxy was focused and present, and they all noticed they were stronger in that area too. Julie's slight limp was gone, her leg and hip completely strengthened. Phil had suffered some intermittent back issues in the past, but they were healed. Those who normally wore contacts or glasses no longer needed them. Their vision was perfect.

They also noticed some more unusual abilities were present within some of them. Roxy had some powerful abilities to help others reach their full potential, but it wasn't fully manifested yet. She continued to learn and grow.

They all felt close to each other and were getting closer. This was a good thing for Phil, as he didn't have a lot of close friends. It was a shift for all of them to be this close and this open. They savoured every moment together here.

They walked for a little bit and came to an area that looked like a garden, beautiful and filled with plants and trees. Everything was beautiful, and every type of plant or tree imaginable was here. All was well groomed and cared for. There was one tree that looked like the others but was darker. It was dead and produced no fruit. Its leaves were falling off. Other than this one tree, everything else in the garden was alive and growing. Everything else was full of life and vibrant, beautiful, and lush.

Phil came close to this dead tree. He touched it, and the limbs were sharp. It had thorns, and he cut himself on a thorn. Not a bad cut but enough to make him pull his hand back. *What good was this tree?* It was dead, produced no fruit, and it had thorns. It was taking up space and had little or no value. It was worthless. Phil wanted to get rid of it. It made him angry. *Why was this tree making him angry?*

Phil could feel something inside of him like a fire brewing. *Was this caused by his anger?* The energy and power building in him were getting harder to contain. He looked to the dead tree and sent a wave of heat and fire that burnt the tree and split it in two. It was lit on fire now and badly burnt. He had disintegrated a huge chunk of it with that heat ray.

"Did that come from me?" Phil asked.

"Yes," Tina replied. "That power resides within you. You have set the fire within you free. You are powerful."

Tina came over to Phil. It was a dumb question. Phil knew where it came from. He was having trouble believing it. It was an ability Phil had begun to manifest. The power resided in him. It was a gift for him. It was a power Phil was now able to walk in. A power from the inside. He was the guardian. He had the power to protect everyone. That ability was the fire ability. The ability to manifest fire at will. Without a spark. Without gas or any type of fuel. Just radiate it out of his being with power. He was deadly with it. Phil felt it inside him like it was there all along and was now able to release it. He felt powerful.

"You have that ability for a reason," Tina explained.

"I know," Phil agreed. "I sensed that too."

"You need to learn how to use it. How to be effective with it. You need to be able to control and channel it to be effective. Use and master your strength."

"Okay," Phil replied.

Suddenly, Phil saw a huge wolf come his way. The wolf was grey with a bluish tinge. Lean and strong. Larger than a normal wolf. They all stepped back, and Phil prepared to use his ability against the wolf if it threatened them. The wolf then changed form, and it was Daniel. The navy-blue clothing fit back neatly onto him. This ability was called the morphasis ability. He could change into this wolf at will. The wolf's name was Spirit. He was also fast and agile. Much faster than any human. He could run faster and jump higher than anyone in the Circle. He was the scout of the Circle. He could scout ahead, and his senses were sharper and keener than the rest of them.

"You are very quick and agile. Use your abilities wisely," Tina explained. "Your abilities are unique. Master them."

"I will," Daniel replied. He was excited.

"Don't let it get to your head."

"I won't."

Tina and Daniel both laughed and continued to talk. Daniel was growing in speed and power quickly. As Spirit, his speed and agility increased tenfold. He had the senses of an animal and was sensitive to his surroundings. He also had a special connection with animals of all kinds. Phil didn't fully understand this connection, but it was powerful.

Jon noticed he was bigger and more muscular than before. Tina and Phil laid hands on him and spoke words over him, and he looked bigger and stronger now. Jon's strength defined him. He picked up a nearby rock that was more like a boulder and threw it with ease. He also broke apart the rest of the tree Phil had split in half. His strength was extremely evident and powerful. He was also a humble guy and didn't talk too much. Phil sensed there was more to him than meets the eye. He was glad Jon was on their side.

Tina was learning about her teleporting ability. She disappeared and then re-appeared in a different spot out of thin air. This ability seemed to deplete her strength, though. It took a lot out of her, so Roxy asked her not to use it unless she absolutely had to. They understood so little of what was happening that they didn't want to take anything too far. She was also able to teleport others in the Circle from one place to another, but that sapped even more of her strength. It was taxing on her, so she used this ability in moderation and with wisdom.

Julie was walking with the power to heal, which was high level from what they could tell. Julie touched the cut Phil got from the dead tree and healed him instantly: no trace and no injury. No scar or mark at all. It had only been a small cut, but he had never seen any injury heal that fast. It was like it never happened. He was impressed by how easily she healed, and she was excited by this ability. She was natural at using this gift, and she seemed to master it with little effort. She loved to help others in any way possible. This ability was perfect for her, so she continued to learn how to use it. She was becoming an expert quickly.

Roxy appeared to have a power inside of her, but nothing manifested yet on the outside. They could tell that she had some ability that would be extremely powerful. Their senses told them that it was strong and hard to control. It would take time to develop it. Tina sensed this strongly. Phil felt it too but wasn't completely sure what to make of this power. Roxy was also their leader. She really stepped up in every way imaginable to bring them all together. Whatever this ability was, they continued to encourage her to ponder it and master it at the right time.

Tina's powers of guidance had brought all of them together, and she really stepped out to bring them here to Overworld. She was a powerful woman; it was evident. They were glad to have her, and she appeared to be the strongest female member of the Circle: bold, confident, and sure of herself. She encouraged and blessed them all.

They continued to grow in their abilities and powers. They took the time to get familiar with their abilities and build them. The Circle had them all intricately connected. As their Circle increased in power, they continued to get to know each other and learn each other's abilities while learning their own. They made each other stronger and confident. It seemed like time was standing still here in Overworld. They had no cares in this world.

They continued to survey the area. Daniel and Tina continued to guide the circle forward. They continued to practise their abilities. They also had no idea how to go back to Jump-Point Alpha, or Earth for that matter. They were concerned but continued to follow Tina's lead. They trusted her insight.

The clothing they had received from Sullivan was more powerful than he let on. When Julie touched Phil's arm, her hand went right through the clothing to his skin. It was an odd feeling. Other parts of the clothing would get tough and hard. It would change into a body armour if Phil touched it too aggressively or with a sharp object. The clothing seemed alive to him. Daniel punched Phil's shoulder, and the clothing thickened and protected him. They played with the clothing for a little to test its strengths and abilities. It was powerful. It seamlessly adapted to their abilities and their bodies. It was aligned differently for each of them. Thicker and stronger for Jon and lighter and more agile for Daniel. It would stretch and adapt to Daniel when he became Spirit, almost disappearing, then it covered him when he went back to human form.

The area where they were looked like it had once been more bountiful with more trees and fruit. It was still beautiful, but they could tell it had been even better before. The dead tree Phil split in half was destroyed and withering away. In fact, there was little of the tree left. It had withered away so fast, it was reduced to nothing.

All the grass they walked on was lush and alive. It sprung back up after they stepped on it like it had never been walked on. It would curl around their shoes gently, but not hinder them from walking. All the grass was green and vibrant. The shoes they were given allowed them to connect with the ground. They could feel every nuance of the surface they walked on. They continued to explore.

There were some paths in the ground where the grass didn't spring back completely. They had been worn in, and it looked like others had gone down some of these paths before. It was a little difficult to tell with how alive the grass was, but it was unmistakable. They were not the first ones here. There must be other people here. Phil wondered about these others and how to find them. *Would they be friendly?*

There were rolling hills and mountains in the distance, but nothing looked familiar. They were excited to explore this new area but kept Sullivan's advice and words in mind. They moved cautiously and slowly because they were not sure what to expect.

They walked to slightly higher ground. Daniel led them and guided them. Tina followed close to him along with Roxy, Julie, and Phil. Jon was a bit slower and would walk behind them all. He was a rear guard for them. They were excited but a little cautious. Julie noticed something ahead.

"What is that?" Julie asked.

"Not sure," Daniel responded.

They could see a more barren landscape in the distance. It was desert-like, with sparse vegetation. They never saw any animals or bugs. In that desert, there were four, huge shining figures that looked like pyramids but were flat on top.

"I'll get closer and check it out. I'll look and let you know what I find," Daniel advised. He became Spirit, the wolf, and ran ahead faster than the rest of them to have a look. He used his heightened senses and vision.

"I don't know if I can get used to that ability," Phil replied.

Phil laughed. Everyone else laughed too. They continued to walk in the direction Spirit had run. He was quick. He was an actual wolf, large and deadly.

As they approached the desert area, the climate was getting dryer and dryer. They hadn't walked that long, but it was noticeably different after only a short walk. Spirit returned and became Daniel again. He was back with the Circle.

"There are four platforms down there made of metal. There is some rock and stone, but mostly metal. The platforms have doors that lead to several rooms. I didn't see any animals or people. I think we should go there, as it will hopefully give us some insight as to why we are here."

"Okay, let's go," Roxy replied.

"It will give us some more answers," Tina explained.

Phil had the same sense. She was right. They needed to investigate.

9
PHANTOM

They made their way to the platforms. The scenic land had rolling hills and many valleys. It was like a dream—a perfect day that felt like it would never end. Overworld was beautiful and mysterious. They admired this world, but at the same time, they needed answers. They continued forward with eyes wide open.

They walked toward the platforms. They appeared to be made from metals like gold, silver, and platinum, with no wear on the surface. They were like a pyramid, but the tops were flat. Each platform had a door. Up close, it seemed like most of the platforms were underground. The structures seemed well built and sturdy with unparalleled workmanship. Perfect in design. They wondered what these structures were and why they were here.

"Should we go in?" Julie asked.

"I don't see why not," Roxy replied. "Tina and Daniel both said it would have answers."

Julie was hesitant. This was the first time Phil saw her pull back. She was nervous. She was sensing something that had her second-guessing.

"You okay, Julie?" Phil asked with a bit of concern.
"Nothing to be afraid of," Daniel said.
"We'll all be together," Phil assured.
"Okay," Julie replied.

Julie began to calm down. Phil would be there to protect her. The whole circle would be. They entered the closest platforms and all stuck close together. They kept their guard up. Julie stayed close to Phil, and they all stayed closer together. Julie grasped Phil's hand as often as she could. Tina was watching Julie's reaction and became concerned as well but agreed they needed to move forward and investigate.

The passage led to a large hall. There were beautiful designs all over the walls. Many images of dragons, lions, and other strange creatures decorated this hall. Some of these creatures depicted were unlike anything Phil had ever seen before or imagined. Even the ceiling was covered with images and symbols, almost all of which were unfamiliar. The colours appeared to be smooth metal in all shades of red, blue, silver, gold, platinum, and grey. The hall felt like a beautiful and regal masterpiece. Nothing on Earth could compare to this quality.

They made their way into an even larger oval-shaped room. The walls and ceiling had the same metallic materials. All kinds of metals like gold, but this gold made the gold Phil had seen on Earth look pale. There were many types of precious metals and jewels all over the walls and on the ceiling. It was hard to find a place that didn't have jewels or diamonds. Every jewel, metal, and diamond looked unique and new. Every one of them looked priceless.

"This place must be worth a fortune," Phil exclaimed.

The room had entrances at either end, and above each doorway hung swords that were bent like boomerangs. The room seemed to glow, although there was no visible light source. The light seemed to come from within the structure itself. There were no shadows and no darkness. The room itself was completely lit up by this mysterious glow.

In the centre of the room, there was an hourglass-type container hanging on a gold chain from the ceiling. The container looked like a candelabra from a cathedral. It was built with gold, glass, other precious stones that shimmered. The container held a black and red cloth that was moving around inside. It seemed to react to them. *Was it alive?* They continued to explore but kept their eye on this thing. They decided to leave it alone for now, but Julie was fascinated. It continued to move and shake.

They exited this room and entered another room that was much plainer and less extravagant. This room was shaped like a dome. Every wall was pure white and looked like it was made from marble. It had a similar glow. This white glow was coming from everywhere. The whole area was lit up. It was amazing how different this room was from the rooms and hallways before. It was like the solitude room on Jump-Point Alpha.

Phil looked around. He had a feeling that they were being watched. Phil knew something was wrong. Something didn't sit right and, his guard went right up. He wanted to make sure everyone was safe first. He couldn't shake this feeling. Phil became cautious. Julie sensed something similar.

"I think we are being followed," Julie whispered to Phil. She had the same feeling Phil had. She stayed closer to him.

"I sense it too," Phil whispered back. "Maybe we should get out of here. "

Julie, Roxy, and Tina were communicating telepathically and looking around. They were all sensing something, but no one could figure out what it was. Nothing could hide in this room; they could see every part and every corner.

"I don't see anything," Daniel said. "I don't sense anything, either."

This room was empty with no objects, tables, or markings of any kind. *How could someone hide here?* They would see them coming, but they saw nothing. Everyone was a bit baffled. *Did their senses trick them? Were they paranoid?* They hadn't encountered anyone in Overworld yet. Only Sullivan and his crew and that was on Jump-Point Alpha.

They dropped their guard and relaxed. They must have overreacted. Surely, they would see or hear something in this room. *Were they letting worry go to their head?*

"False alarm," Phil assured everyone. "I guess we need to relax."

Tina was still in a panic and looked around frantically. She was sensing something. "Whoever is following us is a teleporter," she responded. "Like me. Very similar ability to mine but much more powerful. Very hard to track. I can tell they are close, but I can't tell where they are exactly."

She could sense someone or something close and getting closer. Suddenly, what was a clear, bright, glowing room was suddenly shrouded in smoke and dark clouds.

The darkness came out of nowhere and descended on all of them. They couldn't see each other any longer. The cloud was that thick and dark. Pitch darkness just like that. Phil couldn't see his hand in front of his face. The darkness covered everything. The glow was gone. Not a trace. They couldn't find a way out of this room. It had disappeared. They were all trapped.

They were afraid and in a frenzy. The darkness was pushing them further and further apart, but Julie pushed through. Phil felt someone grab his arm. It was Julie. He knew her touch anywhere. They scrambled to find the others. They couldn't see anything because of the darkness. They did their best to find each other.

Then, they heard a voice all around them. They couldn't tell where it was coming from. They couldn't locate the source. They were still trying to find the other members of their circle. The voice spoke: "You would be wise to turn back. You don't know what you have gotten yourself into. Go back to your comfortable, meaningless life. You don't even know why you are here, do you, Cobra? Are you ready for a war? Do you even know what you are fighting for?"

Cobra was the name Sullivan referenced when he spoke of Phil. They sensed this enemy's name was Phantom. *How did Phantom know all this?* Phil wanted to attack but had no idea where Phantom was.

Roxy took Julie's hands, and they both pulled Phil with them. They were locating the others and joining them all together. As they grabbed hands, it became easier to find the others, but they still couldn't tell who was behind this attack.

Who was this voice? Was he telling the truth? A flood of questions overtook them. Phil also wondered why this foe was hiding himself in the clouds. *Why shroud himself? And why confront them? What could they possibly have that he wanted?*

"War?" Julie said to Phil. "Maybe we should turn back. Maybe we shouldn't be here. No one mentioned anything about a war. This is not for us. I'm scared. Do we really know what we have gotten ourselves into?"

"Either Sullivan's lying, or this person is. Right now, I trust Sullivan more," Phil responded. "Something doesn't add up here. Let's stand our ground."

The darkness grew thicker, and the floor was now shaking with strong tremors. There were also flashes of lightning and rumbling like thunder. This person had some type of power over the elements and the environment. They were in a full storm, and Phil could sense that Julie and Roxy were both afraid for their lives. Phil was scared too but more concerned about the others of his circle. No one could find the other. Tina was trying to locate this enemy but could not.

"He does go by the name Phantom," Tina shouted confirming their senses.

They could all feel this Phantom probing their minds, looking for something and forcing himself into their thoughts and imaginations. His mind ability was powerful. He was keeping them disoriented and separated, giving him the advantage. They needed to get everyone together and fight back.

Tina grabbed Phil's other arm, and she had Daniel and Jon with her. They now had the whole circle connected. This increased their overall strength tenfold. It gave them the ability to resist this enemy. They were more powerful together than apart.

Phil thought about Sullivan's words and believed them. His job was to protect everyone. Phil knew he needed to step up and do it. With that thought in his mind, he was no longer afraid. His fear gave away to anger. Phil decided to challenge this enemy.

"Why don't you show yourself?" Phil taunted. "Why do you hide behind clouds and darkness? Why are you so scared of us? I think you are lying. Why don't you come out in the open? How do we know you are telling the truth? I don't believe you."

Phil could feel Julie and Roxy's surprise at his actions and words. They wanted to back off and leave. They were questioning Sullivan's words. They wanted to make peace and not cause trouble. They thought about backing off.

The clouds and darkness started to clear. The storm dissipated and revealed their enemy. His name was Phantom. Tina was right. He had a hood that covered most of his face. Phantom was dressed in white. His identity seemed to be shrouded in mystery. They could tell his eyes were blue and that he had blonde hair, though most of his hair was covered. He had a slender, muscular build. He was similar in shape to Dan but had more muscle. Phil could sense the Phantom's energy coming. He was strong and imposing. Phil could get a read on his circle and his motives. He was the only one in his own Circle. He was a divider, a guardian, and a healer. *So, why attack them?* Clearly, he wanted something. He was taking a great risk attacking them. Knowing a bit about this enemy revealed his scheme, and they were no longer intimidated.

"Sullivan is an old fool. He is barely hanging on to Jump-Point Alpha. He is a liar. I wouldn't believe his words if I were you," Phantom declared. "He is senile and out of his mind. Only an idiot would listen to him."

"It's good you're not me, then," Phil replied with a sarcastic tone.

Phantom was not impressed. He got angry. They felt all the energy moving toward him pushing them back even harder now. He was gathering it, and the room was changing colour and temperature. Another storm was brewing in this confined space. He sent a flash of lightning straight at Phil. He covered up as best he could and was able to generate a force field type shield around their circle. It was merely a reaction. Phil had no idea how he did it. The lightning deflected off the shield, narrowly missing him. The shield weakened, disappeared, and Phil felt suddenly weak because of the force of the lightning. He dropped down to one knee to catch his breath. Phantom was gathering power again to send another blast of energy at him. Phil needed more time to recover. He was a sitting duck.

Phantom saw Phil's weakened state and made eye contact with him. His eyes changed colour, and it was like he was inside Phil's head, looking through his thoughts and imagination. Phil fell to the ground clutching his head. Daniel saw what was happening and moved faster than any of them had ever seen anything move and became Spirit in mid-stride. He bit Phantoms arm hard enough to draw blood. He became Daniel again and struck Phantom on the jaw all in one swift, smooth motion with an uppercut, stunning him.

Phantom was surprised by Daniel's power, speed, and his control of Spirit. He was also surprised at Phil's shield power and resilience. Phantom sent a quick charge against Daniel which pushed him back and sent him flying. Daniel hit the ground but got up quickly. Phantom gathered himself together again, recovering from the bite. By now, Phil had recovered and was standing. He focused on Phantom and gathered power to send a heat ray straight at him. The heat ray hit him directly in the chest. He had a burn on his clothes. Phantom surrounded himself with dark clouds and smoke so they could not see him, and then the darkness disappeared, and he was gone. He vanished without a trace, and the room was back to its original peaceful state. Phil calmed down, and his power dissipated back to normal levels. They could now see the exit to the room again.

"Is everyone okay?" Roxy asked.

"I'm fine," Phil replied. "Just a little shaken up."

Julie came over and looked at Phil to make sure he was good and then hugged him. She went over to Daniel and checked on him. He was wounded, but Julie healed him back to full strength. They left the room and returned to the bigger, oval-shaped room. They didn't want to stay in that room after Phantom's attack. They also had more questions than answers. They exited the room.

"What was Phantom trying to do us?" Phil asked.

Phil was still angry. He didn't know what was going on. He was hoping to get some answers but only had more questions. *Why was he a target?* He wondered what Phantom wanted.

"He was trying to read your mind," Tina replied. "We all felt him prying and looking for something. I'm not sure how you were able to resist it, but we are safe now. He took a big chance, and we stopped him. Seemed like he's desperate. You must have something he really wants."

Their group was now much more serious and focused on this strange world they were in. Something big was happening, and they were an important part of it. They must have an important part to play. *Otherwise, why would they be attacked?* They moved with more caution and vigilance. Everyone was taking Sullivan's words a little more seriously, especially his warnings. At least, now they had confirmation that Sullivan had a reason to rush them to Overworld. Something was afoot.

10
RED

The golden container in the center of the room was now swinging and moving. This red and black thing was frantic like it was trying to break out. Everyone watched it as it shook. Julie was especially fascinated. It was getting more and more active. They all kept their distance.

This thing looked familiar to Phil. *Was it from another dream?* He considered the possibility. He couldn't figure out why it was familiar as he had never seen anything like it before.

"Should we do something about that thing?" Tina asked. "Or should we leave it alone?"

Julie was curious and moved closer.

"We need to set it free," Julie responded out of nowhere.

"We don't know what it is," Phil said with concern to Julie.

Julie looked at Phil with a little disappointment. She was going by her gut instinct. She had a strong feeling that the red-black thing was something they needed.

They could at least help it. Julie believed it was alive and trapped. Phil was surprised as Julie had originally been afraid to even enter this platform.

"I think Julie is right. We should set it free," Tina advised.

Roxy looked at them both with a little confusion. She was surprised that they both wanted to free this thing. "Are we sure we want to do this?" Roxy asked.

"Yes, we are," Julie replied, speaking for everyone.

"Okay. Let's set it free. Be on your guard Phil, Jon, Daniel," Roxy advised.

"I'm not sure this is a good idea," Phil replied, but to no avail.

Julie's instinct that it was a good idea did relieve Phil. He wanted to make sure everyone was safe. Julie and Tina were sure it needed to be set free.

"Let's be careful," Roxy cautioned. She looked over at Phil to make sure he was ready.

"Ok. I'm ready," Phil assured.

They moved closer to where the container was swinging and shaking. As they got closer, it got more still. The thing inside stopped shaking the container. It reacted and responded to them. They moved closer but were slow and cautious. It was right above them now.

Phil looked for a safe way to release it. He concentrated on the chain the same way he had on the dead tree. Phil sent a heat ray straight from out of his chest and hit the chain holding the container. The chain disintegrated, the container fell, and he caught it. Phil took a closer look, and it was alive. It was a living creature. Julie came to see, and it responded to their presence. Phil tried to break the container, but it would not break. He tried pulling it apart. He tried to open it without hurting the creature inside. He then tried banging it on the ground but didn't even scratch it. Julie got annoyed that he had slammed it so hard.

"Don't do that. You'll hurt it," Julie shouted with concern.

Phil gave Julie a look. He gave it to Jon to try to break it open more gently. Though he was the strongest, he could not even dent it. The thing inside was moving slowly and seemed like it was watching all of them. It wanted out. They all wanted to set it free now.

Jon gave it back to Phil, who took hold of the top and bottom of the container holding this creature. He used his fire ability to heat his hands up and start burning through the container. Phil gripped it tightly. It was working. This container started to buckle and crack as Phil got a much better grip. He began pulling it apart, and the glass started to slowly crack. It took all his strength and the fire ability to break it open. Phil could see the creature inside going to one side giving him a clear shot through the glass with his heat ray without the risk of hitting the creature itself. He lifted it up and sent a heat ray right through the glass part and lost grip of the container, and it went flying to the other side of the room. It now had a crack in it large enough for the creature to escape. The creature inside pushed against the glass, and it shattered, and the thing inside went flying and expanded and was quite large. It was free now.

This creature looked like a cloth or ribbon. It moved like flowing water. It had black and red stripes, and it glided smoothly and silently through the air. It began to move toward them aggressively. Phil wondered if they should have set it free. He stepped back, as did all of them except Julie. She was not scared at all. It began to approach her, and Phil began to panic. It was moving fast towards her and Phil decided to intervene. He sent a heat ray and hit it directly. The heat made a hole through this creature, but the hole disappeared. It appeared to heal itself and absorb the injury. Phil couldn't hurt it. It began to move faster in erratic patterns. Daniel became Spirit and tried to grasp it and pull it back but was unable to do so. It slipped right through his teeth and through his fingers when he changed back and tried to grab it. Jon couldn't grab it either when he tried. Phil, Roxy, and Tina pulled Julie back, but the creature wrapped itself around her arm and lay there trembling. It did not harm her. It was quivering. It clenched to her arm gently but firmly. Julie pet it as one would pet a dog.

"Stop!" Julie exclaimed. "He's not trying to hurt us. His name is Red. He told me when he touched my arm."

"Red?" Phil asked.

"Yes," Julie replied. "I think we were meant to find him. He seems to know me. I think that is why it approached me. I wouldn't try to attack it."

Tina came close to Red, and it moved to her arm and back to Julie's arm. Phil touched it as it moved. It felt like cloth or fabric of some kind. Smooth like silk. It flowed gently and smoothly on Julie's arm and stopped trembling. "Guess we have a new friend," Tina said.

Red stayed on Julie's arm. She took care of him. They appeared to be communicating on some level. The rest of the Circle watched with interest. Phil still had some concern about this creature and kept an eye on it with

Julie. He wasn't sure if it was safe and they still knew little about it. They didn't even know what it was.

They noticed the large metal doors to this room had shut, and they were not sure how to open them. They tried to force them open, but they would not budge. There was also some damage on the wall from Phil's heat rays. Phil had put a small hole right through this metal. He was still learning to control his ability. The power of his heat ray was more intense than he had planned. The doors would still not open.

These doors blocked the main entrances in and out of the oval room. They were large and had similar designs to the walls and hallway. It seemed like all the doors were built to keep this creature contained. The doors were seamless and wouldn't budge even an inch when they tried to open it.

"How do we get out of here?" Julie asked.

"This door won't open," Jon answered. "I tried everything."

He tried to pull it open again, but it would not move.

"Maybe Red can open it," Julie suggested. "Red, can you open this door for us?"

"Would he be able to? He was trapped here until we came along," Roxy replied.

Red gently left her arm and went to the door. Red touched the door and moved through it like it was made of a liquid. He flowed like water and passed right through it.

The door swung open, and Red came back to Julie's arm.

"Thank you, Red," Julie said.

She went through the door first with Red on her arm. Everyone else watched her exit the room.

Red was handy. Julie gave him a kiss, and it responded by squeezing her arm a little tighter. Red made getting through that door look easy. Phil wondered why Red couldn't break through the container like he did the door. Red seemed to have the ability to break out. *Why didn't he?* They were free to leave this room and make their way back out of these platforms.

Phil noticed Red didn't leave the area until they left it. He seemed to have the ability to do so whenever he wished. He was powerful enough to break free. *Was he waiting for them?* He was powerful enough to move on from here. *Were they supposed to free him before Phantom attacked them?* These thoughts crossed Phil's mind. Red had no trouble getting through this door, and it was much more secure than the container that originally held him. *Was Red held, or was he waiting for them?*

They were back outside, and it was starting to get dark, but they had no idea what time it was. They walked a bit further and decided to stay and rest for the night. They would discuss and plan what to do for the next day. They were not too keen on staying near the platforms because of their encounter with Phantom. They didn't see a need to check the other platforms and decided to leave that area.

They chose a spot in the grassy woodland forest area to set up a basic camp. Thankfully, the grass was vibrant and cushiony to lay on. They made this spot their camp. They gathered some dry wood to set up a fire. The fire was more for light than heat, but they appreciated both. It was getting dark fast. Red made a covering for them. He could make a cloth tent over them from tree to tree. Once that was formed, he separated from the tent cover and continued to float and move among them. After gliding around everyone, he would go back to Julie's arm. He was playful with Julie. He was like a pet to her and didn't seem to mind.

Everyone was comfortable, and they began to absorb everything that had taken place. *Had it only been one day?* They still had more questions than answers.

They all began to relax, and the mood lightened. They were all a bit shaken by the encounter with Phantom. Once the tension had eased, they stopped worrying, and in turn, they began to see what was going on. There was a battle coming, a major battle. They had to be ready. They could sense it and almost feel it. *What had they gotten themselves into?*

"How are you doing?" Roxy asked Phil.

"I'm okay. I think Phantom was searching for something in my head, but I'm not sure what. I blocked him somehow. The attack had something to do with my fire ability. I believe Phantom wanted it for himself. He may have been trying to steal it. I think he has stolen abilities before."

Tina came and sat with them.

"Do you know where we are supposed to go next?" Phil asked her.

"I'm feeling compelled to head outside this forest to the desert we saw. I think we are headed into a battle. We can overcome our enemies, but we will need to be strong," Tina said with authority.

"Are we ready for this?" Roxy asked.

Phil was wondering the same thing. They didn't have the gear to travel through a desert. *How long would they have to travel? Wouldn't they need provisions?* None of them could be sure. Phil was no expert, but it seemed like a daunting task.

"For some reason, things have become desperate, and I believe we were brought here perhaps prematurely, before we were ready, but we are needed. Time is no longer our luxury. We have to act while there is still time," Phil explained.

Jon and Spirit joined them. They had been scouting and surveying the area. They were also checking to see if there was anything they could eat. Julie was hungry, but none of them wanted her wandering around alone. Julie, along with Red, Jon, and Spirit, found some fruit.

"We found some interesting fruit and Julie said it was safe to eat," Jon said.

"It looks like a mix between an apple and a raspberry. It's really good," Julie explained.

"Well, how would she know?" Phil asked a little annoyed. He was still concerned about the implications of Phantom's attack. It was distracting him. He was also wondering how Julie would know what to eat.

"What's your problem?" Julie asked.

Phil didn't answer.

"Red guided me to it. You should try some," Julie replied.

Phil was a bit guarded about Red. *Could he be trusted?* They didn't even know what Red was. He had helped them get out of the platform building, but they knew so little about him.

Julie left and came back with more of the bright red fruit. It did look delicious. She dropped off a bunch of fruit for everyone to eat and took off running again. She was being chased by Red. He flew by swiftly in the same direction as Julie.

Everyone else tried the fruit; they were amazed by how satisfying it was—a complete meal packed into a few bites. Those who ate it calmed down and relaxed with ease. It was filling but light. Very satisfying.

"Red is right. This fruit is awesome," Phil said. "Thank you, Red."

Red came over and brushed against Phil's arm gently and went back to chasing after Julie. Red was playing with her, and Julie was having a great time. They really lightened the mood with their antics. Everyone else was concerned about the situation and what to do next, but Julie and Red did lighten the mood.

Julie ran by again and stepped through the fire. A piece that was burning flew out and caused some dried pieces of wood to catch fire. Phil put it out using his fire ability. He could feel the heat and warmth of the flame. They watched as the fire burned up the wood. The flame burnt the wood until it was black and charred. Phil used his ability to make it burn faster and slower. It went out with only a glowing ember and then burst into a full out flame. He was getting better at controlling this fire ability. Julie was close by and called out.

"Phil," Julie called from several metres away.

He heard her calling. He couldn't see her, but he could hear her voice. Phil got up to search for her. He found her near the large trees in this forest not far from camp. Red had tied her up between two trees like a hammock. She had teased Red enough, and he got back at her by tying her up. It looked like they had been playing a game of tag or hide and seek before Julie got caught. They all had a good laugh, including Julie. Phil set her free, and she was laughing and filled with joy. Red was gliding through trees watching overhead.

"Okay, Red. You win," she conceded, looking around for him.

Red came back to her and wrapped himself around her arm. Red was moving and becoming more active with everyone in the circle as well. Red was an amazing creature. He could move through any object. He would usually be on Julie's arm when he wasn't floating around. He would stay in a cloth-type form since it was light, and he could move effortlessly and smoothly in this form. He also had other forms he could appear as. Phil wondered if Red could be the missing member of the circle. Phil was curious to know. He stayed with them all the time, and it looked like he would be a useful ally. Julie was obviously the closest to him. The rest of the circle was getting used to his presence and enjoying him.

11
DAMIEN'S CIRCLE

They all turned in for the night. Julie lay on the ground next to Phil. Roxy and Tina were on the other side of Julie. Jon and Daniel were on Phil's other side. It was a quiet, calm night. Red hovered above guarding them all. He created blankets and covering for them all in addition to the larger covering he had already made. Daniel and Phil were also keeping an eye out. They didn't have to worry about the fire staying lit since Phil had power over it and would not let it die out or burn out of control. It kept them warm and cozy in the quiet of the night. He watched Red floating above and then fell asleep.

That night Phil had another dream. He was in the dark and walking toward three shadows with nothing else in sight. He sensed they were sinister and had bad intentions toward him. He was being pulled towards them, drawn to them. He was afraid but could not stop the pull they had on him. As Phil approached them, he realized he was dreaming. He realized none of this was real. He was no longer afraid, and his fear disappeared.

He realized he could change the dream, so he switched it to a beautiful beach and started flying. The shadows had disappeared. He surrounded himself with all the colours of the rainbow like a bubble and flew over the beach at a thousand miles an hour. Phil had transcended the situation. The three shadows disappeared in the light. He woke up shortly after with the dream fresh in his mind.

It was still night, but he was encouraged and filled with vibrancy and power. The dream energized him. He found it a little odd that they could sleep and dream in Overworld. Everyone else was fast asleep. *Was this all a dream?* Phil continued to ponder as he fell back asleep.

The next morning dawned bright and glorious. It was sunny and mild, but in the distance, it was cloudy. The horizon in the distance was overcast. They were sensing today to be a day of challenges, a day of unknown troubles. What they had seen yesterday was only the tip of the iceberg. There was more. They were being led out of the forest area toward a desert. They all knew it would be much drier and hotter there, but they all sensed that they had to go. Something was calling them forward.

Spirit now was leading them. Tina was guiding them as well, but Spirit took the lead most of the time. They communicated often, discussing what they were sensing. Spirit was a natural scout. He had the keenest senses and could see far ahead. He would always be ahead watching and determining the best way to proceed. He worked well together with Tina.

Phil continued to practise his abilities and develop them. He was getting stronger. The fire ability was becoming a part of his being. Phil was powerful and could draw from everything and everyone around him and channel it out in the form of fire. It manifested in powerful bursts, streams, in the form of a heat ray, or by increasing his body temperature. He could also light his hands-on fire and touch stuff and light them on fire. He continued to develop this ability and master it. He could also draw energy from heat or light and use it to strengthen himself.

Phil could sense he had other abilities but didn't understand what they were or how they worked. He was still trying to grasp what changes were happening to him and the others in the circle. He had a feeling there was much more available in Overworld.

They continued to walk out to the edge of the forest and head toward the desert area. It was now getting cloudy and cooler. Fog rose around them from every direction. What odd weather for a place so close to a desert. It was hard to know what was unusual for this world because nothing seemed normal or typical. Spirit went ahead to make sure they were safely heading the way his senses were directing him to go. He came back and became Daniel.

"I am sensing another Circle, a powerful one with many members, not too far from us," he announced.

"I sense it too," Tina advised. "I'm not sure what their intentions are. They can't be good, though, since they haven't tried to communicate with us. They were hiding themselves from us until now. They used some type of cloaking ability to hide, but now they are too close to hide."

Their guard was up, and they all drew closer together. It was hard to see in the fog. It was getting thicker. They were close to a hill and walking on thick, green grass. The weather changed abruptly and quickly. They could barely see the desert ahead.

"I am sensing the other Circle is very close to us now. They are all around us," Daniel explained. "I can sense them in every direction."

"That's because we're surrounded," Tina responded. "Get ready, Phil. They are focusing on you."

Julie drew closer to Phil. She was afraid and came close. Phil tried to comfort her. Red was wrapped tightly around her arm. He was comforting her as well. Phil was watching, but it was getting more difficult to see ahead. The fog was thicker, and it looked like they were being purposely blocked and limited in their visibility. It was getting thicker and harder to navigate. They couldn't see the desert at all now.

No need to be afraid, Cobra, a voice inside Phil's head said suddenly. It caught him off guard. *Where did that voice come from?* It wasn't from Phil himself. He was sure of that. The rest of the Circle could feel the presence.

"Who are you?" Phil asked.

"I am Damien, and this is my Circle. I am all around you. Co-operate, and no one gets hurt. As you can see, I am much more advanced with my Circle than you are with yours. I wouldn't try to fight," the voice replied.

Tina's senses were confirmed as they were surrounded. Damien's Circle came forward. The fog cleared to reveal about two hundred members circled around them. There were men and women in this Circle of all ages. They were all under a spell, under Damien's control. They barely thought or moved unless he told them to. They had no will of their own. They were brainwashed and completely subservient to Damien. He made them mindless, and in turn, he channelled their individual abilities and used them as his own. This made him extremely powerful and dangerous. The strength of this circle was hard to measure. There were so many members with unique abilities joined together. Analyzing and understanding another Circle was easy. It was apparently an ability of the Circle, to read other Circles and understand them, but what they had learned about this Circle was not comforting. It was alarming that this power could be used this way.

Damien and his Circle closed in on Phil's circle. As Damien drew near, it was like a weighty presence had been placed on top of Phil, and it was heavy. His whole circle's ability to breathe had been altered: it was laboured and difficult. They had to fight it, but it was hard. It was hindering them from doing anything. It felt so heavy and burdensome. Phil had to respond.

"What do you want?" Phil asked with a stern voice. "Why are you surrounding us? We will defend ourselves by any means necessary. I am the guardian of this Circle. I will defend as I see fit and by any means necessary."

"I just want to talk," Damien answered calmly and cold.

Tina and Julie were worried about Damien's Circle and the people within it. They could sense what some of the members were feeling. Some felt used, some felt abandoned, and some felt they could not escape. Some wanted to be there and avoid any responsibility, but that was few of them. Many of them believed Damien was helping them, but it was a deception. It was not a good Circle to be a part of. They sensed a lot of deception and hate. All these feelings were taking its toll on this Circle. It was hurting this Circle more than anything else, not making it stronger. These members were being worn out little by little. Phil sensed that some members were trying to get out but could not escape. He also sensed that some members had escaped, and this Circle was hunting them down. They were in pursuit of several members who had escaped.

Phil's Circle, on the other hand, simultaneously realized they encouraged people and built them up and helped them walk in their gifts. This was their strength, the individual growth and development of each member of the Circle. Damien's Circle weighed its members down with pressure and guilt. They could never work the way Damien's Circle did.

"I am Damien, and my Circle is the most powerful here. I will give you the opportunity to join and fight with me. Some battles are coming that we cannot fight on our own. We can share abilities and work together. There are some that want to destroy the Circle, but we can work together to help it grow. We can protect it together. Do you understand?" Damien proclaimed.

His intentions seemed honourable, but Phil could tell Damien was lying. He didn't need any special abilities to know he was not telling the whole truth. He was cunning and trying to deceive them. He wanted something. His Circle was in trouble. Phil sensed that he had been given some power but had wasted it and now was paying the price of his irresponsibility. He had been powerful in the past but now strayed from the right course. He had lost some of his more powerful members and was searching for them. They had to get away from Him. His Circle was desperate.

He was right about one point, though. Some did want to destroy the Circle. *Who would want to do that?* Phil hadn't seen anything negative about the concept of a Circle until he encountered Damien. He was using it only for his own gain. Come to think of it, Phantom also represented the use of a Circle for selfish gain. He was trying to adopt all the roles himself without possessing all the qualities needed to be successful. He was taking others' abilities and using them for his own purposes.

Damien wanted something from their Circle. That much was clear. He really needed something they had that he was lacking. Because he oppressed most of his members, they never reached their full potential or realized their full abilities. Despite this handicap, he still chose to take over their abilities and use them for his own purposes. His Circle was a twisted version of what a Circle should be, a parasite Circle, not truly living or free. Truly *dead*. The members of their Circle were living in a state of limbo, and many of them were desperate to be freed from Damien's control.

"Sullivan sent us on a mission, and we have a job to do," Phil declared. "Do not interfere with our mission."

It wasn't completely the truth, but it wasn't far off. Phil was looking for a peaceful way to resolve this situation. *Would Damien take no for an answer?* Phil was sensing that he wasn't asking them but telling them. He was used to getting his way, even if he had to take what he wanted by force.

"Okay, Cobra," Damien replied with a sly grin. "We can do this the hard way or the easy way. Your Circle has some abilities I need. You have that fire ability, and I need it. Your girlfriend there has a healing ability that I can't do without. You are outmatched and outnumbered."

Damien looked at Julie, and the rest of his Circle also looked at her. Julie was getting uncomfortable, and the

Circle could tell she was worried. They all drew closer together, and Phil wanted to guard Julie. Damien's entire Circle closed in on Phil and his Circle. Julie and the others were frightened now.

Why would one of the most powerful Circles need Julie's ability? Was she really that powerful of a healer? It looked like Damien's Circle did need healing. Phil wondered what abilities this circle already had. It seemed to have many.

"I can't let you do that," Phil replied. "I am a guardian, and I will protect this Circle with my life."

Phil took ownership of his position in the Circle. The rest of his Circle looked at him with a sense of pride and adoration. He stepped up as a leader. Phil meant what he said and was ready to back it up. He was getting angry as well. Phil could feel those emotions rising, and it was making his abilities increase in strength and power. His Circle and Damien's Circle detected the sudden increase in Phil's power, and they drew back from him. His power had increased three-fold in that short amount of time. The situation was getting tense now. No one was backing down.

"This may just cost you your life," Damien responded. "I tried to reason with you. Have it your way. You'll wish you had listened to me."

Damien meant those words. There was no sign of bluffing in his voice. He teleported everyone else in Phil's Circle behind all his members. Now it was only Phil surrounded by the 200 members of his Circle. They all closed in on Phil and laid hands on him. With each person that touched him, Phil felt his strength fade. He was getting weaker and weaker. The members closest to him touched him, and the other members that could not reach him touched the members touching him directly, creating a chain intent on draining Phil's power. It was sapping his strength. He could barely move now with the weight of all 200 members pressed against him. Phil attempted to break free, but his strength was being drained too fast. He was weakening faster than his power had originally increased. Damien was getting inside his head. He was trying to steal away his fire ability and any other ability he found useful. He also wanted to get Julie's healing ability but wanted Phil's fire first. Once they had that, his Circle would be completely defenceless. Damien would become impossible to stop.

Damien was working hard to absorb Phil's fire ability. He used a technique like the one Phantom had tried on him earlier. Phil could resist him because it turned out he had a similar ability that had not been developed yet. He reflexively used it to block and resist Damien. His newly recognized ability to resist was enough to stop Damien from taking the fire. Phil could tell the ability he was using to resist was the same ability Damien had. He could take another's ability and use it against them. Damien was surprised Phil could resist him. No one had ever stopped him before from what Phil was sensing. He became incensed and tried even harder. Phil was quite adept with this ability. He didn't even know he had it until now. Phil couldn't hold him off forever, though. Damien was getting through, and Phil resisted. He was also doing a power drain which weakened Phil's resistance to his attack. This ability was draining Phil's strength and resolve while making Damien stronger. Phil was weakening fast.

During this connection, Phil gained intimate knowledge of Damien's Circle. A transfer of information in great detail. Damien also became familiar with Phil's Circle. This knowledge would pass between both Circles. This would take some time to digest as it was two hundred different people that they would now know extremely well. The Circles had exchanged the most intimate of details and knowledge.

Julie, Roxy, Jon, and Tina began pulling through the Circle members to get to Phil. Spirit would tear people out of this formation one by one. Red pulled and separate Damien's Circle members to get try to get to Phil, but there were so many members in the way. Phil could sense his Circle all fighting to get to him. Some members were harder to pull off than others. Jon could pull many members away without being affected by their influence. He freed Phil more than the rest of the Circle combined. It was not fast enough because Phil wouldn't be able to resist much longer. His strength was weakening too quickly. Damien was slowly breaking through, and Phil's Circle knew it. Phil thought Damien had already drained some of the fire ability away because he knew he had lost power of some sort. Damien was now winning this battle.

Tina touched one of Damien's members and was trying to guide Phil and strengthen him so he could break free. Phil had an idea or got the idea from Tina. He would increase his body temperature to the point where they would have to release him to avoid being burned. He concentrated and caused those who were in direct contact with him to let go due to the heat. The fire flowed right through him and burnt their hands, and they released their hold. Phil had to give up some level of his fire ability to get free, but he had no other choice. It was the only way to break free. Everyone fell back to the ground, and Phil was released. Tina, sensing that Phil was free, immediately teleported Him back, reuniting him with his Circle. They were all together again and had some room between themselves and Damien's Circle. Phil was with his Circle again. He was drained; he could barely stand for the moment. Tina was exhausted as well after using the teleport ability. Damien's Circle was also weakened in the exchange, but they recovered quickly. Much faster than Phil and his Circle did. The members of Damien's Circle that were torn away from the group were back and recovered.

Damien was recovered and got up. The rest of his Circle was back on their feet now and re-grouped. They were recovered and ready to attack. Damien did manage to absorb some of Phil's fire ability. Phil was still drained as well and needed more time to regain his composure. Phil was drained physically and mentally from fighting off Damien's entire Circle. He noticed Tina was still drained from teleporting them to safety. It took a lot out of her, and she needed help, even to stand up. The rest of the Circle helped Phil and Tina, and they were also making sure Julie was safe. They were defenceless. Damien was closing in.

Damien's Circle was preparing to attack again. Phil saw them posturing to strike, and he responded. He absorbed all the energy around him and channelled a heat ray at two of Damien's Circle members who were closest to him with full force. They put up a force field that protected them and the rest of Damien's Circle. Phil now got angry and increased his fire intensity to break through their shield. He hit them directly, and the heat vaporized them to nothing. The two members were gone, and Damien was enraged. With his anger and rage, he sent a white beam of energy from his body towards Julie, which completely caught her off guard. Before it could hit her, Tina pushed Julie out of the way and took the full intensity of the blast. She reacted without even thinking about it to protect Julie. Phil didn't know how she managed the strength to get in the way after being so drained. Tina went unconscious, her heart stopped beating, and she was motionless. The purpose of that attack was to stop her heart, and she was already weak. She was not breathing or showing any vital signs.

 Phil stepped forward to strike again, but Damien's Circle was backing off, and they disappeared. They used the teleport ability to get away. Phil and his Circle lost track of them. The fog and darkness subsided, and all was calm again. The Circle was more concerned about Tina's well being. Tina would have been the one to find Damien's Circle, but she was down and out. The cloudiness cleared, and Julie pushed everyone out of the way to get to Tina. She still wasn't breathing and was unconscious. Her heart was still not beating. The attack accomplished its purpose of stopping Tina's heart, but it had been meant for Julie. She held Tina close and hugged her tight. Julie began to glow, and the Circle could see energy emanating from her being. Tina began to breathe again, and her heart started beating again stronger than before. Her eyes slowly opened, and she was awake again but still drained. She took a deep breath and seemed okay. Red curled around Tina's arm to comfort her. She needed to rest and recover, so the Circle stayed put. They all needed to recover.

They were in a clearing of the forest close to the edge of the desert. The desert area was not far. They knew they were being drawn in that direction. They pondered if they should continue forward. They almost lost Tina. *Were they ready for this?* That question kept coming up. *What other battles lay ahead for them?*

This world was not so much fun anymore. Now they were all worried. *What had they got involved in?* They didn't sign up for this. They needed some clarity. It was early in the day, but with the day's events so far, they all decided to discuss what was happening before moving forward. The recent events were making them question everything now. Roxy came over to speak to Phil.

"You should have kept our force field up before Tina was hit," she said firmly.

"I wanted to stop Damien's Circle. I didn't realize they were going to go after Julie or anyone else besides myself. I thought I was the target," Phil responded.

Phil didn't realize he oversaw the force field. He barely knew how to control his own abilities. As guardian, Phil should have known that his priority was to protect the Circle members. To defend first. Not to attack. One of the Circle's members was in trouble, and Phil was more interested in revenge for Damien's Circle attacking him.

"I'm sorry. I should have protected Tina and Julie first."

"Yes, you should have," Roxy replied.

"Is Tina okay?" Phil asked.

"She's shaken up, but she'll be alright. She's tough, and Julie is more powerful than she seems. They chose to attack her over you. She is a powerful healer. I'm not sure why Damien chose to attack her, but she is fine too. If she was killed, we would have lost our healer."

"Good that she is okay," Phil replied.

Phil also thought about the two people he had killed. He didn't mean to hit Damien's Circle so hard and kill the two members. He wondered what the repercussions were of his actions on Earth.

"If someone dies here, is it for real?" Phil asked.

Roxy was unsure, but Tina came over after she heard Phil ask the question. She was clearly not at full strength and should have continued to rest. She knew what Phil was asking, and she had the answer.

"You try living without a spirit," Tina replied. "Everything here has implications in the natural realm. In many ways, this world is more real than our world, which is temporary when it comes down to it."

It just shed some light on their situation. It implied some serious implications. Judging on what had happened so far, Phil would never be the same again. None of them would ever be the same. Phil pondered Tina's words and wondered if they should continue. They all had many doubts.

Phil pulled Tina over and gave her a hug. He held her close. Julie came to them and joined in on the hug. Jon, Roxy, and Daniel also joined in, and they were all connected again. It seemed that every time they came together, they would get closer and stronger. All the doubts would disappear. Red completed the Circle by surrounding them and blanketing them in comfort and support. He was as much a part of this Circle now as anyone else. This made all their connections even more deep and powerful. They all knew they should keep going. They couldn't stop now.

"We will keep moving forward. Nothing can stop us," Roxy proclaimed. "I want to know why we are so important. I believe we must keep going."

"Agreed," Phil replied.

"Are we sure about this? We almost lost Tina, and I was the target," Julie replied.

After more discussion, they all agreed. They were connecting at a deeper level. This gave them more insight and wisdom. The battle with Damien and his Circle showed them that they had a reason to be here and that they were being opposed. It made them want to push forward harder. Something bigger than all of them was at stake. They tried to stay positive but were also concerned about what lay ahead. They didn't want to lose anyone in these battles. They were all a bit nervous and scared, so they proceeded with caution.

Phil noticed Jon getting stronger in his abilities. His strength was increasing. He was powerful. He was also quiet and preferred to stay in the background. He had all their respect, especially after how he helped set Phil free from Damien's Circle. He never said much but was always with them, and they knew how important he was. He had become a trusted and important part of the Circle. His contribution wasn't going unnoticed. Phil wouldn't have escaped the grip of Damien's Circle without him. It was a team effort to get free, and Jon was a bigger part than even he realized.

Daniel was getting faster. His quickness had increased than ever earlier in the day. He was adapting to his abilities and taking the lead more often in guiding the Circle. His increased senses of their surroundings made him an asset. He could become Spirit fast and was comfortable in both forms. Daniel seemed to be the most proficient of all of them with his abilities. He was already a master of his power and getting stronger all the time.

Phil was still pondering what had happened during the last attack. A couple abilities had come to the surface that Phil didn't know he had. The first was called the mindsonic ability. It was like mind control, and he had inadvertently used that skill to protect his mind twice now. It was also the reason he couldn't communicate telepathically with other members of the Circle. Every Circle they encountered had someone with this ability from what he was sensing. It also enabled him to hide things in his mind from other members of his Circle and other Circles. They would find that he wasn't as easy to read as other members of the Circle. They had to talk to Phil to know what was going on and what he was feeling. Roxy and Julie didn't like this fact, but they worked with it. He made sure he was as open as possible with them. He wanted to be connected with them. He tried to stay open and honest with them. Phil didn't want to hide anything. He wanted to master this ability but wasn't sure how to practise or improve it. Phil continued to ponder on how to use this power.

Phil had another ability that came to the surface when these attacks occurred. He had an absorption ability. He was able to draw other abilities out of them and use these abilities as his own. Phil could use this power against the person he drew it from although he didn't really know how to use it. Most Circles also had someone with this ability, and it was usually the guardian who would walk with this power. It would help him defend this Circle and all the members. He could take whatever he needed to accomplish his goal. Phil could use the attacker's ability against them to defend his Circle. He was beginning to understand how these abilities worked and how Circles worked. This ability was already on top of the Circle member's ability to draw from one another. Phil was starting to see how this power could go to go to his head. *Who would be able to stop him if he gathered all this power?* It was tempting but he chose not to go that route like Damien or Phantom did.

Red was more involved and moving closer to everyone in their Circle. *Could Phil absorb power from him and how much power would be available?* Phil was curious. He continued to test and play with his abilities to see where his limits were. Phil was also increasing in strength and power. He was more focused and confident. He was stepping further into what he understood was his calling. He was growing in understanding and revelation. The entire Circle was increasing, and it was awesome to see everyone walking in their gifts and strengths. Not like Damien's Circle, where it was more oppressive. Everyone in that Circle was held down or held back. Damien controlled them and their powers to do as he wished. Phil's Circle allowed people to become who they were meant to be one step at a time. They wanted to see everyone reach their full potential.

Tina had recovered enough to continue. Julie continued to heal her, and she was getting stronger. She was a fighter and wasn't scared or ready to quit. The rest of the circle made sure she rested enough. She wanted to keep going and there was no keeping her down.

Julie was still a little shaken up but wanted to move forward. She stayed closer to Phil from now on. He would guard her closely. Phil was more alert and keeping an eye on the entire Circle. Red continued to stay around Julie's arm most of the time. Red would move around with the rest of the Circle but was usually with her. He would comfort her more than anyone else, especially after these last few attacks. Julie needed extra comfort and protection as it shook her up to know she was the target of one of the attacks. It was still baffling the Circle why she would be a target, but they took extra precautions to ensure her safety. Damien seemed desperate to have a healer in his Circle, so they would have to be extra careful. Julie took comfort and appreciated all the Circle did to keep her safe. The Circle considered her the weakest member, so they would all watch out for her. She was rarely left by herself from then on.

12
THE RETURN OF SULLIVAN

As the Circle moved forward, they encountered an old man walking alone. He was covered in rags and old worn garments that barely covered him, but he was covered well enough to conceal his identity. He turned to them, and he looked like Sullivan. In fact, it was Sullivan.

"Sullivan?" Julie asked.

"Yes, it is I," Sullivan replied.

"I thought you never left Jump-Point Alpha," Phil pointed out.

"I don't. Well, I'll explain later. Keep pressing forward. Don't fear. You all will make it. Be strong and courageous. What are you afraid of? Don't be afraid," Sullivan advised with his usual charismatic tone. He spoke his usual encouraging words to all of them. He looked a bit frail here but spoke with enthusiasm and gave them some hope. They all hugged him and were glad to see him.

"Why are you here?" Phil asked.

"To help you guys," Sullivan assured them. "You all need me. You need my help."

"Yes, we do," Roxy replied.

Red would come to him and wrap around his arms.

"Hello old friend," said Sullivan to Red.

"I see you found Red. Keep pressing forward. Don't give up. Watch out for the destroyer. Don't let him deceive you. Walk in who you are. Don't be anything less. You will be amazed at what you can accomplish. You are dangerous to the enemy. Your power knows no limits."

These were powerful words he spoke once again. Phil couldn't even get them all in. There were too many words, and every word impacted them on a deeper level. They took in as much as they could. They did their best to believe what he said. They wanted to ask Sullivan so many questions.

"Well, I got to get going now. You know how it is," Sullivan said. "Here today, gone tomorrow. Busy, busy, busy."

They had no idea what he was talking about. He was cryptic. But his words were still enlightening and ignited something within them. They all loved to hear him speak.

"What do we do now? Phil asked. "We need help. We have more questions than before. We have encountered many enemies. Tina was almost killed. Some have targeted Julie."

Phil needed some answers. The direction they were being led didn't seem like the easiest way to go. They were all sensing more and more enemies, and the warnings they were getting from the ones they had encountered made them want to turn back.

"Trust yourself and trust each other. You have all the wisdom and knowledge you need. Prepare for more. Prepare to go deeper. You are ready. You are on the right track. Trust your gut feelings. You have many on your side. More than anyone you will ever face. Trust the one who brought you this far," Sullivan reassured.

With this last statement, he vanished in a mist and was gone. Phil had to take some time to ponder all the words he had spoken. Phil tried to make sense of what Sullivan spoke. What he did pick up he continued to ponder. Sullivan seemed to be right and who were they to doubt him. He had earned their trust. They all wished he could have stayed longer. They still had so many unanswered questions.

13

THE WILDERNESS

Daniel led them out of the forest to the desert area. The ground was rocky and sandy. The sun was bright overhead, and the sky was clear. They were not sure how they could navigate this type of terrain without supplies or water, but they continued to move forward.

Daniel became Spirit and continued to lead the Circle to the desert area. He was ahead of them, guiding them again. He was doing what he was meant to do in the circle, leading them forward. Tina was also up ahead while Julie, Roxy, Jon, and Phil followed closely behind.

As they moved forward, Spirit began to sense that something was off. Something was not right where they were going. They all had been walking on a level plain with sparse vegetation, and Spirit sensed they were walking into a trap. Tina also noticed the ground they walked on was not normal, but she couldn't put her finger on what it was. Phil's guard was up as well. He was sensing what the others were feeling and moved more cautiously. They all felt like they were in danger.

They continued the path they were on slowly. The ground did feel different. It was softer and felt more unstable. The ground would sink a little when they stepped, which caused them some concern. They felt a slight tremor, which startled them. They all stopped briefly, and Spirit became Daniel. The ground shook for a second or two then stopped.

"What was that?" Julie asked. She was worried now.

"Stop," Daniel shouted. "No one move."

Daniel became Spirit again to get a better sense of what lie ahead. All his instincts were telling him not to proceed. They all felt as though they should stop going forward because it seemed too dangerous.

"We're not alone. Someone is watching us, but I can't get a sense of where they are. They mean to attack us."

"I sense it too," Tina replied. "I can't pinpoint a location."

"Which way do we go then?" Roxy asked a little frantic.

It felt like the ground around them was about to give way. They moved slowly and carefully with each step, but the ground felt fragile. Every direction felt unsafe now. They felt another slight tremor. Julie was the most nervous of them all. She was scared, and Red stayed on her arm tightly to comfort her. They were unsure whether to move forward or go back, but they decided to continue forward slowly. Their guts were telling them to move forward, but every sign around them was telling them to go back.

Another tremor hit, but it was more intense and lasted a bit longer. They stopped moving again. Phil could only sense that the ground was getting weaker and more fragile, but he could sense nothing else. They weren't sure if forward was the right way, but they figured any direction they moved would be dangerous.

They felt a stronger tremor, and Red came off Julie's arm. He pushed them east, and they started to move in that direction. They started to run, but the ground started to give way. The ground all around them sank, and it became a pit that was almost eighty feet deep. They all fell right down into it, but they landed safely. Phil was the only member of their Circle who had been harmed in the fall.

"Aaaahh!" Phil screamed.

Phil had landed off balance because he put too much pressure on his ankle. It wasn't broken, but he sprained it because he had landed on it awkwardly. Phil was in pain, but he was okay. Jon came and helped him up while Julie began to heal his ankle. Red was in the air floating and came to them. Red surrounded them protecting the entire Circle.

"Phil, Are you ok?" Roxy asked.

"I think I twisted my ankle," Phil replied in some pain.

"How do we get out?" Julie asked.

"I'm not sure," Jon replied.

"Could Spirit scale this wall?" Tina asked.

"Not eighty feet up. It's got to be at least eighty feet," Daniel replied. "Maybe a human ladder?"

"This is going to be fun," Julie said. She had lightened up a little and tried to find some fun in the situation.

"I don't think we can make a human ladder that high," Phil replied. "Could Red help us out?"

Suddenly, Phil was attacked by another mindsonic, and his head pulsed with intense pain. Because he had experienced this attack before, he was sure someone was trying to penetrate his mind again. They wanted to steal fire or some other ability of his. Phil also knew once they had his ability they would go after Julie's healing. Phil refused to let that happen. It was like the attack Damien tried on Phil earlier.

Outside the pit, Phil could sense two people attacking him with their minds. Close, but hidden, he could tell their abilities were powerful. They were concealing their location and identities while attacking Phil, which trapped the Circle and made them more vulnerable. They could not locate the attackers.

"There are two behind these walls somewhere," Phil shouted.

"Where? Which side?" Daniel replied.

"I'm not sure," Phil replied in pain. "I can't tell. Whoever is doing this is concealing their location."

Julie came over to him to try to help. Everyone could feel a measure of the pain Phil was feeling because they were all so intricately connected that they could tell what he was feeling. Julie tried to comfort him with little success. Phil was getting an idea of where these attackers were.

"There," Phil cried.

Phil pointed to one of the walls that seemed to be weaker than the others while Jon and Daniel began digging into it. Jon punched the wall, and it began to crack. Daniel became Spirit, and he began to quickly dig into the cracked wall. It was chipping away. Tina was trying to figure out who was attacking but was having trouble locating whoever was behind this. Red and Roxy comforted Phil while he continued to fight off the attack as best he could. He could only get a sense of where they were.

It was two women attacking them: Scarlet and Violet. They were both mindsonics, and they were quite powerful. They were working together and were stronger than Damien and Phantom had been with this type of attack. This was the only thing Phil could sense because most of his energy was spent defending from this attack. Tina was getting a similar sense and attempting to help Phil locate them.

Phil was weakening and could not resist much longer. This was a stronger attack, and Phil was still a little weakened from the previous attacks. Jon and Spirit were not getting through fast enough. Julie decided to send Red through to stop the attack.

"Red, if you know where they are, stop them, please," Julie shouted.

This was the first time they used Red in a fighting situation. Red moved fast toward the spot where Jon and Spirit were digging. Red travelled right through the wall and made them aware of an underground passage on the other side. Violet and Scarlet were there attacking Phil's mind with their own mindsonic abilities. Violet was focused on Phil's mind and extracting the fire ability for her own use. Scarlet was confusing everyone so they would not be able to locate where Violet and her were and attacking from. With Red coming towards them, Scarlet turned her attention to Red but was unable to stop him. Scarlet tried to strike Red with an ability called *push* but missed him completely. It was a powerful ability, but she did not have the same focus and control that her sister had. Red surrounded her, and without hurting her, he knocked her unconscious. Violet, seeing what happened, turned to Red and hit him with an attack, mixing the push ability with fire, cutting Red to pieces. He was badly hurt, and Julie immediately screamed and collapsed because she was closely bonded to Red. Phil noticed Julie's reaction with surprise.

With Scarlet unconscious, Tina could locate where they were attacking from. Violet took her attention from Phil, and he immediately knew where they were exactly and absorbed some energy back. He sent a heat ray that hit Violet flush in the chest. Right through her heart. It killed her instantly, and she crumpled to the ground. Scarlet's body trembled when Violet was killed, and Red felt the vibration directly. Red was still on the ground from Violet's attack. They all felt it and found that odd. They had a connection of some kind to her.

Phil hit the spot in the wall where Jon and Spirit were digging with a heat ray and broke the wall wide open. They rushed in. Once Julie was recovered, she also rushed in to gather the pieces of Red together. She held the broken pieces of Red to her chest, and healing flowed out of her to restore Red completely. He was healed and back to normal in no time because Julie's healing power was strong, but Julie could do nothing to help Violet. She was dead, and Scarlet was unconscious but alive on the ground. Jon carried her out. They found the pathway where Violet and Scarlet hid that led back out to higher ground. Julie attempted to help heal Scarlet because they desperately needed her to answer some questions.

Phil's ankle was tender but better thanks to Julie's healing. Red was as good as new after Julie healed him. Her healing was a key ability for them, but she was still learning how to use it and getting stronger all the time.

Red became a blanket that they put Scarlet down on and wrapped her up in it. Julie had healed her, but Scarlet was still unconscious. Most of her physical injuries were healing fast. She was sleeping. She appeared to be in a coma, but they could not wake her. She looked peaceful and appeared to be dreaming. She looked like she was in a rem type sleep mode. They moved everyone to a more solid area of desert and rested there. Red provided more blankets and places to rest so they wouldn't get dirty. He also used the few sparse trees around and made some shelter in the form of a covering.

"She is connected to us," Tina explained. "She is a part of our Circle. She is strong. She will recover and become even stronger."

"How come Sullivan never spoke of her?" Phil asked.

"I'm not sure. Could she be the other he said was missing? It looks like there are many things he never told us," Tina responded.

"Could she have come to Overworld another way besides Jump-Point Alpha?" Roxy asked.

"I believe there are other ways to get to Overworld, so yes, she could have. We'll have to find out from her," Tina replied.

They let her rest and recover, knowing she might give them some answers about what was going on here. Phil could sense that her mindsonic ability was extremely strong. Stronger than his, but he didn't even know how to use or develop that ability. He could sense through Scarlet that her sister Violet managed to steal a level of fire ability from Phil to use against Red. That was how she was able the rip Red to pieces. She must have been well versed on how to use this ability because Phil has used it with no effect on Red before. Scarlet also had other abilities that were still growing but powerful. She had an abundance of skills and abilities from what they could sense in her. They sensed that she was much more powerful than anyone in their Circle. It appeared Scarlet and her sister shared their abilities, but it was hard to read her while she was still in a coma.

Scarlet wasn't quite as strong as her sister, but she was also less developed and less familiar with these abilities. She may have been deceived by her sister as well because she did attack them. It did appear that Violet had suppressed some of Scarlet's power. If she had known they were all part of the same Circle, she would have acted differently. None of them would ever attack each other. Not with what they knew about the circle. *What had happened to Scarlet that would cause her to attack?* They wondered if they had connected to Scarlet earlier, if this could have been prevented.

Phil was also a bit troubled that he had killed Violet. That was three people now that he had taken out. It could be argued that it was self-defence, but it was a hard pill to swallow. Phil took some time by himself to ponder this because he needed to make peace with himself. He needed to be sure his motives were pure and that he was clear. Phil needed to learn better control of his abilities because he didn't want to hurt anyone unless he had to.

"You okay?" Julie asked as she came and sat beside Phil. She leaned in close and put her arms around him.

"I'm fine," Phil replied quietly. "Just making sure my motives are right."

"They were," Julie responded. "You just need to be patient and use these gifts with wisdom and understanding. You also need to learn control."

"How will I explain this to Scarlet? I don't know how she will take this," Phil replied.

"She will understand. Besides, she attacked us. They set a trap for us, and you defended us. You did what you had to do. You do need to learn to control your abilities, especially when you get angry or scared. Your power increases, but you can lose focus and concentration. That will make any of your abilities hard to control," Julie explained.

"You are right," Phil replied. "Okay."

"We'll work together," Julie responded.

She was right. It didn't make sense. *Why would one of their members attack their own Circle?* They had so many more questions to discuss with this new member. They knew little about her, and when they touched her, they couldn't read her like they could read each other. It could have been because she was unconscious, though. They weren't sure. They needed to find out more about her, how she got to Overworld, and why she attacked them. She had some keys they needed that would be critical to the survival of their Circle. She could also give them further insight on Overworld, what was happening, and why they'd all ended up here.

Phil wondered why they couldn't sense her like they did with the other members of the Circle. *Was it because of Violet?* It appeared she could have been hiding Scarlet from their Circle. *Or did she choose to hide?* Why didn't she have a connection like Roxy, Julie, and Tina? With the power she appeared to possess, she could have easily found the Circle. It was odd that they couldn't find Scarlet on Earth either.

Roxy, Tina, and Julie kept a close eye on Scarlet. She was getting stronger and healthier. She was recovering fast. Red didn't hurt her too badly. Killing Violet was more traumatic to her. She was becoming more vibrant and alive but was still unconscious. She was still in a coma, but she appeared as though she was asleep. They were deciding if they should enter her dreams, like Julie did with Phil to get answers, and wake her. They were sure she was a part of their Circle, so they needed to know what she was doing in Overworld before encountering them. It wouldn't hurt her or them, but they didn't know her as well. This would be a good way to get to know her. There were some risks, but Julie wanted to try. They let her give it a try, but they warned her to be cautious.

Julie lay down close to her so that she could enter her dream. It would bring Scarlet into her dream and set up something calm that would cause her to relax. Once relaxed, Scarlet would be able to trust Julie more, allowing her to eventually exit this world and return to Overworld to come back to consciousness. It was the only plan they had at this point. They also thought she would have some valuable knowledge they could use.

Julie fell fast asleep. Phil did the same as they didn't know what to expect and didn't want to take any chances. When Phil fell asleep, Julie pulled him into the dream. This was possible because they were all part of the same Circle, at least the way they understood it. It was another benefit of having such a close connection. Scarlet was part of their Circle just by the fact that they could connect with her this way. They wouldn't be able to share dreams with her if she wasn't. The connection with her was strong. She was important, and she was a key to their role in Overworld.

14
DARK DREAM

Phil was suddenly in a desert, but it was dark, dry, and barren. It was like the spot where they had fallen asleep in Overworld, but there was a shroud of darkness around and against them. Julie found him. She drew Phil close and hugged him. They were having difficulty finding Scarlet because something was preventing them from finding her. It was powerful, but they had to free her. From what they could sense, she was hiding because she was afraid. Something was after her, and she didn't know how to deal with it. Scarlet ran and hid. She was good at hiding, and they were in unfamiliar territory. She wasn't as open as Phil was in the dream state, and the surroundings showed it. It appeared she didn't want to be found. They would have to navigate her unconscious to get her free. *But why was she hiding?* She must have known on some level that she was part of this circle.

There were hills and sparse vegetation. Phil could also see some small shrubs and trees, but it was almost too dark to see. There was a moon which shone some light that allowed them to see a bit further. Phil used his imagination and created a firefly-type creature that shone light and gave them more visibility. His idea worked perfectly. He could manifest it. Phil was being creative with his abilities, and Julie was impressed to see he had grown since the last dream they shared. The firefly flew ahead of them and lit the way. Phil created several of these things to help them see. Julie looked at Phil and smiled.

"You are learning," Julie advised.

"I'm getting the hang of this," Phil replied.

Phil knew he had some creative power here. He used it to help them find Scarlet. She was hiding, but there were enough clues to lead them to her. She could not conceal the fire ability from Phil, or she didn't want to. She was scared and didn't know what do. Julie could detect she was once a part of Damien's Circle. She was used because of her abilities and trapped. She wasn't treated well during that time and not much better by Violet. Those same abilities also helped her escape. She also was aware that Violet was dead, and she didn't know how to handle it, except only by hiding and burying it. If they let her do that, it would pull her and the whole Circle down. It appeared that she had never been separated from Violet until now and was having trouble dealing with the situation. She was isolating herself and felt completely alone.

They looked around, but it was still hard to find anything here. They knew that Scarlet was close, but she remained hidden. It may have been because of her various abilities, like the one she used to attack them with. She was good at hiding herself, but they could tell she was afraid and hurt.

Julie noticed there was a cave close by. They continued to look, and Phil could sense a fire. Scarlet had made a fire to keep warm right outside the cave. Fire and heat also comforted her and helped her relax. She found the heat relaxing and comforting as it was cold. Phil followed his senses to the cave. He relied on his instincts and could find the cave through the darkness. It was well hidden here despite the area being barren. He sensed the heat from the fire. The fire ability stolen from Phil was used to make this fire. These abilities worked in the dream like they did in Overworld. Scarlet must have known that creating a fire, even in a dream would lead them to her. Perhaps a part of her did want to get found. Phil found Julie and the cave.

"She is in there. She is scared," Julie advised.

"I agree. You go in first. I think she is still afraid of me," Phil replied.

"Okay but stay close to me."

"Okay."

Julie proceeded. She also pulled Red into the dream, and it worked. Red was here with them as well now. Red stayed with Phil since that might be too much of a shock for her. Red was the one who knocked her unconscious. Red was curled around Phil's arm and stayed hidden until needed.

Everything in this dream and area were signs of fear and hiding, signs of looking for comfort. All of them had to be careful not to make Scarlet shut down. She was hurting, and she needed their help. They had the sense that she would never wake up if they didn't intervene.

Julie proceeded, and Phil followed with Red tight on his arm. Red stayed hidden under his sleeve. They reached the opening of the cave, and there was a fire lit as they expected. That was the one Phil sensed. He could tell that it was created using the fire ability for sure now that he was so close to it. Phil didn't believe Scarlet had access to the fire ability before encountering him. If she had the fire ability before, he would have detected the exact location much sooner when they attacked. Phil wasn't completely sure what abilities were taken from him or what they were looking for when he was attacked. It was amazing how he could detect these things, even in a dream.

Julie froze for a second. She held Phil still too. "Don't move," she whispered. "Scarlet is watching us. Don't act threatening."

"When do I act threatening?" Phil asked.

"Quiet," she said back with a slight grin. "Where is Red?"

"On my arm," Phil responded. "Out of sight."

Phil rolled up his sleeve more, and Red was tightly fastened around his arm still. He could feel Red moving softly on his arm, assuring Phil of his presence.

Why are you trying to find me? Scarlet asked Julie telepathically.

Phil knew immediately that Julie was communicating telepathically by her reaction and the look on her face. He couldn't sense what she was saying but knew they were communicating, and that Scarlet was close.

We're here to help you. Don't be afraid, Julie replied telepathically.

Scarlet was outside the cave in the darkness, watching them. She was quiet and didn't make any noise. She was more cautious than guarded. She was still missing the presence of her sister. It was odd that they sensed she was in the cave, but she was outside the cave. *How did she do that?* Even in a dream, it was odd. They totally misread her location. It was an ability she was good at.

We need you to come back. We mean you no harm. We are wondering why you and your sister attacked us, Julie said telepathically.

We need your powers to fight Damien's Circle. To fight for the other Circles. There is a battle coming. Damien's Circle was after us until they encountered you, Scarlet explained telepathically to Phil and Julie at the same time.

Phil heard her words in his head, and it was a shock. It was a weird feeling. It was something he would have to get used to if he wanted to learn to communicate this way. Scarlet was particularly good at communicating this way.

Phil thought he saw her, but it was just a shadow. Scarlet was closer but still hidden. She was skilled at concealing herself. She made use of the dark well and appeared to control the light so that she could stay hidden. They stayed by the campfire, but it was slowly going out. Phil added wood and used his ability the make it burn again. Phil made it burn even brighter than before, and the new light made it easier to find Scarlet. She was still using the dark to conceal herself from the light of the flame.

Phil felt the flame. It was comforting and almost like a source of energy for him. He controlled the brightness and strength of the flame. He had more control over his powers in the dream than he did in Overworld. Phil could tell Scarlet had taken notice of how much power and control he had over fire. She was impressed and fascinated by his abilities.

"Let's talk about this and go back to Overworld. This is a dream. We will work together. Please come back. We will not force you, but we need you." Julie explained.

Scarlet could sense Julie's sincerity and came closer. Julie sat with Phil by the campfire. Scarlet came out from the darkness. She was like a little child although she was in her mid-twenties. She was quiet and shy. Phil could now sense how powerful she was. She had several abilities and powers. Her mindsonic ability was off the charts. *Why did she need anything from him?* She lightened up, and the area they were in became bright and sunny. The clouds and darkness were gone. Phil put the fire out. It was now like daytime in the dream—beautiful and clear.

Julie and Scarlet were establishing a strong connection. Julie altered the surroundings, and they were now at a beach. It was like the dream Julie and Phil shared before. Scarlet had control of the dream and the environment but let Julie take control and change it.

"The desert was getting too dry for me," Julie said.

"This is beautiful," Scarlet replied.

Scarlet was now much more open and comfortable. It was like Julie's love broke through her barriers. Scarlet was still reserved. They knew she would take time to open herself to them, but she was trying.

"Aren't you angry at me for attacking you both?" Scarlet asked.

"No, we're not," Julie replied. "It was a misunderstanding. You are part of our Circle. I'm sure of it. We're all not sure what is happening. There is a lot of confusion. We're glad no one else got hurt."

Phil wasn't completely in agreement with that. Her attack did hurt him, and he wasn't so eager to welcome her in yet. Phil wanted to know her a bit better. His defence was still on high alert. Phil wasn't as trusting or forgiving as Julie, but he did kill her sister and wanted to make amends.

"I am your healer, and Phil is your guardian. We know that you are a part of our Circle," Julie explained.

"Is that why I know everything about you guys? I knew your names and abilities before we even met. I know who Roxy, Daniel, Tina, and Jon are," Scarlet asked. "I know so many details about you guys. Too many to mention."

"Yes, you are right," Julie replied.

Scarlet was encouraged by this. She was developing a sense of belonging. She knew she needed to be healed from her sister and from Damien's Circle. Part of her was still a bit guarded, but she was much more open now. She was noticing their Circle was nothing like Damien's Circle, and it made her interested and curious. She has been oppressed by Damien and her sister, and now was free.

They relaxed in the beach setting and watched the waves splash on the shore, but they all knew they needed to get back to reality and what was at hand. They needed to know all that she knew. Scarlet appeared to be keeping her distance from Phil. Almost ignoring him. He leaned over to Julie.

"We should go back now," Phil whispered.

"We have to go back," Julie said to Scarlet.

"Okay. I will return with you both," Scarlet replied.

With that last thought, Phil woke up, and Julie woke up shortly after. They watched Scarlet as she woke from the dream they had shared.

15
SCARLET

Scarlet was wide awake now. She got up, came to Julie, and they embraced. Scarlet was a member of their Circle. She hugged everyone one by one and apologized for any trouble she caused. She was so humble and sincere. The rest of the Circle became aware of her past and knew much more about her. Julie knew the most and shared the knowledge after being connected to her in a dream.

"I am sorry for what I put our Circle through," Scarlet said remorsefully.

"You are forgiven," Roxy replied.

Touching her flooded them all with so much knowledge and understanding about what was happening that it would take them a while to fully grasp all of it. The connection with her was more intense. Scarlet understood a lot about what was happening in Overworld. She had so much insight that it was overwhelming. There was much more information on Damien's Circle, Violet, and other ways to get to Overworld besides Jump-Point Alpha. Scarlet's understanding would require her guidance to make use of it. She was overflowing with power and knowledge because she had been to Overworld several times. Scarlet and her sister had been part of Damien's Circle for a long time but were able to escape. Being part of that Circle was traumatic.

Scarlet wanted to see Red. He was still tucked away on Phil's arm. Red had gone to Phil's arm before she awoke. Red didn't want to startle her. Scarlet was aware of him now and a little afraid, but she understood that he was as much a part of this Circle as she was. She wanted to confront him. Others in the Circle thought it might be too soon, but Scarlet insisted.

"Can I see Red?" She asked.

"Are you sure you want to?" Phil asked Scarlet.

"Yes, I do," Scarlet replied.

Red came off Phil's arm and wrapped himself around her arm gently. Scarlet touched Red and got along with him quickly. She was no longer afraid. She embraced Red, like best friends. Phil still needed to talk with Scarlet about what happened to Violet but waited for the appropriate time. She had a right to know the truth.

Scarlet fit right into the Circle. She got along with everyone and was easy to connect with. Her abilities were like Tina's. In fact, they were the two most similar members. Phil thought it was odd to have them both, but he figured the Circle needed a lot of guidance. There were no hard feelings or ill will in the circle toward Scarlet. They all made her feel welcome and it helped her open up. She appeared to have no ill will either.

"We are being led to the east," Tina explained to Scarlet.

"You are going in the right direction. Keep going," Scarlet assured.

"Ok, we will," Roxy replied.

Scarlet looked at her and smiled.

"Where will that lead us?" Phil asked.

Scarlet looked at Phil with a puzzled look. She was surprised by his question.

"You don't know?" responded Scarlet. "We are going to see the Creator. The Maker of all things. He is the reason we all found each other. He is guiding us to Him. He is the source of all our power and the reason we're here."

"The Creator?" Phil replied. "Are we ready for this?"

"We'd better be," Scarlet replied. "There is a battle going on for control of the Circle. Everybody here wants control of it. We can win. We must win."

This was news to Phil, but it wasn't completely unexpected. They knew there was something at stake but not of this magnitude. "So, this will affect our lives back on Earth?" Phil asked.

"Of course," Scarlet replied. "Every action has a consequence. Everything that happens here will affect everything everywhere."

"What about the people I have killed in battle? How does that work here?" Phil was concerned.

"We all entered a battle, and there will be casualties. Who did you kill?" Scarlet asked.

Now, this was making Phil nervous because she didn't seem to know what had happened to Violet. *Was it the right time to tell her that he killed Violet to protect the Circle, or did she already know?*

"I killed two members of Damien's Circle. I'm not even sure who they were. They attacked us before we found you. You were once part of their Circle, right?" Phil was changing the subject. He didn't feel it was the right time.

"Yes, I was. But I needed to get out of there. It was killing me. That Circle was killing me. Violet helped me escape. She is my sister. Where is she? I don't sense her like before."

Phil was confused now. He thought she knew Violet was dead, but it appeared she didn't, even after they were all connected in the circle. Phil looked at Julie, and she shook her head, saying *no*. Roxy was nodding, encouraging them to tell her. She did need to know. Julie took Scarlet's hands.

"Violet is dead," Julie said as gently as she could.

"Dead?" Scarlet asked.

"Yes."

"How?" Scarlet said as her eyes teared up.

"It was an act of self-defence," Julie replied. "When you and she attacked us...."

"I hit her direct and hard with a heat ray," Phil said, cutting Julie off. "I didn't mean to kill her."

Scarlet turned away with tears in her eyes. She was hurt and couldn't contain the sadness she felt. Julie comforted her while Red wrapped himself around her arm as well. She used Red to wipe her tears away.

She needed some time to deal with what had happened. Tears came to Phil's eyes as well. It was a sad moment. Scarlet looked at Phil briefly with a sad look, and a little bit of anger. Phil didn't know what to do.

"I'm so sorry," Phil responded. "I didn't mean to."

She didn't speak, but she continued to cry. Tina and Roxy went over to her. Phil stayed back to give her space.

She was upset. It was clear she wasn't handling the news of her sister's death well.

Jon, Daniel, and Phil continued to stay away while Scarlet got the attention she needed. Jon and Daniel were concerned about Phil.

"You okay, Phil?" Daniel asked.

"I'm fine," Phil responded. "I think I need some time too."

"You did what you had to do in that situation," Jon assured.

Phil was silent now and didn't know what more to say. He needed to talk with Scarlet alone. Julie looked over at Phil with a straight face and knew what he was thinking. Scarlet felt the same way too. They needed to talk before they went any further. This issue would not go away by itself and they both knew that. With all of them so close, none of them could bury or hide these feelings. Scarlet must have known what Phil felt, them both being in the same Circle. Hopefully, she could see that he never meant to kill anyone.

Julie, Roxy, and Tina continued to minister to Scarlet. She was no longer crying and was ready to speak to Phil. It had to be done, but Phil felt like a failure as a guardian. His job was to protect, not to kill. They had to deal with this before they could move forward.

Scarlet came over to Phil, and everyone else moved aside to let them talk. It didn't really make sense because everyone else in the Circle could sense what they were feeling and saying. Out of all the members of the Circle, only Scarlet and Phil could hide things from the other members. Tina and Roxy had some of this ability, but Phil and Scarlet had most of this power. This was an ability of the mindsonic.

"I didn't mean to hurt her. I didn't mean to hurt anyone," Phil explained. "I'm still learning to control these abilities. The fire ability can be difficult to control. I never planned to kill anyone."

"I understand," Scarlet replied. "I believe you. I can read you, and you are telling the truth."

"So, you believe me?" Phil asked. Phil was shocked. He thought she would be angrier because of the way she looked at him earlier.

"Yes, I do," she replied.

The rest of the Circle were overjoyed. It was a relief. Tina thought Scarlet may not be telling the whole truth, but she seemed sincere. Julie was sure she was being truthful. Scarlet accepted Phil's apology, and they embraced. She was truly a powerful woman. Phil was relieved that they were all going to move forward together. They would all need some time to heal but were willing to press on.

Now that they were ready to move ahead, they needed more information on the situation at hand. *What was their next step?* Tina with Scarlet's help would figure this out. With both guiding them, they would be back on track in no time.

It was now in the late afternoon. It was still a bright day but what a day full of activity and challenges. Days in Overworld would pass by like days on Earth. Phil thought at times he would wake up and go back to normal life, but it never happened. They awoke to Overworld because it was the only reality they knew at that moment. Going back wasn't an option They all shared the fear that they might be trapped in Overworld together without any hope of getting back to Earth. Phil wondered how they could leave if they needed to.

Their Circle was closer than ever now after working through that major issue, and they had moved forward with a shared purpose. All eight of them huddled together, including Red. They were feeding off each other's energy and power. They were understanding the power of the Circle together. It gave them hope and strength. They all knew they needed each other. They were connected even deeper than they originally thought. Having Scarlet connected increased the Circle's power ten-fold. Damien's Circle must have been powerful when it had both Violet and Scarlet.

All their abilities were increasing exponentially. Scarlet was a catalyst to them because she was able to take them all deeper. She had a special gift that was being realized with all of them together. They also increased in understanding. Things became clearer. They also understood there were challenges ahead. They would need each other and would have to rely on each other at times. They all needed each other and knew it.

They were also developing a deep love and respect for each other. None of them were perfect. They accepted each other as is. Few secrets existed between any of them. Little, if anything was hidden. They were completely transparent and needed to be. They didn't want anything to hold them back or make them hide from each other.

They were headed to see the Creator. The maker of all things. The one who brought them here. There were many unanswered questions they all had, but they were patient. *There must be a reason and purpose for all of this,*

Phil thought. *But how do you prepare to meet with the Creator?* He continued to ponder these things.

"Why are we going to see the Creator?" Phil asked.

"It is a tournament," Scarlet replied. "We are fighting for control of the Circles. Control of it is up for grabs. Whoever controls the Circle can change it and use its power for good or for evil. They can also destroy it. They would be powerful."

Phil thought about how powerful someone would be who controlled the circles. It surprised everyone to know that a tournament would be used to determine who would get control.

"A tournament?" Phil asked.

"Yes. All battles are individual. One on one to the death. It's all or nothing."

This shocked everyone. This was the first time any of them had heard about this, and Scarlet was surprised they didn't know about this. Phil was also wondering why this was being decided by a tournament. *Was there not a better way?*

"I'm not sure I'm ready for this," Phil protested. "And to the death?"

"Well, you better be by tonight. We will reach the Creator by then. Most of the contestants won't think they are ready either. But time is no longer on our side. We had all the preparation we would get. The Circle is worth fighting for. There are some who want to destroy the Circle and all its power. We had to act now."

Phil was getting an idea of what he was capable of after the past few confrontations. He was getting better at using the fire ability and had grown more powerful and dangerous. A few enemies had tried to steal his abilities and failed but fighting in a tournament to kill or be killed was another level. He continued to practice with this ability.

These battles were to the death? Phil wondered if he or the rest of the circle was willing to risk their lives. Phil wasn't okay with killing more people. This concerned everyone and had them all thinking twice about what was happening and whether to proceed further.

Phil was noticing he had another ability involving absorbing power and using it. When he did it, it seemed to drain him until the power was fully absorbed then he would be stronger than before. It was taxing on him. He could absorb energy from around himself, but that took more time, and he felt weak when he sent out the pull for energy until that power returned to him. It was the absorb ability. It could be used as a power drain so that Phil could use the power outside of himself and not use up his own strength. It was a different but powerful ability. He was slowly learning to use it.

All members of the Circle continued to increase in strength and power. They were being prepared for something much bigger than themselves. It had to be the tournament. It had to be the upcoming battles, and they had to be ready. Phil was getting a sense of urgency and had to walk in his power. There was no other way he would be successful. They all had to work together because they knew they couldn't do this on their own. It would take all of them together and they knew it.

Phil's determination was increasing. It wasn't a time to draw back but to step forward. He didn't want to sit back and wait for more enemies to attack, but he wanted to take them out first. That was a better plan to him:

to be proactive. They were tired of always being on the defensive.

They now had a deeper understanding of how the Circle worked. There were abilities to move things with only their minds. They could also read and hear each other's thoughts, although some of them were better at this than others. They could also use each other's abilities to a certain extent. Daniel, Jon, and Phil had some martial arts experience, so others in the Circle knew it as well because of their connection. Julie and Roxy were focused, and that helped Phil focus and concentrate better. Jon's strength made the whole Circle stronger. Daniel's speed made everyone quicker. They couldn't share the fire ability unless they came in direct contact with Phil because some abilities required direct contact, like fire and healing, and some didn't, like concentration and focus.

Fire worked differently for some reason. It was harder to get access to fire and to share. Probably to prevent it from getting into the wrong hands or misuse. Fire was powerful and the most dangerous ability they had experienced so far. The other abilities they were able to share in the circle made them all stronger. It balanced them all and helped them work together.

The mindsonic ability could not be shared. Only Scarlet and Phil had this ability. Roxy had some abilities that were not completely clear, and they could not be shared either. The absorption ability Scarlet and Phil had could also not be shared. Scarlet had a level of the fire that she took from Phil. Violet and her used the absorption ability to gain, stealing the powers they needed at will. They were powerful and proficient with this absorption ability. They knew how to use it as they had used it several times. Most of this experience was with Damien's Circle as Damien used that ability quite often. He was one of the more powerful users of this skill.

    Scarlet was proficient with the fire ability she had taken. She taught Phil how to use fire more efficiently. Roxy began to wonder how Scarlet was picking this stuff up so fast and how she knew so much. She was developing and gaining power fast. She was comparable to Phil in power now. She also had similar power and ability to Tina. Her sister Violet must have been powerful too. Violet must have taught her a lot and well. Tina was learning from Scarlet as well. Having Scarlet in the Circle was increasing everyone in every way fast. *Possibly too fast?* It was hard to tell. They continued to follow her advice, but they were cautious. With a grain of salt so to speak. They had no reason to doubt her, but they still didn't know her as well as they knew everyone else. It was evident that she had been to Overworld before. Several times perhaps. She was familiar and comfortable here. She knew the ins and outs of Overworld with intimate detail. She understood all the Circles abilities well, including all the strengths and weaknesses. She knew about the Creator and the tournament. She also knew about the enemies they had faced and would be facing. She helped them and gave them a deeper understanding and insight. She had a vital understanding of their purpose and reason for being here.

    They took their time moving forward. They were all fascinated with Scarlet and her wisdom. They asked her questions about everything, and she answered with wisdom and deep understanding. She herself had grown and become more powerful even since she joined their Circle.

Her abilities were stifled by Damien's Circle, but now she could grow and flourish, and it was powerful to see.

    Julie and Scarlet were developing a close bond. They were close, although Julie was close to everybody, especially Phil. They had a deep connection. Julie was like the glue that kept the Circle together and helped everyone grow constantly. She was always around and open. Available to talk or just give a smile. She truly loved everybody. She always walked in love. She was always talking with the other members and making sure everyone was okay. She spent any extra time she could with Red and Phil.

16

PRESSING FORWARD

Phil was getting better at using his fire ability but needed more practice. He knew he could be more proficient with it. Julie and Red would help him. Scarlet would help and advise him to master it. Phil needed to control it more consistently, and the circle would assist him anyway they could.

"You will need to control your power if you are going to succeed," Julie advised. "You are not quick or accurate enough with fire yet."

Phil was sensing what everyone in the circle was thinking—that he needs to learn to control his power. They were concerned that he could hurt himself or others with this power. He agreed that he was having some trouble but hoped he wasn't sparking fear in the others. Julie had an idea.

"Try this," Julie explained. "Try to hit Red."

"Hit Red with my ability? With fire? Won't I hurt him?" Phil protested.

"You weren't able to hurt him before. He wants you to try. Don't go full out but just get your accuracy up to par."

"Okay," Phil replied with some hesitation. He was still a little gun shy.

Red was off in the distance floating through the air. An easy target, or so Phil thought. He sent a heat ray at Red. He moved quickly for an instant, and Phil missed.

"You'll have to do better than that," Julie advised.

Phil looked at Julie, and she smiled as usual. Phil looked back at Red, and he was moving slowly not too far away. Phil sent another heat ray towards him. A weaker faster blast, and it grazed Red, leaving a slight burn. Red healed himself instantly. He was moving a little faster now.

"Not bad," Tina said with some interest. She watched as Phil continued to practice his fire ability on Red.

She came closer to get a better look. Red decided to be more aggressive. He moved faster now and charged toward Phil in waves and twists through the air. This caught Phil off guard. He sent another heat ray at Red, not expecting him to come so fast. Red dodged it easily, and he moved around Phil's leg and tripped him. Other members of the Circle found it amusing, but Phil did not. Some members of the Circle laughed at him. Phil was annoyed by their reaction.

"That's not funny," Phil said to the whole group. He was embarrassed and a little angry.

Red went into the ground and out of sight. Phil looked around but could not see him. Now he was toying with Phil. This annoyed Phil more, while the rest of the Circle was finding this funny again. Red came out of the ground right under him and sent him falling onto his back. Phil landed awkwardly but was fine. Julie got a bit concerned that Red and Phil were taking this a bit too far but didn't interfere. Now Phil was getting angry. He could feel his body temperature rise. He could also feel the fire ability increase in himself. Red started to move a little faster and dodge and go by Phil and around him. Phil sent some medium power heat rays towards Red, and he moved fast and fluid and dodged them all. Phil sent a more powerful heat ray, and it hit him dead on and hurt him. Red was injured and went over to Julie, and she healed and comforted him. That last heat blast almost cut Red in half.

"Red, I'm sorry. I didn't mean to hit you that hard," Phil responded with concern.

Red came over to Phil after Julie healed him and wrapped himself around Phil's arm. He was trembling a little.

"You got to take it easy," Julie replied. "You could have hurt him."

"I got a bit angry and lost control for a second. He was asking for it, though," Phil responded.

Phil noticed his ability was stronger when he got angry but also harder to control. It also got more powerful when he was scared as with Damien's Circle and the battle with Violet. He had to keep this ability under control; otherwise, Phil could hurt or kill someone again. He didn't want to do that. Being part of a circle with focused people helped with his control, but he could still lose it. Phil knew he needed to be aware of his emotions as well as his power.

The fire ability seemed to revolve around Phil's emotions. His mood would dictate its power and strength. It would also be trickier to control at times depending on how emotional he was. Phil found this a little odd as he wasn't an overly emotional person. He did have a lot of anger buried on the inside, and it did affect the fire ability. He did know that when he was pushed too far, he could get angry and lose control, but that rarely happened. He always tried to make sure emotions didn't get the best of him.

They moved forward together as one. They were moving toward the Creator. They could sense He was waiting for them and expecting them. Phil wondered if any of them were ready for this. Probably not but they had to be now. The time for preparing was over. It felt like they had no preparation, but they had come too far now to stop.

17
FIRE

Scarlet and Tina began to sense a stronger presence coming toward them. The presence they sensed was more than likely an enemy, and they would encounter him soon. The entire Circle could feel the negative energy circling them and preparing to attack. They all were having feelings urging them to turn back or return to Earth, but they had to fight back these negative thoughts if they were to continue. Sullivan's warnings and encouragement echoed in all of their minds. With the enemy's presence getting stronger, they had to find a way to stand their ground.

Phil noticed his fire ability was growing, even more than before. He found this odd because he wasn't doing anything to increase it. The Circle could sense his power escalating. From what Phil could tell, his power had increased two-fold in an instant. He had not absorbed any surrounding power. He wasn't even thinking about it. It was intensifying at an astronomical rate. He never felt so powerful. It was a good feeling, but he wondered what the source of this power was. *Where was this power coming from?* Phil felt unbeatable. Nothing could stop him. Even with all the doubts and insecurity they were feeling, Phil's power continued to increase.

Scarlet noticed her power had gone up as well even though she had a low level of fire. She was nowhere near as strong as Phil, but she could feel the difference. The whole circle could feel the energy, but it caused more concern than anything else. No one knew what to make of this.

Whoever was closing in, he knew the fire ability at a high level. Even higher than Phil. They had not encountered an enemy that used the fire ability, but there was no mistake. This enemy was powerful, and Phil's fire ability was reacting to this new enemy. *But why would Phil's and Scarlet's power get stronger as this enemy approached?* Well, at least this enemy wouldn't try to steal his ability, *but then what did this enemy want from them?* This enemy must know the fire ability well to cause this reaction. The whole area was being affected by this being.

Phil didn't want to overestimate or underestimate this enemy. He wanted to use everything he learned up to this point to beat this opponent. They could tell this enemy's intention was not good. He remained vigilant.

Phil used his mindsonic abilities to see what he could sense or detect. He was still new at using this ability. He was expecting an enemy to get in his head or try to attack his mind, but nothing came. They could sense this enemy, but he was nowhere to be seen. They could not pinpoint him. It felt like he was right next to everyone in the Circle, but no one was there.

"You sense anything, Cobra?" Scarlet asked.

FIRE

The rest of the Circle looked at Scarlet and Phil with a little confusion. Scarlet was concerned.

"I don't sense anything," Phil replied. "Did you just call me Cobra?"

Scarlet looked confused and was surprised at Phil's response.

"That's your name. Well, the name your enemies know you as."

"Well, you don't have to call me that. You know my name is Phil. You are not my enemy."

"That's true," Scarlet replied. "I'll refer to you as Phil from now on."

Phil liked the name as it sounded dangerous and powerful. *Was he letting power go to his head?* Phil wanted to stay humble because he knew the power was not his own. Still, he liked the ring of that name.

"Tina is known to our enemies as Stinger," Scarlet proclaimed. "She is more dangerous than even she thinks. She is quite powerful. I'm a little surprised you don't know this."

"It seems there are many things we still don't know," Phil replied.

"Really?" Tina replied to Scarlet. "I certainly don't feel powerful. I feel like I am one of the weakest parts of the Circle."

"You are definitely not weak. On the contrary, you are stable and powerful. You have a solid foundation."

Scarlet was speaking with boldness and power. Even with an enemy bearing down on them now that was strong. This was a deeper authentic boldness they had not seen from anyone in their Circle. She encouraged and empowered them all. They all needed this. This was helping lift some of the doubt and fear they had with this new enemy bearing down on them.

"What does the enemy call you?" Phil asked Scarlet.

"They call me the avenger," she answered. "I always get even."

"The enemy won't want to mess with you," Daniel replied.

"Do I have a name known to the enemy?" Julie asked. She said that with her usual sweet tone. Everybody looked at her and at Scarlet.

"Yes, you will hug and love the enemy until they are sick of it and leave," Phil responded sarcastically and with a laugh.

"I don't find that funny at all," Julie replied. "I can be very dangerous."

She said that with an angry tone. Angry for her, which was only slightly peeved for the rest of them. Phil was like her in the same way. He never really got upset or emotional over things. She got emotional but never really upset. He hadn't seen her that way.

"Actually, you do," Scarlet replied.

Julie eyed Phil's reaction with a smile and a giggle. Phil smiled back at her. She was once again trying to lighten the mood. It was appreciated, but they were still concerned about what they were about to face. Julie was trying to cheer everyone up but was unable to hide her fear.

"You are the most powerful healer here in Overworld. You can heal any injury with little effort, and it won't drain you too much. You are also known as Serpentine. You are also deadlier than you think. That's why Damien's Circle went after you. You are also one of the hardest to kill. You are feared by the enemy. You have many more gifts that have yet to be realized. You are getting stronger and more skilled all the time," Scarlet proclaimed.

"Thank you, Scarlet," Julie replied. "I thought so."

Tears had welled up in her eyes. She gave Phil a look as she hugged Scarlet. Those words, much like Sullivan, ignited something in her. A spark and fire that would not easily be snuffed out. Phil knew she felt weak and that she might be a burden to the Circle because she needed to be protected most of the time, but she had a valuable ability. Her power could not be overestimated. Scarlet's words were a comfort to her.

"Jon, you are Megadeath. You are the power and the glory. You are the strength of this Circle. You are pure power. Many will live and die by your strength. You are a rear guard for Cobra and everyone else in the Circle," Scarlet proclaimed.

Jon was shocked and amazed by the words. It gave him hope and power to play his part. He thought his part was small, but it was important. He had already earned all their respect. Phil would never forget how Jon helped free him from Damien's Circle.

"Daniel, you are the Spirit. The Spirit is within you as you already know. You are a rear guard for Cobra. You are also the forerunner," Scarlet proclaimed.

Daniel agreed with everything she said. The words went to his heart like Sullivan's words in the past. Daniel was on a new level and increasing as well. He took these words to heart.

Roxy gave Phil a look for a different reason. They were still amazed at how powerful and advanced Scarlet's abilities were and how strong they were increasing. It worried them, but at the same time, they were glad she was on their side. She knew exactly what they were thinking as well. She kept that to herself. Phil could sense that she was aware of these thoughts, but he thought nothing of it. They had bigger challenges at hand. Scarlet was the youngest and yet was the most mature and skilled with what she possessed. The Circle continued to rely on her instincts and abilities. It was difficult to tell if they were relying on Scarlet's abilities too much. They continued to trust her insight and wisdom.

Scarlet and Phil had a unique connection unlike anyone in the Circle because of the mindsonic ability. Others could sense it in the Circle, but it was a powerful connection. Both she and Phil were aware of it. He wasn't sure how to use it or how it worked yet, but Phil knew this connection was there.

They all continued to keep their eyes open. Spirit was watching over them and making sure everyone was safe. He was keeping an eye out for anything that would threaten them. Tina was in control of their force field and kept it up. Jon and Phil were ready to fight. They were ready to do whatever it took.

Phil's abilities continued to grow in every way. His strength was again multiplying. He had never felt so powerful and so full of energy. No need to absorb any outside energy. All the power was coming from within him. It felt like a limitless source of energy flowing from within him. Phil's fire ability had doubled again in the last few minutes. It was clear to the Circle how powerful he was becoming. Scarlet continued to increase in power but not at the level Phil was increasing.

"The destroyer is closing in," Scarlet advised. "An enemy with a high level of fire. Higher than yours. He controls fire. He is extremely dangerous and powerful. Ready or not, we must face him. He is the creator of fire. He is fire itself."

Phil remembered that Sullivan spoke of this enemy. In his cryptic rant, he did mention something about this enemy and that they needed to be prepared. This was that enemy.

"Are you sure?" Phil asked. "That must be why my abilities are increasing so much. But why would I get stronger as he gets closer?"

"He is a higher-level fire user. You won't be able to use fire against him," Scarlet explained.

"I won't?" Phil asked.

"No. He designed the fire ability that way. A lower level member cannot attack a higher-level member." Scarlet responded with a serious tone. "It doesn't matter how powerful you go with fire, and it will increase the closer he gets or when any fire users come closer together. You still won't be able to hurt him with that ability."

This fact made everyone nervous. Phil and the Circle had relied on this ability to get this far. The whole Circle was concerned since their primary weapon would now be useless. *What would they do against this enemy?* They have never needed to defend against fire before. It was a scary new challenge. As powerful as Phil now was, there was nothing he could do against this enemy. He wondered what else he had to offer. Their Circle continued to worry about this foe.

They sensed the enemy getting closer, and they could feel the weight of his presence. His power and strength were almost without measure. It was that immense. They also saw the grass dry up and things around them began to smoke. Plants and trees that were once so vibrant were now dying. Life was being sucked away from them. The temperature all around them was increasing. The only reason their Circle could stand this heat was because Phil was a fire user and member of the Circle. Phil knew the fire ability without which they would have been too vulnerable to stand against this level of power. Phil could protect them and absorb enough of the heat to make it bearable for the rest of the Circle. Scarlet helped too with the fire ability she did have. She helped bear some of the weight, but it was getting harder and harder. Between the two of them, they could keep the others safe, *but for how long?*

Fire was approaching. Phil wondered what an enemy of this magnitude could want with their circle. Phil couldn't think of anything he would need from them. He didn't need fire. *Did he want Julie's healing power or even need it?*

They prepared to meet him head-on. Training and play time were over. This was a serious moment and an unpredictable situation. They were as ready as they could be. They chose to be on this journey, and there was no turning back now.

The whole environment was changing. This enemy was powerful. He was approaching, but they couldn't tell from where. He was already trying to absorb energy from them. They had to resist him but were not sure how to do that. The weight was heavy upon them, but they held their ground. Phil wondered why this enemy was absorbing energy from them. They had many questions. They did their best to resist. Phil was still getting stronger because of the heat and the presence of this powerful enemy, but it wouldn't be any good if he couldn't use his ability.

FIRE

The sky went bright and then dark again like a light was switching on and off. The temperature around them was continuing to increase, and they all knew they couldn't survive the rising heat much longer. Even Phil and Scarlet—the keepers of their Circle's fire abilities—were starting to get uncomfortable. This was the first time Phil was uncomfortable because of heat and fire.

Having Fire close in affected Phil physically. His eyes had a slightly reddish tinge now from the fire ability being fully activated within him along with his strength and power. He was also more on edge with this power arising. Phil kept it under control, but it was hard to keep it at bay. The power within him continued to increase.

Scarlet was affected physically as well by Fire's presence. Her strength and abilities were increasing. She also had a red tinge in her eyes, and her already red hair was redder. Her energy and strength were at new levels of power.

They didn't feel ready, but it wasn't about how they felt. A lot of things didn't feel quite right here in Overworld, but other things were meant to be. They knew that. There was a lot at stake.

Smoke appeared around them, dark and thick. The cloud was thicker than when they encountered Phantom. This smoke was choking them, making it hard to breathe. They had trouble seeing anything around them, like they had gone blind. Fire was now close, and the smoke was dark like charcoal. They couldn't tell where Fire was approaching from. Phil could sense him using the fire ability, but since he had control of fire, Phil didn't want to rely on it too much. He wondered if he should even use the fire ability at all facing an enemy like this. Phil considered all his abilities he could use. He considered all his options.

The smoke cleared, and Fire was among them. With a large frame, he was bigger and more muscular than Jon. He had long hair and a short rough brown beard. Covered in leather and spikes, his clothing gave him a rough appearance. He also wore dark sunglasses to conceal his eyes. There was something about his eyes he was keeping from them, and they couldn't get a glimpse through the dark glasses. They could tell his eyes were extremely bright and fiery—even under the sunglasses his eyes were different and hard to look directly at.

"I am fire," he announced. "I am the creator of fire. I am more powerful than you can imagine."

"What do you want?" Roxy asked, interrupting him abruptly.

She was not ready to listen to Fire's speech or agree with his statement. Fire looked at her with surprise and anger. Roxy cut right to the chase. She spoke with boldness and was direct. Fire was not amused, and the circle felt his displeasure in the form of heat.

"You better pray I don't destroy you for not showing proper respect," Fire replied to Roxy in disgust.

Roxy showed that she was a leader and refused to be pushed around by any more enemies. She had the same attitude the Circle felt as well. They were a bit tired of being attacked and were ready to go on the offence. To be less reactive and more proactive, regardless of how powerful this enemy was.

"I like your spirit," Fire replied. "I have a deal for you. We can join forces, and we will wipe out all the remaining competitors. The tournament the Creator is staging is a waste of time. With the power I can give you; you could destroy them all now. Otherwise, you will continue to be attacked, and you will eventually lose. Aren't you getting sick and tired of it? I can provide all the safety and comfort you will ever need. No enemy here can defeat me. I am unbeatable. I am god here. This world is mine. Remember, I can take your fire ability away, but I can also give you all the power you will ever need. I can increase your fire ability beyond anyone or anything here."

Phil wondered if what Fire said was true. He wasn't sure he believed Fire. He seemed powerful, but something wasn't right. Everything he said seemed to be lacking in truth and sincerity they were used to in their Circle. He clearly wasn't telling the whole story. Everything he spoke Phil took with a grain of salt. Something didn't add up, but Phil could not put his finger on it. Still, he paid close attention. Fire seemed to enjoy boasting and showing off his power.

"Thanks for the offer, but no thanks. We are fine right now, and we must be on our way," Phil replied with some boldness of his own. "I think we got everyone and everything we need. I want to meet with this Creator and find out what this is all about."

Fire nervously watched as Red moved from Phil to Julie, wrapping around their arms. Phil wondered if Red was who he was really after. Once he noticed that everyone was watching his reactions, Fire spoke in a much louder and harsher tone.

"I'm not giving you a choice," Fire replied angrily. "Make me part of your Circle, and no enemy will be able to stand against you. I have all the power, and I will give it to you to rule all of this."

Nothing that Fire said was making sense to Phil. If he was so powerful, he wouldn't need their Circle at all. Fire's deception became quite clear at that moment to many of the members of Phil's Circle. Once they observed what he was trying to do, they all suddenly became much more confident in their place in Overworld.

"No thanks. I think we are fine without you," Roxy replied.

They turned down his offer and started to move forward, but he was not happy with their decision. He was especially unhappy with their disrespecting him and not fearing him. He assumed they would take his offer, and their refusal made him angry. They could feel his presence and power increasing again. *What was he doing?* It looked like he was absorbing power to himself from everything all around him. They could feel the heat coming off him.

"Okay, have it your way," he responded.

18

THE DESTROYER

Fire removed his sunglasses, and his eyes were pure fire. Like the sun, nobody could look directly into his eyes for long. His body became like a flame but did not damage his clothes. He let out a flash of light, and it temporarily blinded Phil and the others in the Circle. Daniel got his bearings back and moved to the side and became Spirit. He moved faster than anyone thought possible. Fire focused on him, and Phil moved forward, sending a heat ray straight at him. A powerful shot that hit him directly, but it had no effect. The circle looked in disbelief when it seemed to make him stronger.

Jon moved close to hit him, and his punch knocked Fire back. Fire hit Jon in retaliation, and he fell and was burned. Spirit attacked him and bit him, but Fire burned him and forced him down. Tina increased the force field, and it struck Fire and pushed him back, but he suffered little damage. It did nothing more than knock him off balance and make him angrier. Phil got set to hit him with a stronger heat ray blast, but he remembered what

Scarlet had said about not being able to injure Fire with this ability. He decided to try one more time anyway.

Phil sent a heat ray and once again hit him directly in the chest, and it had no effect whatsoever. It didn't even singe his clothing. Even with the additional power Phil had gained, Fire didn't even budge. It once again only made him stronger and angrier. Fire had taken all their best shots and was still standing strong. Phil took a second to recover his energy, but Fire sent a heat ray toward him, stronger than any heat ray Phil had ever seen. This blast hit Phil right above his heart and came inches from killing him. Phil's clothing moved to protect him from the blast, but it got through their force field easily—through the protective clothing and through Phil. He was badly injured. Phil fell and screamed in agony. He couldn't move. He clutched his chest because he was in so much pain. Julie rushed to Phil when she saw what happened, but Fire cut her off. He grabbed her and surrounded himself and her in a fire circle. Fire surrounded Phil in a fire circle as well, and he could not escape. Phil was still hurting on the ground, and his wound was burning with no relief. He was trapped in this fire circle unable to escape. Jon and Spirit tried to penetrate the fire circle but could not and got badly burnt in the process. They were each trapped inside a fire circle with no way to escape and at Fire's mercy.

Phil could barely move, and his wound continued to burn. He could not get up. Fire could cause his injury to burn at will, paralyzing Phil with the pain. Julie was trapped with Fire and unable to reach Phil to heal him. Fire pushed her to the ground face first and held her. Julie screamed and was tearing up. Fire was too strong for her and for all of them. Julie had burns on her neck and arm from Fire. He pushed her harder to the ground, and she screamed louder. He burned her again. She could heal some of the burns but could not break free. She might not have survived if it wasn't for her high level of healing. He was burning her faster than she could heal. Phil wanted to help her, but he could not do anything.

Phil had never felt so helpless because he could barely move and couldn't help Julie. She was in so much pain and agony, listening to her screams without being able to help, tortured him. The whole Circle was immobilized. Phil was injured and trapped in one fire circle, Julie was trapped with Fire in another fire circle, and the rest of the Circle was trapped in a third fire circle. Tina was unable to use her teleport ability as the fire circle seemed to block it, so she couldn't get out of the fire circle she was trapped in or rescue anyone.

Red came out of nowhere and knocked Fire back. Fire got angrier and grew stronger in the process. Julie was freed by Red's bold move. Fire was surprised at how powerful Red was and backed away from him. Red went back to Julie and around her arm. She was okay but injured. It would take some time for her to heal of these wounds. Injuries from Fire appeared to be difficult to heal. Phil was still in pain and on the ground. Red left Julie and came to Phil and wrapped around his arm. Red's presence gave Phil some strength and comfort. Red prevented Fire from killing them all and was able to move in and out of the fire circles with ease. Julie was still trapped in the fire circle with Fire. Fire was gathering more power and preparing to attack. He was targeting Red.

Then, out of the blue, they all heard a voice. It came from the direction they were originally going. It was the voice of the Creator, and He was speaking to all of them. His voice sounded like many waters like it was coming from everywhere. Everyone stopped and listened.

"Enough," the Creator said with a voice that shook them to their core. "Fire. You are bound. You shall cease."

Fire's power diminished immediately. The fire circles were extinguished and disappeared. Julie, seeing this, got up and came to Phil as quick as she could with her injuries still healing. The rest of the Circle followed. Julie healed Phil as best she could. He was getting better, but he was still badly injured. It would take some time for him to recover.

"Why do you choose such weak vessels for your tasks?" Fire said to the Creator. "They are weak and useless without you protecting them. What do you hope to accomplish with them?"

Fire was angrier now. His anger was directed at the Creator as well as the Circle. His power was being limited, but he was still powerful. He wanted to attack again but would not challenge the Creator's authority.

All their doubts about the Creator existing were gone. There was no doubt now that there was a Creator and that he was watching. They wouldn't have survived without his intervention.

Out of the sky came a golden flame and it landed near them and became an angel. This angel shone brightly, much brighter than Fire, and he stepped back. The angel stood between Fire and the Circle. This angel provided them with protection and gave them a sense of safety and comfort. They were out of danger for the moment.

"I am Ariel," the angel announced to all.

Ariel was a tall angel with large wings that could envelope her completely. She looked female from what they could tell. She had many colours all over her but blue was the most predominant. She also glowed with the radiance of the sun at times. They could all feel her power, energy, and light. Red also began to glow and exhibit more power and light. Fire drew back and tried to shield himself from the light as it made him uncomfortable. As bright as his fire was, He hated the light and could not stand in it. The Circle wanted to draw near, and Ariel wanted them to come closer. They were in awe of Ariel, and her power made Fire seem weak in comparison.

"This far and no further," Ariel proclaimed to Fire. "Your time is short. Don't make it shorter. Don't make your end come sooner than it must. Blackest darkness is reserved for you."

Ariel stepped back and began to glow even brighter. Fire backed away even more from the light. Ariel was now like the sun, and the Circle had to cover their eyes. Her power was much greater than Fire's. He was weakening more, which made him even angrier.

"I am Ariel. These are the Creator's children. They shall not be touched. I am Ariel. I dwell in the presence of the Creator. I move and act at the Creator's command. I walk in the authority of the Creator. There will be no more conflict until the tournament ends. I will be watching. Break any of these rules and risk everlasting punishment. Don't make the little time you have any shorter."

Ariel spoke with a bold power they had never ever seen. She spoke with clarity and wisdom that was unmatched. No one dared defy her. Her power seemed to have no limits. She spoke once more in a voice that was almost as strong as the Creator's.

"I am Ariel. I am always in God's presence. Remember I will be watching with all the power and authority of the Creator himself. Pray that I don't reappear before the start of the tournament."

With that last proclamation, Ariel became a flame and flew up in a flash, disappearing into the sky. The Circle all gathered back together, and Red stopped glowing. Ariel was gone, but they would never forget the words Ariel spoke.

Julie continued to heal Phil, but she was not able to fully heal his injury. The mark above his heart would remain there for a long time, and it looked like it would never completely heal. It still caused Phil some pain, but he would have to deal with it.

"She is going to the Creator," Tina explained. "She is always in the Creator's presence."

"Ariel is one of the most powerful angels," Scarlet advised.

Their Circle re-grouped and re-focused. From what the Creator and what Ariel said they could not be touched by any enemy. Fire was not allowed to touch them. It was also a confirmation that the tournament was on, and there was no turning back. They were on the right track, and this would be their defining moment.

19
WALK WITH FIRE

Fire stood up and regained his composure. He looked so weak compared to Ariel. He was not happy and seemed to be drained of some of his power. He was still a dangerous enemy, and they did not want to take him lightly, no matter how he appeared to them. He was still much more powerful than their Circle, even in his weakened state. He had made physical contact with Julie, so she had some insight into his intentions. That was an ability of the Circle—reading the minds of those they encountered.

"He just wants to kill all of us," Julie advised. "He wants to destroy the Circle. He wants to destroy the Creator and this world. His power over us is being limited by the Creator, but we still must be vigilant. Fire hates the Creator with a terrible passion. I mean really hates him. I have never felt this much hate. All he wants to do is steal, kill, and destroy. He is the destroyer. That's all he knows. He is also the deceiver. He wants to trick us and lead us down the wrong path. Don't believe anything he says."

They all huddled together, and everything Julie sensed about Fire was transferred to all of them. The enemy's intentions were much clearer now. They were preparing to venture forward to where they believed the tournament would take place. Fire was still there with them, and he followed them, taunting them all the way. He was determined to use and deceive them. They could not get rid of him.

"You think because your healer touched me you now know all my plans?" Fire announced, singling out Julie. "You think it is all that simple? You know nothing. You only know what I let you know."

"That's a lie," Julie replied telepathically to the rest of the Circle.

She looked at Phil and shook her head and he knew immediately what she meant. Fire was good at lying, but they were getting wiser to his scheme. If he was able to deceive Julie that easily, it would be hard for their Circle to go up against him and understand his intentions. Julie seemed sure about what she sensed, and no one believed that Fire deceived her.

"Never been wrong yet," Tina replied. "The power of the Circle and the Creator has brought us this far. We trust it more than you. You looked very weak when that angel came."

This made Fire angry at them yet again. His slightly friendly tone was gone and replaced by bitterness and hatred. His madness and aggression were tangible again to the Circle. It made the Circle give themselves more space between them and Fire.

"Before all this is over, we'll see who you really trust," Fire declared. "The Circle isn't as powerful as it seems.

There is power unimaginable available to me. There are much more powerful abilities and beings than the Creator. He is weak. You haven't seen true power yet. I will show you what true power feels like."

Fire mocked them with laughter. If he were right about the Creator, He wouldn't have been so interested in their Circle. The Circle was their major source of strength. It connected them to each other and gave them all strength and power beyond what they had individually. He was still trying to deceive them. If Fire had as much power as he wanted them to believe, he would have proven it with force instead of taunting them. He walked along beside Phil. He continued to taunt and cast doubt.

"Why are you afraid of the Circle then?" Phil asked. "Why do you want to destroy it? You wanted to join our Circle earlier. Do you even know what you are doing? You sound confused."

Phil wanted to annoy him, so he was being sarcastic and condescending on purpose. Phil wanted to kill him for the attack on Julie and himself and the injuries to the other Circle members. Phil's chest was still hurting every time he took a breath or touched his wound. It continued to bother him. Phil wanted revenge for all he had done, and he was filled with hate for Fire. He was getting angrier, and Fire turned to him.

"You think I want to destroy everything. I want to make things right here. Aren't you the one who killed three members of the other Circles? You tell me who the destroyer is here? And your Creator allowed you to do it. He brought you here and allowed you to have the power I gave you, knowing you would do this. And you trust him still?"

Fire knew a lot about what Phil had done. He was right from a certain point of view because Phil did kill those people. He felt like there was no other way to defend his Circle at the time. Phil wanted to avoid confrontation, but he didn't mean to kill them. It wasn't on purpose, and he never intended to hurt or kill anyone. Phil was confident it was self-defence, but he had no answer for this accusation. Phil had no defence or argument that could justify what he had done.

"It was self-defence," Phil replied. "We were attacked. I would never kill anyone."

Fire was getting on Phil's nerves now, and Phil was getting angry. Fire was good at making accusations. The rest of his Circle listened on as Phil was getting more defensive. He could feel the fire ability rising again as he got angry. Fire knew how to push his buttons. Phil thought he'd already worked through his guilt by making amends with Scarlet for her sister's death, but Fire was getting under his skin and causing Phil to doubt himself again. Fire was skilled at causing dissension.

"Evidence would suggest otherwise," Fire responded. "Judging by your reaction, you are guilty. You won't last long here without my help. Your enemies will play on that. They will look for any weakness and strike quickly and accurately. I can increase your Fire ability so high that no enemy can overpower you. You would then control the Circle. Isn't that what you want? I'm only offering an easy way out. A guaranteed win. With my power, you cannot lose. Imagine all the power you would have. How many enemies have tried to steal the fire ability from you? No enemy would be able to stand against you. You would never lose ever again. Isn't this what you want? Aren't you sick of being attacked without any help from your precious Creator?"

Fire said all this with a smile. Phil would be lying to himself if he didn't admit Fire's offer was tempting, but he had no way of gauging his sincerity. The rest of the Circle was silent. Red came and curled around Phil's arm. *Wouldn't it be wise to take his offer?* Phil was already injured going into this, and he had no idea what to expect. He wasn't a hundred percent. All the enemies they faced so far were tough, and as a Circle, they had trouble with all of them. It was Phil's fire ability that chased many of them away. Phil would have to rely on this ability heavily no matter what. The increased power of this ability with Fire close was intoxicating and Phil's fear did subside with this much power available.

From Phil's limited understanding of what the tournament would be like, it was a one on one battle to the death. The designated weaker opponent would get the option of setting the environment where the battle would take place. Scarlet enlightened Phil and the rest of the Circle on details of the tournament. It made Phil nervous. He wasn't completely healthy either after the short battle with Fire. His wound was healing, but it needed time. Fire had increased Phil's abilities merely to give him a taste of the power he possessed. Phil was even more powerful now with the fire ability. He also put Phil in his place by demonstrating that even with increases to his fire ability he still couldn't injure Fire. He was still in control. Phil couldn't even harm him slightly. Roxy stepped in.

"Phil doesn't have to justify himself to you," she explained. "He did what he had to do, and it was in self-defence. We all stand behind him completely and trust him. We don't need you or any of your power. We don't trust you."

Roxy was right, but Phil did like his power. He did like how powerful he could be with that much fire ability in his possession. It was like a drug to him. It felt better than the constant pain in Phil's chest, which was inflicted by that same fire ability. Phil now knew what it was like to be attacked with this ability, and it made him see why it was one of the most feared weapons. It was also a difficult and slow process to heal injuries inflicted with this ability, even for Julie, one of the most powerful healers. The energy and rush were inviting, but Phil couldn't accept it. Something wasn't right with his offer. Fire was giving Phil more power even though he refused. Phil started to doubt their ability to compete in the Creator's tournament. He wasn't sure whether they stood a chance against Fire or any other enemies they might have to challenge.

"Suit yourself," Fire replied. "You are welcome to try this on your own strength then. You won't get help from anyone else. You will not be enough yourself against the coming battles you must face. It could cost you your life. I wouldn't depend on the Creator either. You can see already how well that's going. He has once again abandoned you. You are alone and helpless again. There is no one else who can help you now but me. "

Red tightened himself around Phil's arm, and Phil looked down at him. The rest of the Circle looked at Roxy and Phil. *Did they make the right decision?* In their hearts, they had peace, but looking at the circumstances, nothing looked good. Phil's confidence was slipping away. He had no answers to Fire's accusations and insults. It was obvious arguing with him would go nowhere and only waste their time and energy. That was probably what he wanted so they would see him as their only option. Relying on him more gave him more control over them, and they were not prepared to lose control over their own destinies.

The rest of the Circle was indifferent. Julie was worried. Scarlet was scared silent, but she was full of information they would need to win this tournament. Jon was ready for a second round with Fire even though he had some burns and scratches from the last altercation. Daniel was burned as well but always up for the challenge. He had a never give up attitude as well. They both wanted another piece of Fire. Roxy was trying to get them all to focus. Jon and Daniel turned their attention to the task at hand—the tournament. They continued to make their way to the area where they believed everything was taking place. All of them were ready to fight in this tournament despite having injuries and scratches in the fight with Fire. They made their way to the spot they were being guided to. Julie came over to Phil.

"We don't need Fire or his power," Julie exclaimed within earshot of Fire. "You are ready, and you are powerful. We all believe in you. I believe in you. I don't care what we face." She meant those words, and those words strengthened Phil.

Fire turned and looked at Julie with an evil look. She was getting on his nerves, but deep-down Phil could tell that she was worried and a little unsure. Julie tried to heal Phil's injury but could not. She knew Phil was strong, but it was a deep wound, and he was still in pain. She held Phil close, and he could feel her trembling. Julie held him close every chance she got. She also healed Daniel and Jon, but using her ability was draining her. Roxy got her to stop and rest for a while. Julie agreed and took a little time to take a deep breath and calm down as best she could.

"Thank you, Julie," Phil replied. "Thanks for everything."

Phil was staying as positive as he could while Fire continued to watch on and gloat. He smiled every time he saw Phil wince in pain at his injury. Fire was enjoying every minute of it, but Phil was not. He was getting angrier every time he looked at Fire. Phil was upset but chose not to show it. Phil sensed his time was coming. He needed to be patient. He needed to focus on healing, resting, and recovering. Phil knew he had to be focused for what was ahead.

Off in the distance were some huge hills and mountains. There was also a roadway that had formed leading to a white mountain. At the base of the mountain was a castle that appeared larger than any other castle Phil had ever seen. It was made of white shining marble. It glimmered like diamonds and reflected the sun, which was much brighter than it had ever been. The castle had many towers and a dome-shaped structure in the middle. Phil could also see different colours and light radiating from this beautiful city. There were gold and other precious stones at the base and throughout the castle. There were gates and statues all around the castle, and the white mountain went so high it was out of view. They couldn't see the peak as the clouds covered it completely.

"The Creator is there," Scarlet advised. "He is expecting all of us."

"He is weak, and his time is running out," Fire mocked. "You just watch. You'll wish you had sided with me. This won't end well for you."

Red was floating freely with excitement. They could tell by the way he was moving that he was ready for the journey ahead of them. Red would pull Julie and the rest of them along toward the castle. It was as if the castle was moving towards them. It was odd because the castle seemed to appear in front of them out of the blue. Phil figured the castle decided to reveal itself to them because they were ready for the tournament. That's the sense they were getting—that they were meant to be here. Currently, in this situation, at this moment, for such a time as this, it was all planned, and they were a part of it. It felt reassuring to be guided and watched over ever since Ariel saved them, and the Creator spoke to them. They all felt special and like guests of honour. They also sensed that Fire was unwelcome, which made them realize they made the right choice by rejecting his offer.

Red led them through the entrance. They saw other angels. The angels saw Red and bowed with respect. They pointed the Circle to a larger room. The angels also saw Fire, stopped what they were doing and watched with curiosity and a serious gaze. Everyone they passed stopped and looked at them with smiles but then looked at Fire with some concern. Everyone in the Circle felt welcome here, but Fire was not.

"What are you looking at?" Fire shouted to one of the angels there. The angel glanced back at him and then went about what he was doing.

The angels did not respond to Fire but kept watching him. The angels saw the Circle and smiled. They also acknowledged Red and bowed. He was well respected by everyone there. Red would move between Julie and Phil most of the time. He was guiding the Circle as well as wanting them to hurry up. He was also shining brighter and glowing here.

They entered a large hallway leading to a banquet hall. The floor was made of pure gold, and there were precious stones in the walls and ceiling. There were also statues and pictures all along the hallway, and the ceilings were high. The whole hallway seemed to be lit, but there were no lights. Everything had a glow and was well lit with no shadows. Everything felt pure and bright. The designs on the walls were of the highest quality and workmanship. They continued toward the banquet hall.

They entered the banquet hall. This was the largest and most beautiful banquet hall of the ones they had seen. The hallway seemed plain and boring compared to this hall. This room had more gold on the floor and walls. There was luxurious, red carpet on the floor that made them feel like celebrities when they walked on it. Tables had wood and gold in amazing detail and quality. There was also a marble-type material for some of the tables and pillars. The chandeliers were gold with glowing gems and stones. This room alone would be worth billions if it were possible to put a value on it. They stood in awe of the room and just took it all in for several minutes. It glowed brighter than the hallway. They were also amazed by the different beings in the room. There were all sorts of creatures and angels.

When they entered, all the activity in the room ceased. Everyone stopped and stared at them. All the attention was directed at them, and they weren't sure why. Tina and Scarlet believed it was because of the abilities Phil possessed. It may have been because Fire entered with them. He was unusually quiet but no less intimidating. They all feared Fire and his abilities. They must have been wondering why the circle was with Fire. Maybe they thought their Circle joined forces with him. Everyone continued to stare, but the Circle thought nothing of it.

They also sensed that their Circle was looked down on a bit because they had more women than men in the Circle. They also had a female leader, Roxy, as leader of their Circle. No other Circle had a female leader. None of them were concerned with this fact. It didn't seem to bother Roxy or the other women in their Circle.

Scarlet guided them and showed them where to go. She recognized most of the people and creatures in the room. She had amazing insight that benefitted them immensely. None of the other members even knew there would be creatures that were not human here. It was a shock. Scarlet gave them as much detail as she could. The level of knowledge and wisdom she had was off the charts.

20
THE OTHERS

There were several beings in the banquet hall. Most appeared to be here for the tournament.

Blue

There was a creature much like Red. He was several shades of blue and black mixed. He moved like water through the air. He was thicker and wider than Red. Scarlet called him a liquid hydra. He controlled water in all forms. His name was Blue. He began to move more aggressively when they entered the room. Phil kept his eye on this creature. Red stayed close to them and guarded them. Blue kept his distance but was aware of their circle.

The Venom Carrier

There was another creature that looked like half man, half lizard. His skin was half red and half black. The two colors were constantly moving and fighting each other. There was some type of internal battle going on in this creature. Phil was sensing this creature had multiple personalities and abilities he didn't want to face. They kept their distance from this creature. His name was Venom. He had many with him, following him and sticking close with him. He was never alone. A better name was Venom Carrier as Venom was a liquid inside this creature, trying to take and keep control of it. This liquid had a black form and a red form in constant opposition.

Chameleon

There was another creature like Red and Blue. He was coloured green, yellow, and black. He moved a bit faster than Red. He also moved differently when Phil and his Circle entered the room. He was in constant motion and active. He would change colour and shape every so often. He never stayed in the same form too long. His name was Chameleon.

Vertigo

There was a half tiger half wolf type creature moving around and watching them. His fur was a brown and black striped colour. He was a strong teleporter. He never took his eyes off them once they entered the room. The Circle decided to keep an eye on him. He had some type of link to Venom as well as a few others. His name was Vertigo.

Layla with Shadow

There was a human female, and she was young. She looked younger than Scarlet. She seemed quiet and disconnected. They could also sense a power in her that was unequalled. Her name was Layla. Daniel sensed she was a morphasis user of some kind, and she could change into a strong creature, but there was something else there that was more power and filled with strength. He couldn't put his finger on exactly what it was. Rumours had circulated that she was connected to a creature called Shadow. In fact, they were one, but no one was sure what it meant. Scarlet knew little about Layla and Shadow. They also knew that she was also connected to the creature Venom. She watched the Circle as well with much interest.

Damien

Damien was there along with several members of his Circle. He saw them and was not happy. He never got the power and abilities he wanted from Phil. They were not sure of what level of fire he got from Phil, but it wasn't much. The tournament was a one on one style battle, and he wouldn't be as strong under those conditions. He kept his eye on Phil's Circle, and their Circle kept their eye on him. He was still a force and dangerous. Some of his circle was with him, but most were not there. No one was sure where they were. Rumors circulated that some, fled, hid, abandoned him, or he killed. No one was sure what to believe.

Jenna Ziatta

Another powerful female was there. She was part of Damien's Circle from what they could tell but she kept her distance. She had dirty blonde hair and was an athlete. Her eyes were a light brown hazel colour. Her name was Jenna Ziatta. She had an ability they couldn't recognize, but she was powerful. Jenna was watching Phil closely.

Julie noticed this and watched her closely. Julie didn't like the way Jenna looked at Phil and kept at odds with her.

Roy and Sabrina

There was an older man there. He was overweight and looked like a hunter or someone who spends all his time in the wilderness. He had the morphasis ability as well. His name was Roy. His ability made him change into a large alligator. He also had a girl with him. She was in her early twenties and a morphasis user. She could also become an alligator but not quite as large and much faster. Her name was Sabrina. They both watched Daniel closely. Daniel was watching them as well.

Phantom

Phantom was also there. He saw Phil and his Circle and continued to watch. He appeared to be watching Scarlet, but Phil couldn't be sure. Scarlet looked at him as well, but the Circle thought nothing of it. Phil was sensing that he would be a powerful opponent in this type of tournament. He fought a lot individually, even against other Circles, so they assumed he would do well. They noticed Phantom was interacting with Blue. They continued to watch. They were not sure what he was up to, but it couldn't be good.

Goliath

There was another fighter named Goliath. He looked like he lived in the forest full time. He was muscular and strong. He had shorts on that were torn up and looked like he had fought a large animal. Goliath used the morphasis ability as well, but no one was sure what he became. He was stronger than Jon from what Phil sensed, and he had other abilities up his sleeve. He was Native American and fast. He was also a loner and stayed away from everyone. Everyone stayed away from him as well.

Saphire

Another angel was talking closely with Fire. Her wings were dark grey and like blades in the way they moved, and there were six of them. She had a mark on her chin, her hair was a strawberry blonde, and she also wore a ring with a large red ruby in it. The red ruby was large and glowed between red, pink, and white. Scarlet sensed that ruby was part of a bigger crystal called the kaos crystal. It had some hidden power they did not know enough about, but it was powerful and dangerous. She watched at times and talked with Phantom and Fire. Her name was Saphire.

Dragon

There was another female with black hair. Her hair was dark, like Roxy's hair, and she looked a little like her. She might have been a morphasis user, but Daniel was finding her hard to read. Her powers were difficult to distinguish. She wore a purple dress with silver lines and markings. She kept to herself and seemed to be at odds with everyone. She was human but had some unknown power within her they didn't want to face. She also had a raven sitting on her shoulder. This raven had some special power as well. She went by the name Dragon. She wasn't allowed to participate in the tournament, and they wondered why. They kept their distance from her as well.

THE OTHERS

Aspen

Beside Dragon was another angel-looking creature that was silver and looked sort of like a robot. It looked intimidating. Its wings and body were silver, and it was larger than all of them. It made weird humming and machinery-like sounds, but it was alive and active. It was not allowed to participate in this tournament either. They weren't sure whose side it was on. It was analyzing everyone and scanning. They were surprised a robot machine type creature would be in Overworld, but there it was. Its name was Aspen.

Dead Wing

There was another angel-like creature with black wings. His wings were dark, and his skin had black fur that was like hair mixed with feathers. He also had some black metal parts on his body. Those pieces changed shape and re-formed as he needed. His name was Dead Wing.

Black

A small cat wandered around. This cat could change size to a large panther-type cat. His fur was a smoky greyish almost black colour. He was not friendly and wandered around Layla and Vertigo. His name was Black.

Spiral

A tiger looking animal wandered around the edges of the hall with strange patterns and markings that were constantly changing and glowing. It would change colour as well. This tiger was known as Spiral, but little else was known about him.

Blight

Another creature was off in the background and was made up of many smaller creatures that were a little like bats. It could form different shapes and creatures. Its name was Blight.

The Black Lion

Back in a corner, there was a lion looking type of creature that had black fur. This lion's eyes were a reddish-yellowish colour. It was larger than a normal lion and much more intimidating. It kept watch of them all. Scarlet wasn't sure of its name. It didn't move or eat but watched them all with determination and interest. It was another creature they kept their distance from.

Their Circle sat close together, and Red stayed on Phil's arm. There was every type of food imaginable. All the competitors were eating. They ate and kept their distance from the other combatants.

There were water and wine to drink. There were fruit and meats of all kinds to eat. A great selection and food for every taste. Phil couldn't think of anything that wasn't there. It was that extravagant. It was a feast in every sense of the word.

A few of the other Circles continued to watch Phil's Circle closely, and they were especially focused on Phil and Daniel. They seemed to find both Phil and Daniel intimidating. Phil found some of them intimidating, but he was a little surprised that there were few fire users. Fire was difficult to control. There were many other abilities, most of which Phil had never seen out there. He could sense a variety of abilities and powers that would challenge his own abilities. Phil was sure to not let anything get to his head because he needed to focus and be clear.

Ariel

There were several angels keeping guard and order in the hall. Ariel was the main one. She was the one that helped Phil's Circle. She was extremely powerful and was sent directly from the Creator for this task. No one dared fight against her. Even Fire didn't mess with her because of her authority. She had the respect of everyone there. All obeyed her without question.

Serenity

Another angel, Serenity, stood in the background. She also kept the order and peace. She had four large wings and was surrounded by a constant flame and fire. She was always glowing. Her power and speed were unmatched. No one dared challenge her authority either. She was where the Creator wanted her, and she also possessed the power of the Creator. Her power seemed almost limitless.

Silver Wing

There was a silver eagle-type creature flying around and landing on Ariel's shoulder. It looked robotic, metallic, and had glowing, blue eyes. The eagle's name was Silver Wing. He was metallic silver, which shone and glowed constantly. It watched everyone with much interest.

Elo

There was another leader among the angels. He was a man that looked human. He was extremely powerful but stayed in the background watching. He had some type of morphasis ability. Whatever his animal form was, it was extremely imposing. He commanded many angels, and they all showed him a huge amount of respect. He had brown hair and a beard. His name was Elo.

As the Circle sat down to eat, Phil drank some wine. Blue silently came over and froze his glass. Phil touched the wine glass, and his hand was partially frostbitten. He pulled back, and Blue arose. Phil stood up, knocking over his chair. Red uncurled from Phil's arm and stood between Blue and him. Red pushed Blue back. Blue tried to freeze Red, but the freeze had no effect. Red shook off the ice and cold. Julie touched Phil's arm and healed it as best she could. Phil used his fire ability to help heal his hand, and the heat helped it get better. This was a scare tactic being used by Blue. Phil had no doubt that Phantom had something to do with this intimidation move. He also noticed the other Circles and competitors were watching how Phil reacted to this move. He saw Phantom watching closely. Others watched at Phil's reaction. It seems they were trying to scare Phil. They were looking for weakness is what Phil sensed in this tactic. Fire watched with little or no interest. He wanted to challenge the winner of the tournament and take over. He was already sick of waiting.

Phil decided to pull a scare tactic of his own. He was tired of the enemy playing with him and showing him up. Fire had increased his fire ability, and he decided to use it. Phil got out of his seat, and he sent a heat ray near Phantom and sliced the table he sat at in half. He also struck the spot where Blue was, and he pulled back. He also destroyed a pedestal right beside Fire. All the competitors were intimidated by the power Phil displayed and took cover. His heat ray and fire ability cut through all those objects with ease. Phil was powerful, and it felt good to show it off. He could tell Fire was pleased because Fire watched him and smiled. Phil got everyone's attention.

Fire also laughed. He was not impressed, but he did like how Phil displayed the power he was given. He loved the fear the fire ability put in all the combatants, and Phil had accomplished what he wanted to do. The rest of his Circle wasn't impressed. Roxy thought Phil was showing off and drawing more unwanted attention. Julie gave a look of disappointment. Jon and Daniel loved it and wished they could do a similar tour de force. Tina and Scarlet watched with interest how others responded. Phantom wasn't fazed or impressed but was a little in awe of Phil's power. Blue didn't bother him anymore and backed off. The other combatants gave Phil more room and space and didn't watch him as closely. They were all thinking the same things Phil's Circle was. *What have they got themselves into?* The angels took charge and put a stop to all these little intimidation tactics and posturing.

"Enough all of you," Ariel proclaimed. "These tactics stop here." The whole room went silent once again. She looked at Phil sternly and smiled.

"Your time shall come, Cobra. Settle down. The matchups will be decided shortly by the Creator. No further conflict or you risk disqualification. Cobra, this is your last warning. Blue, this is your last warning." She meant what she said, and Phil didn't argue or challenge her statements. She was bold and powerful. Blue backed off and kept his distance. No one dared question or argue with her.

21
THE TOURNAMENT

This tournament was simple—one on one battles for complete control of the Circle. The fight was to the death, or a competitor could also lose if they left the tournament battle area or surrendered. The Creator would decide who gets to choose the location of the fight. Fire, Red, Saphire, Aspen, and Dragon could not take part in this tournament. Several others chose not to participate and backed out. Many left when they learned of these details choosing not to risk their lives. Some didn't think the Circle was worth all this.

"May the best combatant win," Ariel announced. She then spoke with more power. "I am Ariel. I was with the Creator from the beginning. I was there when the heavens and the Earth were created. I am Ariel. My judgment is absolute and final. Pay heed to my words. I am Ariel. The battle is for full complete control of the power of the Circle. Now, go prepare yourselves. Now is the time."

THE TOURNAMENT

The format of the tournament was easy enough to understand. Phil didn't have any questions, and neither did his Circle, except to know who his first opponent would be. He was expecting a battle either way.

Phil was prepared to battle. The time for talk was over. His injuries were still a concern but not enough to make him want to quit. With a new intensity and drive, he saw some of the fear he put into the competitor's hearts when he did a scare tactic with the fire ability. It made him realize that he wasn't the only one who was a little scared.

Phil was getting better at controlling his abilities. His practice, although limited, had paid off. Phil also felt powerful and was curious about what he could do against these opponents. He was feeling strong and wanted to stand up for himself, which was something he had not done too often in the past. Now was the time to act.

From his Circle, Jon, Daniel, and Phil would be fighting for control of the Circle. Roxy and Phil decided none of the female members of the Circle would take part in the battles, and they agreed. There was no point in taking unnecessary risk. Only Scarlet wanted to take part, but she did listen to Roxy and Phil and agreed not to pursue.

Phil understood finally the power of the Circle and how it brought them closer together. They would have never found each other without the Circle. They saw the value of the Circle, and Phil did not want the power falling into the wrong hands. He had to make sure it didn't, whatever it took. Phil wasn't sure why he felt so strongly about this, but he did. There was something here so powerful, and he didn't want it lost or destroyed.

Phil had felt the restorative power of the Circle and how it changed lives, including his. This was one of many benefits of the Circle. It was worth fighting for. The journey ahead would be one of the biggest challenges in Phil's life, and despite his doubts he was ready to proceed.

22
THE CREATOR

Phil wanted to meet the Creator, and he wanted to understand why things had to be done this way. *Why have battles to determine control of the Circle?* He wondered if there was a better way. Surely there must be a way that didn't involve killing each other. The person with the most bloodshed gets control of the Circle wasn't making sense to Phil. He needed a reason and justification for all this. He had to have some answers.

Phil left the rest of his Circle to go on a quest for the Creator. Julie thought he was going crazy. She and the rest of his Circle wanted Phil to prepare for his match. Not go on a quest, but Phil had to do this. He proceeded to find the Creator.

"Where are you going?" Julie asked.

"I need to talk to the Creator," Phil replied. "If He really knows everything and planned this whole mess then He should know that I need to have these answers before I risk my life for control of the Circle."

Phil was determined to find answers to all his questions. He didn't care what anyone thought. All this must be for a reason. There must be a rational explanation. *Was Phil missing something?* Phil was going to get answers and some understanding.

Red was back with Julie, and he came off her arm to lead Phil out of the banquet hall. Red led him down another hall even more glorious than the previous hall. The ceilings must have been over twenty feet high. All the halls had gold and a more luxurious form of marble. It was perfect and beautiful.

As Phil proceeded, he saw a room with blue marble walls and another high ceiling. The trim was gold that shone in the light that seemed to illuminate from everywhere. The floor was also marble. The room had what looked like a chessboard. There were several pieces, but it was not the typical pieces for chess. One piece was glowing red like it was on fire. That piece was cornered and outnumbered. That side was going to lose to the other pieces that were a glowing gold colour. Phil took a closer look at the board before moving on.

The hall led to a staircase that led up to a throne room. The Creator was in the throne room. This area of the castle glowed even more brightly than all the other areas. Every new place Phil was exposed to was more beautiful than the last. As Phil got closer to the throne room, he could tell the source of light for the entire castle was coming from the Creator himself. This light penetrated everything, and it shone so bright and beautiful without any shadows. Serenity was there, guarding the entrance to the throne room. There were other angels around as well, but she was the strongest and appeared to be a leader.

"You shouldn't be here, Cobra. You are not allowed to come any further," Serenity said. She spoke gently

THE CREATOR

but firmly. She then saw Red and turned to look up the staircase. She seemed unsure what to do next and was looking to the Creator for some guidance by the looks of it. Phil was sure he wasn't allowed to be there, but it was too late to turn back now. Red was also pushing him forward, but Phil hesitated and resisted Red's push. It was clear to Phil at that moment that he had gone a bit too far, but it was too late to go back. He wanted to go forward.

"Let him come. Phil. Come up here," a powerful voice announced from all around. It was the Creator. Phil had heard his voice before when he spoke during the altercation with Fire. His voice was unmistakable because he would never forget the sound of the Creator's voice. He wanted Phil to come forward, and Phil felt a bit nervous.

Serenity let Phil and Red by with a welcoming smile, and Red led Phil up the staircase to the throne room. Red waited for Phil and guided his every step. They entered the throne room area and saw how beautiful and elegant it truly was.

Now, Phil was getting nervous. He was allowed to enter the throne room of the one who created him, his enemies, Red, the Circles, the heavens, and the Earth. Phil had to ponder this for a moment. *Did the Creator want him here?* He allowed him to come. He also must have known Phil wanted to talk to Him directly. *He was supposed to know everything, right?*

The one who sat on the throne was glorious. He was surrounded by pure white light, but the light was coming from Him. He was the source of this powerful light. He appeared to Phil as a man, who looked like a king. An older man with brownish grey hair and a beard. Phil approached him along with Red by his side. Red was not shy or nervous and urged Phil closer. The Creator spoke.

"Welcome Phil," He said. He spoke with love and a tender tone. "You are always welcome here."

"I am?" Phil replied. "You see all my screw-ups. Aren't you mad at me?"

"Of course not," He answered. "I brought you here. I brought you all here. It was my doing."

"You did?" Phil asked.

"Yes, I did," He responded. "Is it so hard to believe?"

"No, I guess not," Phil answered, feeling silly and awkward. "Why must this tournament take place for control of the Circle? Is there not another way? I had hoped there might be another solution. This doesn't seem right to me. To fight over the Circle."

"There is no other way," the Creator replied. "If there was, I would use it. You are in a fight for the Circle, not just here, but in the Earth realm as well."

"I'm not exactly sure what I am fighting for?" Phil exclaimed. He wasn't clear what the Creator meant. *What did the Creator mean by fighting for the Earth realm and how would all this affect Earth?* The Creator smiled at what Phil thought was a dumb question, and he answered with wisdom and love.

"You are fighting for this ability to connect. This power to share abilities. To help each walk in their destinies and My calling for their lives. To know there is a greater purpose. To join as one and leave no one behind. The enemy wants to separate everyone, to steal, kill, and destroy. I had put the power of the Circle into one person's hands, but he abused it and used it for his own gain. Now it is being reclaimed, but it must be fought for. Are you willing to fight for this?"

Phil was starting to understand. It was slowly sinking in. The Circle was more powerful than all he had experienced so far. It had a power worth fighting for, and Phil had taken it for granted. To affect the lives and destinies of people here and on Earth. There was more going on here with a greater impact.

"I am willing," Phil answered. "I don't understand everything, but I am willing to trust you. If you are saying it is the only way, then so be it."

The Creator looked at Phil with a proud look and smiled. He was overjoyed. Red was overjoyed as well. The rest of Phil's Circle was getting a sense through him of what was happening. It was empowering them and getting them excited as well. It was challenging, but Phil was getting a feeling that he could overcome the challenge. That he needed to. That so much was at stake.

"I will never fail you," the Creator replied. "I am always with you. I will never leave you nor forsake you. It will not be easy, but you will overcome. The choices you now make will echo in eternity. Many will be affected here in Overworld and back in the Earth realm. Never forget that. Overworld is getting closer to Earth all the time. My kingdom is coming to the Earth realm."

"It is?" Phil asked. "Are we ready for this? I'm not sure I am."

"You will be. I will make sure of it. I complete everything I start," the Creator proclaimed. "I know the beginning from the end. Who can undo anything I have done? Whatever I say is done, and that's the end of it. Go and prepare yourself. You are ready, Phil. The Cobra will defeat all the enemies. Walk in the power you were given. Do what you were meant to do. Do what you were created for."

With that last remark, Phil looked at the Creator, and He nodded to Phil and smiled like a father who was pleased with his son. Serenity had entered the throne room and was guiding Phil back to where the rest of his Circle was. Red also pulled him along. Phil found everyone back in the banquet hall. There was a lot of fear in the air. Ariel also watched on and kept everyone in line. Phil looked for other combatants.

23

A BATTLE TO FIGHT

"Where is everybody?" Phil asked. He was surprised at how many had left before the tournament had started.

"I made them leave," Fire replied, approaching Phil out of nowhere. "I plan to challenge the winner. I want control of this pitiful Circle. I will wait until the tournament is over then kill the winner. I am patient. You should have joined me when you had the chance. Too bad. You would have made a good apprentice Cobra. You have some anger and hate I could use. I could have made you the most powerful, but now you will suffer and die just like everyone else will tonight. Good luck. You'll need it."

Phil was speechless. Several of the combatants had gone, leaving few to fight. He guessed they weren't willing to risk it all for the Circle. If the other combatants knew the value of the Circle, they would be willing to kill everyone to win. They needed to be strong enough to defeat Fire if they wanted to succeed. Phil and his circle were almost killed by Fire once already. Fighting in the tournament would be tough enough but facing Fire after all that would be much harder than competing in the tournament. If the Creator was aware of this, Phil thought He would have stopped Fire by now. Surely, the Creator was more powerful than Fire. This was a dire situation, and the whole Circle was having second thoughts. The Creator must have known all of this and yet he chose to do nothing.

"We have a room we can prepare in," Tina advised. "We will find out everyone's opponents soon enough. Round one will begin shortly. One of the angels will let us know once the matches have been set. We better hurry and get focused. Time is short."

"Yes, Stinger will prepare you for your battles," Fire scoffed. "But nothing can prepare you for me. You will eventually serve me. You will bow down. Pray that I have mercy on you. You could have joined me. Never forget the chance I gave you. You will regret it."

Fire was trying to scare the Circle, and it was working. That battle with Fire would be in the back of all their minds for the rest of the tournament. They had to focus and not let Fire distract them, but it was difficult. Fire referred to Tina as Stinger. It was her name to her enemies. It was her warrior name. She could have participated in the tournament but opted not to and preferred to help Jon, Daniel, and Phil get ready. Scarlet could also have taken part but chose to advise the men of the Circle. She especially wanted to help Phil because he needed all the help he could get if he wanted to be successful. She had intimate knowledge of several of his abilities.

They went down another hallway that led to rooms where they could talk in private and prepare. It was almost time. Tina was finding out who would face who. The rest of them were stretching and loosening up. They had no idea how to prepare or what to expect. Roxy came to talk to Phil. He was just trying to relax and focus as much as he could. It was difficult and nerve-wrecking, but Phil did the best he could.

"Can we talk alone?" Roxy asked.

"Of course," Phil replied.

Everyone else left them, and they took a moment to talk while they awaited the first-round matchups. She really needed to talk to Phil. He could sense a level of urgency in her.

"You know you don't have to fight, right? No one is forcing you. This must be your choice. You could refuse to fight and then leave you know. No shame in living to fight another day," Roxy advised.

"We can't do that. I spoke to the Creator, and our actions here affect Overworld and Earth. There are bigger impacts to us all. We need to do this. There is so much at stake," Phil replied.

"I know," Roxy replied. "I am a little worried about Jon and Daniel. They don't possess the abilities you have. This may not end well. I'm giving them the same speech, but I wanted to talk to you first."

"Well, we'll have to do our best to see that we all get through this," Phil responded with a sudden burst of confidence.

"Yes, you are right, of course," Roxy replied.

Julie found them and came to talk to Phil.

"This connection is powerful. It is available to everyone on Earth. If we have control of it, we can share it. No more loneliness. A deeper connection for those who want it. You must decide if it is worth for. Worth putting your life on the line for. I believe it is worth fighting for," Julie explained.

Julie was right, but Phil was surprised she supported them fighting in the tournament. They were wondering what they had gotten them all into. Roxy didn't know it would be a tournament with so much at stake. Phil wasn't sure Roxy would have made a different choice if she had known. Julie was second-guessing herself as well. This entire tournament could be fake, or it could be a plan the Creator devised to convince them to fight for a deeper cause. They were already in too deep to question what was about to happen. Phil was here for a reason and had to press forward. There was no turning back now. It was all or nothing. It was time. Everything that had happened up to this point was preparing him for this moment. Phil was ready. He felt sure of this.

The rest of the Circle re-joined Roxy and Phil. Julie came back and hugged him close. Red wrapped himself around Phil's arm. Red then went around to the other members. Julie looked up at him.

"How is your injury?" She asked Phil.

"I'm fine. A little pain, but I will live," Phil replied, trying to encourage her. He could tell she was still worried.

Tina came into the room in a rush. She had news of the first-round opponents. "Phil. You will face Blue in the first round," Tina announced as she rushed back. "The other matchups are not set yet. I will let you know as soon as I find out," Tina advised Jon and Daniel.

Everyone looked at Phil, and Red once again came to him and wrapped himself around Phil's arm. Blue was the one that froze his drink. He had tried to intimidate

Phil. He was expecting to face a human opponent, but now it didn't matter. Phil had his target and focus. Blue would be a harder target, but Phil was ready.

"Ok. What do we know about Blue?" Phil asked.

"Blue is a liquid hydra. He is a type of snake, but he controls water in all forms, and it allows him to bend and twist into his own shape. He can flow like water or glide like the moisture in the air," Scarlet explained. "This makes him hard to hit. It also makes him faster as he can alter the moisture in the air and flow with it. He knows you possess the fire ability, and he will try to limit its effectiveness by lowering the temperature. He wants to freeze you. He may try to drown you or cause hypothermia to kill you. He wants to turn you into an ice cube and shatter you into pieces."

This got Phil's attention. He was starting to face the reality that Blue might be stronger with his water ability than Phil was with the fire ability. Going up against Blue wouldn't be easy, but Phil knew what was at stake in this tournament. He had to try.

"Okay," Phil replied. "How do I beat him? What is our strategy?"

"It's good that you know the fire ability. There's no better ability against this enemy," Scarlet explained. "He will be hard to hit, but with your level of fire and power, a direct hit could do a lot of damage. He will not be defeated easily, though. Water is a good ability to dodge and deflect fire with. It's one of the best to defeat fire with."

Tina came back. She was out of breath again. She caught her breath and spoke up.

"Phantom is working with Blue to prepare him to face you," Tina said with a surprised look. "I guess they are working together."

"Great," Phil replied sarcastically. "What is Phantom up to? I thought he worked alone. What could he possibly have in common with Blue?"

Phil found this odd from the little he knew about Phantom, so he figured that something more was going on there. Phil kept that thought in the back of his mind. If Phantom was willing to work with anyone to have a place in the tournament, there must be something bigger happening.

"Blue will want to face you in his home world," Scarlet advised. "He will pick that as the battleground. He's comfortable there, and you won't be as comfortable, especially with the low temperature and dangerously sharp ice."

"Why does he get to choose the battleground? I thought I would get the choice," Phil responded with much surprise.

"You are favoured to win," Tina explained. "You are more powerful, they believe. You have greater potential and power. Don't you believe this? The Creator and His angels have set the battle, and they believe you are favoured to win."

"They do? I thought I would be the underdog." Phil responded. He never looked at himself as a favourite, even with the power he possessed.

"Well you better start now," Roxy replied. "Blue is going to treat you like that and will come even harder at you to win. You must believe in how great you are. You are amazing. With or without these abilities."

"The Creator wouldn't give these powers to just anyone. He chose you," Tina advised. "He must have a really good reason. He knows you better than any of us, and we know you well thanks to the Circle. You must be very special."

Tina gave Phil a hug. They were all encouraging him, preparing him for a deadly battle that was coming up. Julie was concerned about this enemy Phil would be facing soon. She was concerned but believed in Phil. Scarlet came over to offer more advice.

"You are a mindsonic. You could steal the water ability from Blue. You would have to come in contact with him to do that," Scarlet advised. "You aren't as powerful as me, so you would need to physically touch Blue to take his power, and it could prevent him from freezing you completely. It's also dangerous to get that close to him as it will be easier for him to freeze you. If you get the water ability, you would be able to resist the cold and the freezing to some degree. It would give you a better chance. Provided you survive touching him."

"That is very risky," Tina responded. "Blue would freeze him to death and kill him. We don't know enough about the mindsonic ability. I don't think we can take that chance here. Phil hasn't used it except as a reaction. I don't think he should try it. It could be disastrous."

"He's stronger than you think," Scarlet responded. "It could end up saving his life. And he would have a new ability. A powerful one. It would make us all more powerful. I think he should use it if he gets the chance. It is worth the risk. I would use that strategy if I were in this battle. I think it's the only strategy we have. Unless someone has a better idea. Blue will be hard to hit directly with the fire ability."

No one had any other ideas or plans nor were they sure how to defeat Blue other than hitting him directly. Tina and Scarlet were a little at odds with each other. They could all feel the tension and concern for each other. They agreed to disagree on the strategy with Blue.

Phil wondered how Scarlet would know all this. She had amazing detail on the enemies they faced and even developing their abilities, the details she knew about Overworld and the various opponents was mind blowing. Phil started to wonder what she had done when she was here before, but it was of little importance with Blue waiting to face Phil.

Tina and Scarlet's discussion was getting a bit heated over what strategy to use against Blue. They had finally started to calm down, and they looked at Roxy who was quietly listening. Roxy then spoke up.

"I will let Phil decide how to use his abilities. Only he can decide, depending on the situation. Phil, I trust your judgement. I am confident in you. I believe you will overcome."

Roxy was right. Phil took everyone's advice, but the bottom line was it would be him in the battle, and he planned to do whatever it took to win. He would use every ability he had at his disposal to come out on top.

Then, they heard an announcement. It was Ariel.

24
ROUND ONE

"Round one has begun. You must head to your first-round matchup," Ariel announced.

Phil was to head to a specific door where he would enter. On the other side was the location where he would face Blue. Tina and Scarlet believed it would be something like Blue's home world. A dark and cold place. Blue was already inside waiting for him. It was now the moment of truth.

"We love you, Phil. Be strong. You're already a champion. You have already won in my eyes," Julie said.

Red wrapped himself around Phil's arm again for a short while. He untangled from his arm and went back to Julie.

"Remember what I told you," Scarlet reminded Phil.

"Let's do this," Daniel said. "We believe in you."

"Keep your body temperature up and take Blue out," Tina advised. "Don't let him freeze you."

"I won't, " Phil replied. "Thanks, all of you."

It was hitting Phil that he would be alone in an unknown environment battling this creature, and it had him a little scared.

"Just be yourself," Roxy said with a smile.

Cobra vs. Blue

Phil looked everyone in the eyes. It would be a lie if he said he wasn't scared. He was afraid but knew what he had to do. Phil proceeded down the hallway to a large dark platinum-coloured metal door. The door was so large a car could drive through it. Phil walked forward, and the door opened automatically. There were a few feet of space and then another door just like the first one. Phil stepped into the space between the doors, and the first door closed. He was temporarily in darkness. Once the first door was completely closed, the second door opened. The door opened to a blizzard. It looked like the middle of the North Pole. There was snow and ice everywhere. It was a dark and gloomy sky, only the glow of a moon provided any source of light. The ground had a slight glow, but that was the reflection from the moon. It looked like the middle of the night.

There were endless mountains and hills of snow and ice. It was a constant blizzard and freezing cold wind. There was also rain and hail everywhere else. It felt like the wind, rain, and snow was all against Phil from every direction. It was hard to move, and hard to breathe. It was difficult to see anything, let alone find Blue in this storm. Phil covered up as best he could to endure the cold. The clothing he was given got thicker and warmer, but he could still feel the sub-zero temperature. No sign of Blue, but Phil could tell this storm was unnatural. Blue was causing this. This was not normal weather on any planet. He would have frozen Phil's hand if it had not been for his fire ability. He did his best to keep warm.

Phil pressed on. He could not quit now. He could not draw back. He had to fight. He needed to encourage himself. He thought about the words of encouragement the Circle said to him, and what was at stake. Those thoughts gave him strength to keep going. It was not easy, but he pushed forward.

Phil used his fire ability to keep warm and attempted to warm the surroundings. Blue was trying to freeze him, but it wasn't working. He would have to do better than that. Phil did all he could to make it warmer. He could shield himself from Blue's power though it was draining. Still no sign of Blue. Phil was getting warmer and stronger. He continued increasing his fire ability and started to see the ice melt. The snow changed to rain. Phil was overcoming the strategy of his enemy. Using this ability was sapping some of his strength, but he had no choice. He had to use it to survive and to get a better idea of the location of Blue. Phil wasn't sure how he would find Blue, but knew he was close. Blue was watching and looking for the best time to strike. Blue was testing Phil's strength to determine how powerful he was. Phil could see what Blue was up to and attempted to counteract it.

The weather began to change. It was calmer now, and it felt like the temperature was going down faster. The snow that had melted was now becoming ice. The blizzard was gone. It was an eerie calm. The environment was now hard ice and more slippery. Phil slipped a few times as he struggled to keep balance. Phil could sense that Blue was closer and getting ready to attack. He wanted Phil on unstable footing making an easy target. Blue was biding his time looking for the right opening.

Phil still had no idea where Blue was. He was closer than before, but that was a gut feeling. The weather was a bit calmer now but still harsh, making Blue difficult to locate. Suddenly, a flash from the sky and a bolt of lightning came down right in front of Phil, forcing him to stop and step back. He was also startled and a bit scared to proceed. It was totally out of place for the current weather conditions, which made Phil wonder where it came from. Phil wondered if Blue had the power to do this. *If it wasn't him then who? Was this a distraction to take Phil's attention from Blue?* Phil got his focus back on finding Blue. He took another glance at the sky then put his focus back on finding Blue. He was getting closer, but Phil still wasn't sure where to find him.

Phil looked around but still no Blue. Phil then noticed some tracks like the slithering of a snake in the ice and snow. Blue had been here, but with all the melting, freezing, and wind blowing, he lost Blue's tracks. Suddenly, Phil felt a sharp pain in his right leg and ankle. Blue had struck him, and it felt like a knife of ice had pierced his leg. Phil was in pain and had trouble walking momentarily. Blue was setting him up for something, but Phil still couldn't see Blue. He didn't even see where the strike came from.

Phil tried to figure out where Blue was, based on where he was hit but still nothing. Phil's mindsonic ability was telling him Blue was much closer but well hidden. Phil didn't think Blue would face him head-on. Phil continued to look but could not see him. Blue sent a blue flash of light toward Phil, and it hit him in the chest. Phil went down to his knees. It felt like his chest was now frozen, and he had more trouble breathing. Now Phil got angry. He sent a heat ray back in the area that he thought the freeze ray came from. He missed Blue, but sensed some movement, and Phil had an idea of where he could be. Phil could see some movement under the ice and snow. He sent another heat ray but hit nothing. Phil thought he had Blue point blank, but he missed. Blue was difficult to hit. He seemed to move through ice and snow like it was water. Sometimes it seemed like all the snow around him was shifting. Blue was on the move, but Phil had to take time to warm himself up a bit and recover his strength. Phil was getting cold again, and his leg and chest were still hurting from the two attacks. Phil's wound from Fire was less painful after the hit he took from the freeze ray. It froze that part of his upper chest and numbed the pain. Phil still had trouble breathing and moving, though. He summoned all the strength he could, but it was difficult. He lost sight of Blue again. Phil again started to raise the temperature as much as he could. Raising the temperature seemed to force Blue to react, *but would he be able to survive any more of these attacks?* Phil didn't want to entertain that possibility and pressed. Blue was trying to wear him down. Phil continued to raise the temperature, and he could sense Blue moving and preparing to attack again. It appeared to be easier to find him when it was warmer. Phil generated as much heat as he could muster.

Phil could sense Blue was closing in. Phil still could not see him because he was blending in with the ice and snow. Phil sensed Blue was behind him, and he turned around. There he was, in proximity. He hit Phil with a freeze ray at close range, freezing him. Phil couldn't move, and immediately began to heat himself up to unfreeze. It was so hard to breathe between the pain and the cold air. Phil sent a heat ray where he last saw Blue but missed. Blue came out flying, but Phil managed to unfreeze enough to get out of the way. Blue missed Phil and quickly went into the snow and ice before Phil could use his fire ability. He lost sight of Blue yet again. Blue was trying to set Phil up for the kill. Phil tried to unfreeze himself, but before he was free, Blue hit Phil again with a stronger freeze ray. Phil was completely frozen and could not move at all. He started to melt himself free when Blue charged at him again. Phil managed to unfreeze his arm enough to grab Blue and stop him from doing more damage.

    Blue wrapped himself around Phil's arm and began to freeze him. Phil then remembered what Scarlet said about stealing Blue's water ability. He attempted to steal the water ability from Blue, but he was getting colder and colder. Blue was freezing Phil. It was getting harder to concentrate, and Phil was losing consciousness, but then he began to absorb Blue's water ability. Blue was tightly wrapped around Phil's arm, but now Phil had Blue in his grip. It was Blue trying to escape as Phil was absorbing some of his strength. Phil was weakening Blue and at the same time getting stronger. Blue couldn't escape Phil's grip and was struggling. Phil was unfreezing as Blue focussed on escaping. He had to give up a level of water ability to escape, and he did. Phil's eyes turned a slight Blue, and his skin had a blue tinge now. Phil was now able to adapt to the cold, and the ice and snow had less of an effect on him. Blue broke free and was moving away from Phil. The battle was far from over and had shifted in Phil's favor.

Phil could sense Blue's exact location now. He could completely unfreeze himself and move normally. Phil could even move faster despite the ice and slippery conditions. He looked at water and ice completely different. He had more energy and some defence against Blue's freeze ray. Phil was still vulnerable to it because Blue was so powerful. He still controlled the water ability, and Phil had no idea how much water ability he had absorbed. Blue hadn't anticipated Phil stealing his ability. It was a strategy he never considered.

Phil hit the area where Blue was hiding with a heat ray and forced him out into the open. He attempted to move towards Phil and attack. Blue sent a freeze ray, and it hit Phil directly. It still hurt him but not as much as the previous attacks. Phil sank back after the hit, and Blue charged forward toward him and was getting close. Phil sent a heat ray more powerful than any he had ever sent, and it pushed Blue right into the snow and ice melting all of it around him and severely injuring him. Phil sent another heat ray hitting Blue directly and concentrated it on him. A sustained burst of fire would certainly destroy Blue. Suddenly Blue vanished with a flash of light. Phil wondered if he vaporized Blue. There was no sign of him, and nothing left behind. The fire ability was too strong for Blue and Phil felt the level of water ability he had increase. With Blue defeated, Phil was victorious. He was still hurting from the freeze ray hits he took, but he would live. It felt like he had frostbite on his arm, leg, and chest. Phil pushed past the pain and started walking back. Even with the water ability level he had, his injuries still affected him, slowing him down.

Phil noticed the water ability was continuing to increase in him. He felt more powerful and much calmer. He was surprised how fast and powerful the water ability was getting inside of him. By killing Blue, he took control of the water ability. If he had full control of this ability, he would need to learn quickly how water and fire could co-exist and help him defeat his next opponent.

Phil rejoined the rest of the Circle back at the hallway entrance. He had a slight limp from Blue attacking his leg, but it was getting better. Phil was recovering but needed some time.

By defeating Blue, Phil got control of the water ability. It was a different ability from the fire ability, but he had no idea how to use it. He was surprised that he still had injuries due to frostbite now that he controlled water in all its forms. Water changed the way he sensed everything around him. It was a different kind of strength. It was a deeper power that flowed inside of him. He had used it only to adapt and heal in battle with Blue, but using it intentionally was a different story, and controlling it was a skill he didn't possess yet. Phil would develop this power quickly because it was much easier than fire to master.

Phil was still limping from the attack on his leg from Blue. He thought he could heal it or heat it up with fire, but it didn't work. Julie saw Phil and was shocked. Phil was still in pain. He looked worse for wear. He was having trouble moving.

"Are you okay?" She cried frantically. "You can barely walk."

"I'll be fine," Phil replied in pain. "Just need to get my leg moving and blood flowing."

ROUND ONE

It was nice to be in a warm environment again. Julie and Roxy brushed off the snow and ice from all over Phil. Tina and Scarlet came over. Scarlet looked at Phil closeup. Her eyes were light brown but changed to a fiery red color when she acquired the fire ability from Phil. It made her stronger. She immediately sensed a difference in Phil.

"Your eyes have a blue glow to them now," Scarlet said. "You have the water ability. You control water completely. I see it all around you and all over you. And it is increasing your strength very fast."

Everyone noticed Phil was calmer and more relaxed. The water ability had a level of healing different from Julie's healing power. Phil was more relaxed and focused, which was an attribute of this new ability. Even his clothes which had adapted to the increase in fire ability by turning a bit red now had a bit of blue as well. Water was becoming a part of him. In fact, it was as much a part of Phil as the fire ability.

"I see that you beat Blue," Fire scoffed. "Now you have the water ability, but I wouldn't waste your time with such a weak ability. What ability did you use to defeat Blue with? You would be dead without the fire ability. Remember that. Just by having this ability you have weakened yourself and the fire ability I gave you. I would lose the water ability if I were you. Aren't you weak enough? My power is absolute, and no enemy can withstand it as Blue found out and you experienced. No one can resist the power of fire."

Fire was right on one point. Phil would have been dead without that ability. He relied heavily on the fire ability to overcome Blue. He also absorbed the water ability from Blue which helped him win that battle. Fire taunted and gloated before he walked away. Fire had no fear of the water ability, and he didn't consider it a threat.

Phil sensed that other combatants in the tournament expected Blue to beat him and thought Blue had the best chance to beat Fire, but most of them got even more discouraged when Blue was beaten by Phil, a lower level fire user. It made the water ability look even weaker. They were all afraid of Fire even more.

Phil also noticed that there were almost no water users in the tournament. Water was not an ability that anyone relies on for these battles. Despite all these knocks against the water ability, he wanted to use and develop it the best he could. You never know when it could come in handy. Julie brought Phil over some water to drink. The water moved in unusual ways and patterns when it got close to him. The water ability was changing everything.

"Whoa," Julie said. "That is amazing. It is flowing with you."

The water in the glass Julie brought would swirl around and then be still. It seemed to reflect, and change based on Phil's moods and thoughts. It became still, even when Julie tilted the glass. Phil could alter the temperature of the water as well. He didn't exactly know how he was controlling it, but it came naturally. This ability flowed with him easily and powerfully. Phil sensed that this ability was stronger than everyone thought but also that it took time to master. Fire came even more naturally and was powerful and easy to master. That would explain why many wanted it for this tournament. Phil continued to practice this ability every chance he got. Phil would have some time before the next round started.

ROUND ONE

Phil drank some water. It felt different now. It seemed to energize him and increase his strength. Drinking the water also helped heal some of his injuries. It was soothing and more refreshing.

"Learn to use this ability," Tina advised. "The water one is extremely powerful with you. You will be extremely dangerous and effective with it. I am sensing this strongly. There is more to this ability and you using it."

"Okay," Phil replied. "I will."

Phil also sensed that he would need it.

Scarlet was surprisingly quiet. Phil knew she could sense his ability, and he did follow her advice.

"Hey, Scarlet. Your advice and strategy worked," Phil said. "Thank God. Water is a powerful ability. Very different from fire. It's powerful in a different way."

"It did work," she replied. "I'm glad."

She was happy for Phil, but she was a little distracted. No one in their Circle could tell why. They were a little concerned, but it would have to wait as there were bigger things at stake.

Phil could sense the Creator watching every battle with interest. He planned all the matches, and He watched over every aspect of the tournament. His angels watched along with Him and kept order. There was also another named Elo who was in the background as well, paying close attention. He was powerful but not directly involved yet. Phil could also sense another evil presence in the background, but it was too hard to tell what it was or its intentions. He could sense it, though. Many forces were at work in Overworld.

Spirit vs. The Alligator

Daniel was preparing for his match. He was to face Roy aka the Alligator. He was the one with the morphasis ability. Strong both as an alligator and a human, Roy would be a challenge for Daniel as Spirit. Roy would decide the environment he would fight Spirit in. As Spirit, Daniel was much faster, but Alligator was much stronger. It was an interesting match as they were similar in ability.

"Use your speed and strike hard and fast," Tina advised. "Overwhelm him. Use your senses and skills. Use your speed. You will need to, and it could be the difference between victory and defeat."

"Okay," Daniel replied. "I will."

Tina gave some great advice. Daniel would have his hands full, but the Circle knew he could overcome.

Daniel made his way down the corridor to the doors that would lead to alligator's battleground. He approached a big door like the door Phil went through when he faced Blue. Daniel entered, and the door opened to a swampy area. It was dark with few places to stand. The water was slimy and hard to move through, even for Spirit who was fast and agile. This was part of Alligator's plan, to slow Spirit down to be able to strike him or grab him and pull him underwater. Spirit had trouble detecting where Alligator was. This environment made it difficulty to track him. Alligator was hiding underwater, and it was hard to see him through the mist and fog. Spirit moved from one patch of earth to another, avoiding the water because he didn't want to get caught. Spirit still could not sense Alligator, but he couldn't be far. He was good at concealing his location. Alligator was patient and biding his time. Daniel believed Alligator wanted to pull

ROUND ONE

him under, and death roll him. Spirit wouldn't be able to survive that.

Daniel stayed in Spirit form. As Spirit, he had a better sense of smell and sight. This was beneficial against a powerful enemy who was good at hiding. Alligator remained hidden looking for an opening. Spirit went to jump across another part of the swamp, and Alligator came out of nowhere to strike, getting part of Spirit's front right paw. Spirit's paw slipped out of alligator's grasp, and Spirit limped to the closest solid ground. Spirit changed to Daniel, and he noticed his right arm was injured. It was a near miss by Alligator but still a damaging blow to Spirit. Alligator came at Daniel, got his left foot, and pulled him into the water. Daniel reached for anything he could get his hands on. He found a rock slightly larger than his fist, and he grabbed it and started hitting Alligator with it on his head and eyes. Alligator would not let go and pulled him right under the water. Daniel changed back into Spirit, and his foot became a paw and was now small enough to get loose and free. Spirit swam back to the surface. He wasn't as quick as normal because of the injury to his paw. Spirit changed to Daniel, and he was now limping a little but found some solid ground again. He also found the same rock he had used and grabbed it again. Alligator chased him and came to the surface, trying to crush him. Daniel dived out of the way. Roy as an alligator was much larger than a normal alligator. Daniel jumped on his back and began striking him with the rock on his head and eyes again. Daniel wanted to get Alligator to change to his weaker human form to fight with him on land. Daniel was on Alligators back, avoiding his bite. Daniel grabbed Alligator's front legs, and he could not move and was severely restricted in his movements. Alligator could not move or roll. He became Roy, his human form. He took a longer time to change than Daniel did. Roy threw Daniel off him, and he started to change back to his alligator form. Daniel again picked up the rock, threw it, and it struck him on the head, and he fell back. Daniel changed to Spirit and bit his arm to get closer to him and got behind him and began to choke him. Roy could not completely become Alligator and went unconscious from the choke and was out. He was out in a half-alligator half-human form. Daniel was victorious. He had injuries to his right arm and left leg but was fine. Daniel exited the swamp area and came back to join their Circle. Roxy ran over to hug him.

"Thank God you are okay," Roxy said. "Are you injured? Julie will heal you".

"I'll be okay," Daniel replied. "A few scratches and bruises."

Julie came over to heal Daniel as best she could. He was tough and rugged, so he wasn't bothered by any of his injuries. Being a morphasis user and having an animal form like Spirit within him made him even tougher. Phil, on the other hand, was having a tough time with some of his injuries. They were better, but he wasn't quite as rugged as Daniel. Phil was ready either way to deal with whatever was next.

Jon vs. Damien

It was Jon's turn to fight. His draw was Damien himself. They were not sure how powerful Damien was. It was a one on one battle, and Damien would not be able to use the abilities of all his members. Jon wouldn't either,

ROUND ONE

but Damien was reliant on those powers and his Circle. Jon would decide where the battle would take place. Jon was ready. He was the physically strongest of the Circle would not go down without a fight.

"You are a powerhouse," Tina said. "You are the strongest one of us all. You can beat Damien. He won't have the rest of his Circle to hide behind."

"I know," Jon replied. "I want to fight him head-on. No sneak attacks. I will choose to fight him on the pedestal. He liked the one outside the castle near the White Mountain."

"Sounds like a good plan to me, "Phil replied. "Take him out. I would have liked to fight him. Have at it."

Phil and Daniel took turns shaking Jon's hand, which gave him the encouragement he needed to confidently go up against Damien. They all came together in a group huddle. Their strength was all renewed, and they were re-focused. It was Jon's time now. Tina came and held him close. Jon then went down the corridor towards the familiar doors to his matchup. He would fight Damien on the pedestal. Jon entered the room for his matchup.

Damien walked by the Circle on his way to the match, and they sensed his frustration. Angry about the format of the tournament, Damien thought it was unfair. He wondered why it would be one on one battles for control of a Circle that by nature helped people work better together. It nullified his Circle's chances of winning the tournament, and he was also upset that he had to face Jon. He was favoured, but he wanted a tougher opponent. What a surprise he would get fighting someone like Jon. Phil figured Jon would crush him. Damien had some major strength and ability from what Phil was sensing.

This would be one of the toughest battles of the entire tournament. Tina was particularly concerned about Jon. She had a good sense of Damien's ability and was worried.

Jon was ready to face Damien in his first-round matchup. Damien entered the room, angry and upset but ready to fight. Jon came straight at him and knocked him down. Damien was hurt but far from defeated. He got up calmly, was winded but recovered, and measured up Jon, searching for his weakness. He was still getting used to not having all his Circles abilities at his fingertips. He knew a form of karate and other martial arts, but so did Jon. Damien hit Jon a few times, but it didn't hurt him at all. Jon punched him in the stomach, and he went down hard. Damien realized quickly how powerful Jon was. Damien was hurt and winded again, but he wouldn't be defeated so easily. He appeared to be toying with Jon but now took him more seriously. Damien decided to use his absorber ability and absorb some of Jon's strength. With this ability, it would make him even stronger while weakening Jon. They continued to battle, and Jon proved he was the better fighter, and he was trying to choke Damien out. He used a similar choke to the one Daniel used earlier. Damien once again absorbed some of his strength, and it was enough to break free from Jon's hold. Once free, Damien sent a white beam of energy that hit Jon direct and made him crumple to the ground. That beam stopped Jon's heart, and the battle was over. Jon had lost. It was the same ability he used to stop Tina's heart. Jon was out, and Damien moved to the next round.

Damien came out of the room with a smile, although he was still angry and annoyed. He was powerful, and his strategy was to steal his opponent's ability to use against them. His strategy worked well against Jon. Damien gloated and left the battle area. He still felt these matches were a waste of his time. He wanted all the power for himself.

Julie ran into the room and healed Jon. He revived and had a steady heartbeat again. Phil continued to stare while Damien watched Jon recover and was impressed by Julie's ability. Damien wanted her ability but would have to go through Phil to get to her. He remembered that he had challenged Phil with his circle and lost two of his members.

"I hope we can go a few rounds, Damien," Phil said.

"Your time will come," He answered. "Careful what you ask for."

"So will yours," Phil replied.

Damien looked at Phil and was silent. He was afraid of Phil, especially since Phil had defeated Blue. A lot of the other combatants were watching Phil. Some were afraid. Some were looking for weaknesses. Phil was more concerned with Jon. He paid little attention to anything else right now. Jon's recovery was the most important thing.

Jon was conscious but weak. Both Julie and Tina stayed with him while he continued to heal. Red stayed on his arm and wrapped around him like a blanket. Tina knew exactly what he went through as she was also hit by that same null ray from Damien. Jon was the strongest and would recover, but he needed time. He would live to fight another day. He was out of the tournament, but Phil was glad he survived.

The strength that Damien absorbed would help him in the next rounds. He had weakened Jon's strength enough to be able to stop his heart. His plan was now obvious: he would absorb an opponent's abilities each round and get stronger, round by round. He would get stronger as the tournament progressed. Phil thought this was a smart strategy, and he realized he could do the same thing, although he was still learning this ability. When Phil defeated Blue using a similar strategy, his confidence in this ability grew stronger. He was sure he could pull it off again.

"Jon will survive," Roxy said. "You two need to get rested and get ready for round two." She was talking to both Daniel and Phil. They had to prepare themselves. They had to be ready and not focus on the distractions. They must instead be focused on the tasks at hand. It took some time to settle down and prepare for the next round. Phil wasn't expecting anything to be easy.

They saw the other winners of the tournament matches. Phantom defeated a member of Damien's Circle. Venom also won his first-round match by ripping his opponent to shreds. Damien tried to take control of Venom and absorb his power, but it failed badly before the tournament. Venom and Damien became bitter enemies as a result. They both wanted all the power. Goliath also fought and killed a member of Damien's Circle. Goliath looked at Phil with an intense look. He wanted to beat Phil specifically. He was even more wild and untamed now. He walked away to rest before round two.

Damien found out that at least three more members from his Circle were killed in the first round. He was even more upset. He used members of his own Circle for his own strength and power that they could not fight individually. They were not effective in a tournament like this. Damien was deciding whether to continue with the tournament. He couldn't afford to lose any more people from his Circle because it was weakening him and his Circle's overall strength. His Circle was getting weaker. Damien's Circle was falling apart.

Fire came over to taunt them and the other Circles. He wanted to intimidate them, and it was working. Other combatants continued to leave because they had an intense fear of the fire ability. They wanted to live to fight another day. There were few combatants left. Others were getting desperate and trying to find a way to be successful in this tournament. There was a lot of fear, which pleased Fire.

Phil had gone for a walk to clear his head because he was a little overwhelmed at the events so far. Jenna Ziatta approached him. She caught Phil alone briefly as he was walking through one of the hallways, looking at the statues of angels and other creatures. There were many strange creatures, even stranger than the ones in the tournament. Phil needed a bit of space and to find his focus. It would help him tremendously to relieve some of the pressure he was feeling.

The Temptation

Jenna saw her moment and came over to Phil. She saw that he was alone and distracted. She was almost as beautiful as Julie, but something was off about her. Her clothing showed a lot of skin, and she left little to the imagination. There was something about her that wasn't right. Her behaviour made Phil think she was up to something.

"We don't have to be enemies you know," Jenna said. "We could join forces. Fire is the real enemy. We could join our abilities. I could join your Circle. We have the strength to defeat Fire. You and I together."

She came close to Phil. Too close. She brushed her whole body against his, and Phil stepped back, a little surprised, although parts of him wanted to step closer. Apparently, her interests went beyond this tournament. The Circle could sense what was going on and were concerned. Julie was especially interested and was getting mad. She immediately didn't like Jenna. Julie was getting jealous and wanted to protect Phil.

"Let's focus on the tournament. The task at hand should be your priority and mine," Phil said sternly. "We don't have time for this."

Jenna gave Phil a surprised look. Phil got an idea of what her intentions were when she brushed against him. She wanted something more, but it wasn't clear. Anger and judgement clouded her intentions, making her impossible to read. Phil couldn't tell where her loyalty was. He originally thought it was Damien's Circle, but she was linked to Venom as well. She also hadn't fought her first-round match yet but was scheduled to fight soon. She was focused on Fire and not her match at hand. The fire ability was useless against Fire. She knew this. *The fire ability could help her in the tournament rounds, but what about beyond?* She spoke slyly. She was deceptive, and it was noticeable. She was hiding something.

"So that's it," she replied in disgust. "No consideration. No discussion with your Circle. We would share abilities, and we would all be successful. Are you so selfish? Do you even see what is at stake here? The Circle is in danger. I am not your enemy. You can have anything you want; you know. Don't miss this opportunity. We can unite and be successful together. We don't have to do this alone."

She again drew close to Phil and pressed herself against him more aggressively this time. Phil had to physically push her back, but she was unusually strong, even though she was in great shape. She was not taking no for an answer. Phil moved away from her again. Julie left Jon and was on her way to where Phil was. She was concerned, so she left the rest of the Circle to help Phil.

"No," Phil replied. "Please stay back. I am not interested."

His abilities were increasing, and he was getting angry. He felt the fire ability rising in himself getting stronger as he got angrier. The water ability calmed him and kept him clear and focused, but it was getting harder to keep his power at bay. Jenna became aggressive.

Phil started to walk away. He had to and needed to calm down. That made Jenna more furious. She gave out a scream that shook Phil to his core. She was angrier than anyone Phil had ever seen. Her mood switched completely to one of anger and rage, losing complete control.

"You will regret this decision," Jenna shouted like she was possessed.

Phil turned back toward her. She moved fast, and she grabbed hold of Phil's shoulder just above his heart and his wound. Her thumb pressed on the wound Fire had given Phil, and he screamed in pain. With her other hand, she pressed it against Phil's forehead. She pushed his back to the wall, and they knocked over a statue, breaking it into pieces. She was trying to steal one of Phil's abilities, but it was different from an absorber. It was also different from a mindsonic. She appeared to be trying to take over Phil with some type of possession and managed to steal something, but Phil wasn't sure what she did. It wasn't fire, and it wasn't water. Phil didn't even have an opportunity to resist or defend. This ability was too fast, and he had never encountered it. Phil pushed her back with all his strength. It took almost all his strength to get her to release as she was sapping his energy. Phil sent a heat that hit her in the chest, and she went down to the ground in a heap. She was badly injured and burned. Julie came over to Phil. The heat ray blast was almost fatal. Phil had enough control to make sure he didn't kill her this time, but he came close. Phil didn't want to disqualify himself from the tournament. Phil wasn't sure what she did to him or what she stole. He appeared to be okay. Phil was weakened from the exchange, but he was still in one piece.

He was still getting used to the increased power of the fire ability he had. Fire wasn't far away, and whenever he was close, Phil's fire ability went even higher to a new level, but Phil had to keep it under control. It felt like Fire would take over control of him if he used it too powerfully. Phil kept the use of this ability in check. He didn't want to depend on it more than he had to.

"What happened?" Julie asked.

Julie held Phil close and looked at Jenna in disgust. Jenna got up slowly and was badly injured. Phil figured she tried to steal an ability but had failed. He believed she wanted something from him to help her defeat Layla. She got the worse end of it though. She was in constant pain now, and her matchup was about to begin. Her opponent, Layla, was in the room, waiting for her. Jenna had been the favourite to win against Layla, but now it was unclear with her injury. Scarlet, Roxy, and Daniel came over. Ariel also appeared in all her power and glory.

"Did I not say there was to be no fighting between the rounds?" Ariel exclaimed in a harsh tone to both Jenna and Phil.

Ariel looked at Phil and then Jenna, who was still in anguish. Jenna had the burn mark from Phil's attack. Julie was healing Phil again as much as she could.

"He hurt me," Jenna cried. "He should be disqualified. I'm in pain," she screamed.

Every word she spoke sounded as though she were in agony. She was hurt badly. There was more to her than on the surface though. Phil knew she was up to something.

"What?" Phil asked. "She attacked me. I defended myself. I warned her several times, but she did not listen."

Phil was upset now because Jenna was trying to get him disqualified. That was part her of agenda, and the game she was playing suddenly became clear to him—to eliminate all threats to clear the way for her victory. She looked at Julie, sensing her healing ability but was in no condition to attack them. Ariel would no doubt get involved if she tried any of her antics again.

"I know what happened," Ariel announced. She turned to Jenna. "It looked like you got what you deserved. You will go to your matchup now or be disqualified. Go now."

Jenna started towards the door to her matchup upset. She eyed Phil all the way to the door. "I will have my revenge, Cobra. I will be avenged." With that last statement, she was gone. She was to face Layla as part of the round one matchups.

Ariel looked at Phil. "You are very close to being disqualified. Keep your power in check, or I will."

Phil nodded as they locked eyes to show her that he understood what was at stake. Happy with his acknowledgment of the rules, Ariel vanished suddenly, leaving Phil alone with his Circle. They gathered around him with intrigue in their eyes.

"What did she try to do to you?" Roxy asked.

"I'm not sure," Phil replied. "It was like she was trying to steal my ability or something from me, but that wasn't all. I am okay, though."

"Do you know what she was trying to do to Phil?" Roxy asked Scarlet.

"I don't know," Scarlet replied. "I couldn't tell what her ability was. She's not an absorber. She's not a mind-sonic either."

"By the way Scarlet, where have you been?" Roxy asked. "We haven't seen you for a little while and had trouble sensing you."

"I was checking who won the other matches and what was to happen for round two," Scarlet replied. "Round two will begin shortly. Round one was delayed because of Jenna. You got to be ready, Cobra."

"Please call me Phil," he replied to Scarlet. "I will be ready."

Phil wasn't used to that name, at least not from members of his own Circle. He didn't fully understand its meaning, and he wanted to remain as authentic as possible with his Circle. He'd learned many times over since arriving in Overworld that his ego had no place in the tournament.

Scarlet smiled at him in agreement and walked away.

"And no wandering off," Roxy advised Phil. "Let's all stick together. Especially after this."

"Agreed," Phil replied.

ROUND ONE

They gathered their entire Circle back together. Jon was getting better, but he still needed time. Scarlet was acting funny but gaining insight on the next round. She was much quieter now and less involved with the rest of the circle. Jon was getting stronger all the time, but Julie continued to stay with him along with Red to make sure he healed as quickly as possible. Roxy and Tina were overseeing and making sure Daniel and Phil were not distracted. They were also keeping a closer eye on the other combatants. She wanted them focused. They all knew round two would be tough.

They all huddled together and held each other close for a little while longer. They once again fed off each other's energy, and everyone's power increased tremendously. It was the encouragement they needed to be strong and triumphant in the second round. The boost in strength gave them the extra push they needed to believe they could win the next round.

Scarlet gave them details on the other opponents and matches happening. She found out that Jenna Ziatta changed her name to Terminal Ziatta. She was dying and thought she had no hope of recovering after she lost the battle with Layla. Terminal was nowhere to be found, so they weren't sure if she died or left, but she was gone. They knew Layla was among the most powerful of the women, but they couldn't pinpoint her actual ability. They were closely linked to Venom as well, and Phil was eager to understand more about her relationship with him. There were rumours Venom could pass and share abilities at will, and Phil's Circle was desperate to learn more about him. They knew he could manipulate them and change them as he saw fit, which made him more dangerous. Many were aligning themselves with him. Their purpose was still unclear, but they wanted control of the Circle. Phil wondered if standing on Venom's side was the key to winning the entire tournament.

Some of Damien's Circle members were allowed into the second round, but his Circle was in turmoil. Some members wanted to leave and fight for themselves while others wanted to leave for good, and Damien was losing the power to keep them bound to his control. It was becoming too much of a strain to hold them and to also fight for himself in the tournament. His Circle was crumbling and losing power. Many members took this opportunity to leave his circle. This was a bit of a shock to everyone because his Circle was the most powerful coming into this battle. Now no one was sure if his Circle would survive this tournament.

With the first round complete, there were few combatants left. Phil was not sure what to expect because many were gone or killed. There was a lot of confusion and fear in the air. Fire's presence still affected everyone and left the value of the Circle in doubt. With such a powerful enemy waiting in the wings, it made some question if it was worth getting control of the Circle after all. Fire made it clear to everyone that he planned to destroy the Circle and anyone who controlled it. Despite that, they proceeded forward. They had to at least try to fight for something so important to them.

Phil was getting stronger with the water ability. It was becoming more natural to use and was easier to develop than fire. He was confused at how much easier water was to develop and control than his fire ability was. It was possible he never truly mastered fire. Either way, Phil decided he would wait to use it in battle again, even though he couldn't deny the good it had done for his Circle.

The water ability flowed so easily through him, and he felt more powerful with it. His whole Circle felt different with it, and it made them all more calm and powerful. It changed the way they all positively interacted with each other. They were all more peaceful and serene. This made their communication by telepathy easier and more accurate.

They were getting a deeper revelation of the Circle and its power again. It could gather power in the form of worship and make its members stronger. It could gather love or hate and change it into pure power and energy. The more members, the stronger the Circle, as in Damien's Circle. He had twisted it to suit his own needs, but in its pure form, it was the strongest. He was selfish, and it was costing him. The Circle allowed them to move between worlds. It gave protection to the weak, and no one was ever alone unless they chose to be, like Phantom. Some used the Circle for power and glory. Some used the Circle for their own gain. How to use it properly was anyone's guess, but it was a powerful tool. It could be used for good or for evil as they had seen. It could be too much power for one person to possess if they lost sight of the Creator's vision.

The Creator had a better plan. He had a better idea. He wanted to use it to help and heal others, share with the less fortunate, strengthen the weak, and to help people work together more closely. It would be essential to make His kingdom more tangible on Earth, to draw everyone to Him so that none would be lost. His power would manifest to help the needy, no matter what the cost was. The people of Earth were His creation and His children. The Circle was to manifest not only in Overworld but on Earth. The world needed healing and the power to overcome. The Creator's vision for the Circle could make all that happen, but so many opposed it.

Many did not understand it while others chose to hate rather than love. There were also people whose God was their belly, and they only lived for their own gain. Who lived for their own pleasures. Pleasure seeking at another's expense. The Creator had a much bigger vision—a greater purpose for the Circle. It needed to be fought for. This was the reason for the tournament, and like anything else good, it needed to be fought for. The Creator thought it was worth fighting for because, in the wrong hands, it would do more damage to an already damaged world. In the right hands, it could save the lost, heal the broken-hearted, and shine a light on the darkness to set captives free. Phil and his Circle were starting to understand the Creator's vision would offer them and the entire world pure power and freedom.

They noticed that few Circles had a healer while theirs had one of the most powerful healers, Julie. Some Circles didn't have a healer and were unable to heal their injuries. They would have to go to the next round with the injuries they received from the round before, but even with the power of healing that Julie had, she could not completely heal Phil. She was still mastering her ability. From what Phil was sensing, a healer was usually a weaker individual, and no Circle wanted any weakness. Julie was considered by some to be one of the weaker members,

ROUND ONE

but they wouldn't have made it this far without her. She was a vital member.

Phil still felt a little pain, but it would not stop him from continuing. He had to fight on. He believed the Circle was worth it. Thanks to Julie, Phil would prove that he refused to give up on the tournament. There was no quit in him. Not anymore.

25
ROUND TWO

Ariel appeared in all her glory. "Round two shall now begin," she announced. "You will now proceed to your next match. May the Creator give you strength and endurance as you fight." With that statement, Ariel vanished. She was back with the Creator Again.

Scarlet was gone for a brief time and returned in a little bit of a panic. She slowed down to normalize her heart rate and took another breath before she spoke.

Cobra vs. The Venom Carrier

"Cobra's next opponent will be Venom," Scarlet advised. "Daniel will be facing Damien. These opponents won't be easy to defeat."

They both had tough opponents waiting in the wings. Both were challenging in their own ways, but they were prepared to fight.

Phil remembered Venom from the banquet when they first got here. He was some type of lizard or raptor that stood upright with sharp teeth and claws. That was all Phil

ROUND TWO

could remember and sense about him. Phil had noticed many combatants had aligned themselves with Venom for some reason. Tina came over with more information, and Scarlet joined her because she also had some insight to share.

"Venom is a parasite-type creature," Tina explained. "He feeds off other creatures. He is fast and powerful. He has sharp teeth and claws, but his tail is his deadliest striking weapon. He is also a strong mindsonic. Stronger than Phantom, Damien, Scarlet, and I. You will need to be mentally prepared as well as physically ready. Venom seems to have some type of liquid in his body besides blood. It's a black-coloured oily liquid that makes him heal and strengthens him. There is also another red liquid besides blood coursing through his veins, fighting with the black liquid. He has other abilities I am having trouble discerning. He is the leader of an unusual type of Circle. His Circle is a perversion of our Circle, like an imposter. His Circle members are all infected with these liquids and under his control. He might have some absorbing-type ability as well. The main thing is to stay away from his tail."

"I understand," Phil replied. "I am ready to face him."

"We're not sure if he can take a direct hit from a heat ray. I doubt he would be able to," Scarlet advised.

"He will use speed against you. He is much quicker, but we believe you are stronger," Tina advised. "Be as quick as you can, but you should be able to overpower him."

Julie was concerned and stayed close to Phil. From what little she knew; Venom was a powerful enemy he would have to be mindful of. He killed a member of

Damien's in the first round, but Phil was victorious as well in the first round against a dangerous opponent.

Phil was considered the favorite, so Venom would choose the battleground. They all believed Venom wanted a battleground that was good for close-range fighting. Venom would want to strike and stay at close range. That was where he would be the deadliest. That thought did make Phil nervous because they still could not determine how well fire would work against him. He was fast, so he would be difficult to target and hit, kind of like Blue, but Venom was faster.

Fire walked by, giving them all his taunting, evil looks. He was watching them slowly wear themselves out right in time to face him when he challenges the winner of the tournament. They were stuck in a difficult situation. Julie and Tina were both worried about what might happen, win or lose. They felt like they were playing right into Fire's hands.

"Let's go, Phil," Jon said. "You can take him. You have the power and the might."

"Yes," Roxy agreed. "You are the overcomer. You will overcome."

"Thanks, everyone," Phil replied. "I needed this."

Phil did need it because he wasn't as sure about this matchup. He was facing one of the deadliest enemies in the tournament. Phil was the odds-on favourite, but that wasn't too reassuring with the battle looming. Only one of them would survive the battle, and Phil started to doubt his chances against Venom.

They all huddled together, and the focus was on Daniel's and Phil's upcoming matches. To prepare themselves, they once again fed off each other's strengths and confidence. They all drew closer to each other and making each other stronger. Their Circle increased as a result of this. They would need all the strength they could muster to overcome these challenges. There was no easy matchup. Not before and not now.

They prepared themselves as best they could. Venom waited for Phil in the battle area. Phil's Circle accompanied him towards the hallway to the large door that would lead the place where he would fight Venom.

"Be strong," Daniel said with confidence. "Venom doesn't stand a chance."

"I agree," Phil replied with some newfound confidence. "I believe I can beat him."

"Avoid the tail and hit him hard and direct," Tina emphasized. "He will come at you fast so be ready."

"Okay," Phil replied. "I'll watch out."

Phil entered through the door. It closed, and he was again in a small area between doors. The other side opened, and it led to a dark temple. It looked like something out of Egypt. Light came in through the ceiling, and everywhere he looked he saw platforms and stairs, even on the ceilings. There were markings and symbols that he couldn't understand everywhere. The large room was mainly sand and stone, but there were parts of metal and steel that were well hidden except for exposed edges and corners. There were torches every so often on the walls. Phil used his fire ability to light each torch he saw, making the room brighter, little by little. In the middle of the room was a small pedestal with a fire pit. Phil lit it, and the whole room became brighter. The fires made it easier to see. Phil didn't see Venom, but he knew he was close because there were plenty of places to hide. Venom must be hiding and waiting for the right time to strike. The room had other small fire pits all over the place, and Phil lit each one, making the room brighter and brighter. Shadows were disappearing, and the small fires throughout the room made him stronger. He absorbed light and heat, and he made the fire in the centre glow hotter and brighter. Suddenly, Phil felt a headache. It was the same pain Phil felt when Phantom, Violet, and Damien invaded his mind, but this time, it was much stronger. Phil fell to one knee and clutched his head. Venom was inside Phil's head, and it felt like he was being attacked from the inside. He wasn't trying to steal Phil's abilities but tried to paralyze Phil so he could have a wide-open attack. Phil could see into his mind when he did this. It was another ability of a mind sonic. Venom moved closer, then slashed Phil's left shoulder and arm. Phil winced and put his right hand on his arm and shoulder, trying to ease the pain and stop the bleeding. Venom partially hit the wound Phil had sustained from Fire, which caused him more pain. Phil tried to heal it or sooth the pain, using his water ability. It helped but was still tender. His healing ability was nowhere near as powerful as Julie's. Venom stepped right in front of him, and Phil was still clutching his head and shoulder. The attack stopped suddenly, and Phil watched as Venom's appearance started to change. His skin turned all black like the oil that flowed inside of him. He changed shape, and like flowing water, began to take shape like Phil. His likeness looked exactly like Phil. The fear of Venom taking over his entire body caused him to panic. He partially recovered from Venom's last attack. Phil sent a heat ray at him, and he narrowly dodged it. The black liquid turned back to black and red and formed Venom again. Phil got up, and getting his bearings back, sent another more powerful heat ray at Venom, and it struck him on his right shoulder. He screamed in pain, and his shoulder was badly burned. His injured shoulder turned black, almost like oil reformed, and was completely healed in a split second. Venom jumped and bounded off a corner and struck Phil with great speed. He sent Phil flying, landing on his back, but he was okay. Phil got up as fast as he could, and he sent another heat ray, but Venom easily dodged it and moved to strike Phil again. Venom was hard to hit. Phil partially blocked the attack, but it hurt him. He couldn't keep taking hits like this. Phil found a spear in the ground with a sharp blade and a wooden shaft. He held it and pointed it at Venom, but it only held him at bay momentarily. The fire ability wasn't quick enough for this battle. Venom was too fast. Phil tried to jab him with the spear and missed. He spun and swung his tail and missed Phil. His tail hit part of a pillar and cracked it, proving how powerful his tail was. He swung his tail again. Phil had to block the strike with the shaft of the spear. Venom's tail slashed the shaft right in half. It shattered. Venom tried to get closer to Phil. His tail was his main weapon, but he wanted to get closer to use his teeth and claws. He moved closer, and Phil caught him in the head with the blade end of the half of the spear he had. Bleeding from his forehead, Venom dived toward Phil to bite, and Phil shoved the other half of the spear into his mouth. Phil slashed him again in the chest with the blade, and it cut him again but broke. He was bleeding the black substance from his chest and healed his injuries slowly. Venom snapped the shaft that was stuck in his mouth. Because Phil's last move unarmed him, he was more vulnerable to his attacks. Venom swung his tail in a quick motion, and it caught Phil in the stomach and cut him. Phil partially blocked it with his arms, and they were cut as well. He swung his tail again, but this time Phil caught it. It cut his hands, but he held on. Phil grabbed hold of his tail as tight as he could. Phil had Venom off-balance, and he was unable to attack. Phil heated his hands as hot as he could to the point where they were like fire. Phil wanted to burn his tail and make it useless. Venom screamed in pain, and his tail secreted a black oily substance onto Phil's cut hands. He pulled his tail quickly cutting Phil's hands again. Venom swung his tail around again too fast for Phil to see it coming. He slashed Phil on the throat just above his chest, and Phil bled from his throat and upper chest. A few inches higher and he would have slit Phil's throat or cut his head off. Phil was in pain. Venom hid to heal himself momentarily while he prepared for another attack. This gave Phil a moment to catch his breath. Phil tried to heal using the water, but it only slowed the bleeding. He needed more practice. Some of Venom's black oil was still on his hands and the ground. Phil burned it off his hands. The drops on the ground started to move towards Phil, so he used his heat ray to destroy those drops. He was weak and tired again. Venom was wearing him out. Phil was also angry now, and he noticed that fire got stronger, and water got weaker inside of him. He could sense Venom was getting ready to attack by forcing Phil to a lower level. It was wider open, and he would be able to use his speed, and Phil would have nowhere to hide. Phil tried to avoid that area, but Venom appeared to him again. He was completely healed and looked like he had just started the match. With no scratches or injuries, he moved even faster. Venom charged Phil again and knocked him into the lower area he was trying to avoid. Phil had nowhere to hide, and Venom charged him again. Phil reacted by sending a freeze ray at him, and it partially froze him. The water ability was much quicker to strike with but less damaging. He was stuck and could not move. Phil punched him a couple times but did little damage, and he couldn't break free. Venom grabbed Phil's arm to get closer and bite. Phil couldn't escape and tried to absorb some of his power. A trick that worked well against Blue, but it made him sick to the point that he threw up. Phil spit up some black liquid that make him choke. He regained his composure and was somewhat recovered. Venom absorbed some of his fire and water ability in the exchange. Phil backed up and hit him with a heat ray and then a freeze ray. Not a powerful blast but enough to push him back. Venom screamed in pain. The heat ray had less of an effect, and Venom used the water ability he had gained to break out of the freeze. He went to charge Phil again. He was most confident as absorbing even a little of the fire ability made him more resistant to Phil's attacks. He attacked more wildly and even faster. Phil couldn't keep up with his speed and pace anymore, and he was resisting all Phil's attacks. Venom, sensing a chance to kill, made a huge lunge forward, but Phil stepped aside and dropped his elbow on the side of Venom's head. It cracked his neck and skull and drove him straight into the ground. Black oil seeped out of him from his whole body, leaving it behind. Red oil also flowed out of his wounds. Phil used a heat ray to destroy the remains, winning the hard-fought battle. This was the last fatal strike that killed Venom; he would not recover. The momentum he used to attack backfired on him with Phil's strike.

Phil was in rough shape. His throat and hands were still bleeding. Phil had cuts on his left shoulder and arm. Venom was close to beating him, but he pulled through. It took everything and every ability in Phil to beat Venom. He was no longer a threat to Phil's Circle.

Phil took one last look. He put the fires out using his fire ability and exited the temple area back to the corridor leading to the rest of his Circle. The door opened, and Julie was the first to see Phil.

"Oh my God," she gasped when she saw Phil bleeding from multiple wounds on his body.

Jon helped Phil walk while Red wrapped himself around him to help. Phil appreciated the help but was fine. Julie held him close, and healing came slowly but surely.

"I'm okay. Really. I just need a little rest," Phil said short of breath. "Let me sit down."

"Can you keep this up?" Roxy asked. "There is at least one more round. You are in rough shape."

She brought up a good point. Phil wasn't sure how long his energy would last because he was ready to collapse. They all huddled together and held each other close. Strength flowed through the Circle, allowing Phil time to recover. Phil continued to rest. Daniel was scheduled for his next match; Damien was ready and waiting for him.

"You ready, Daniel?" Roxy asked.

"Yes, I am. I believe I can take him," Daniel replied.

"Okay. Watch out for the ray he can send that will stop your heart." Tina explained. "He will try to stop you dead. A dead stop. You are the quickest, and you should see it coming. You should be quick enough to avoid it."

"Take him out for me," Jon advised.

"I will," Daniel replied. "I am ready."

"Yes, you are," Phil agreed. "Your speed is the key. Not sure if he'll try to absorb your speed or if he even can."

"Ok," Daniel replied. "He won't get the chance."

"You get choice of where to face Damien," Tina explained.

"I'm fighting him in that desert area we walked through. I want a wide-open spot to fight," Daniel said.

"Good choice," Phil replied. "He won't be able to hide from you."

Daniel and Phil shook hands. All of them huddled together once again. The focus was on Daniel because he needed all their strength to give him more confidence. It would be a battle for him. Damien almost killed Jon, and he would have if it hadn't been for Julie's powerful ability as a healer. Daniel knew the risk, and Julie was preparing and resting herself in case her healing ability would be called upon. She was a little exhausted but was always ready to help. They were all ready.

"You are the warrior," Tina exclaimed. "You can win this. You are more powerful than you realize. Don't be discouraged."

Daniel was encouraged and strengthened even more. He was ready to go and proceeded down the corridor to the doors of the match. He entered the room that would lead to the area he wanted to fight in. The flat plain of the desert where there was no place to hide. Damien passed by them as he headed to the match. He looked at Jon, then at Phil. It was clear he wasn't happy to be up against

Daniel because his Circle was in even more turmoil. They could all sense and feel his aggravation. Another member of Damien's Circle was preparing to face Phantom, so he was angry and distracted. That gave Daniel an advantage in the battle. Damien was heavily favored for this match because he had many more powerful abilities than Daniel, but Daniel was a force that could stop him. He would not be intimated or undermined.

Damien vs Spirit

Damien entered the room leading to the battle location specified by Daniel. It was wide open for the battle, and Daniel was waiting for him. He wanted to face Damien in a closed area with no chance for hiding or sneak attacks. That was why he chose a flatland in a desert environment. Daniel also wanted to assert himself as a force in their Circle and not merely a shadow behind Phil. He didn't need to earn Phil's approval. Phil knew how tough he was and was glad he wouldn't have to face Daniel. Damien was not impressed because he didn't mind a direct battle. He had defeated Jon, one of the Circle's strongest members, earlier.

Damien was expecting to walk all over Daniel because he thought he would be a pushover. Daniel became spirit and charged Damien to catch him off guard. Damien sent the null ray at Spirit but missed. Spirit was much too fast to be caught by Damien's attack. He grabbed onto Damien's arm and pulled him off balance. Spirit changed to Daniel and hit Damien with his forearm. The hit sent Damien down and drew some blood from him. Damien was angrier now. He fought toe to toe with Daniel, using a form of martial art. After he hit Daniel a few times in

ROUND TWO

the chest, Daniel went down. He got back up and was ready for more. They had both drawn blood.

Daniel stayed in human form and moved quickly to strike Damien. Daniel's speed continued to startle him. Damien took a right fist to his face and a punch to the stomach. He was winded but far from done. Damien came back with a hard left that caught Daniel on the jaw and a right to his upper body. Daniel stumbled back. Damien hit Daniel with a right kick, and he went down hard. Daniel struggled to get up. Damien was getting tired but was ready to finish him. Damien sent a powerful null ray that hit Daniel directly, and he went down. Daniel changed to Spirit as he fell, and he was visibly weakened by that last hit. Damien thought he had won, but Spirit began to rise. He was recovering from the null ray and was able to resist it to some degree. Damien was in shock because no one had ever resisted his null ray. Damien hit Spirit with it again, but Spirit kept rising and was no longer affected. Damien was beside himself and was filled with fear. Spirit had taken his best shot and was still there. Spirit became Daniel and prepared to attack again. Daniel had taken more hits during this match but was ready for more, but Damien was not. He backed away from Daniel and teleported out of the match. Damien had conceded the victory, leaving Daniel victorious. Daniel took some powerful shots but was tough. He had nothing left to prove.

Daniel left the battle area and returned to their Circle. Roxy ran and embraced Daniel. The rest of them also ran to embrace him. He had won a serious battle and proved he was a powerful member of their Circle. He was not under Phil's shadow; he was beside Phil as a leader and meant to be. He was a bit worse for wear but fine and ready to fight again. He was a warrior to be sure and tougher than Phil in some ways.

"You are amazing," Roxy said. She kissed him on the cheek.

"Good work," Jon said.

Julie healed Daniel, and he recovered well. He was regaining his strength and was off with Phil to round three. They all huddled together and held each other close. They were proud of Daniel, and everyone was proud of Phil.

Phantom was to face a member of Damien's Circle, but the member was forced by Damien not to fight, and Damien's Circle was gone from the tournament. They no longer had any representation. Phantom was automatically through to the third round. Damien and his circle were nowhere to be found.

Phantom was considering his options. He believed he could defeat Spirit or Phil, but he didn't want to face Fire because he didn't think he could defeat him. Fire continued to follow the tournament with much interest.

Fire was having a major effect on the tournament because many were afraid of him. Everyone knew Fire hated the Circle and planned to destroy it. That was why the tournament had less combatants than originally expected. There was no way to counteract the fire ability Fire had. It was the most powerful ability. There wasn't a participant that couldn't be killed with this ability, and other fire users couldn't use this ability against Fire. He wanted control and wanted to keep control to himself.

The remaining match from round two was Layla against Goliath. Layla was angry, and Goliath was going

ROUND TWO

for broke. Layla was disheartened by the fact that Venom had been defeated. The Circle was not sure of the relationship they had. Layla was the odds-on favourite to win. Goliath was already in the room. Layla looked at the Circle and Phil specifically when she walked by. She knew Phil killed Venom. She was angry. When she stared at Phil, he could feel the presence of her power and energy. The power she possessed wasn't coming directly from her. It was something that moved with her and latched onto her. That didn't sit well with Phil. Whatever power she had was not good. It was slowly killing her as well as being used as a deadly weapon. This power was known as Shadow, a powerful controlling spirit. That's all Phil and the Circle could sense from her.

Layla entered through the large, grey, metal doors. She was favoured and was facing Goliath in a closed dark room. Layla called on Shadow to become a black panther who was massive and deadly. Goliath was ready. He was powerful as well and a morphasis user, even though he was considered an underdog because Shadow was considered more powerful. Layla was still disappointed that Venom had been defeated, and she wasn't able to get focus to use the full strength of Shadow. She was almost killed by Goliath. She left the match and the tournament, leaving Goliath as the winner. Goliath was through to round three.

Layla exited the match with no injuries but was upset. She looked at Phil and his Circle as she left. It was a look of curiosity and some intention. The circle wondered how she was connected to Venom. She knew that Venom was defeated. Venom's followers were in turmoil now that he was eliminated. Layla left dazed and confused, the rest of Venom's followers all also left in disarray. They were all angry at Phil and not sure what to do next. They were now leaderless and had no guidance.

A little while later, Goliath exited the room of the battles and walked out. He looked at Daniel and Phil, ready for the next round. He didn't appear to be afraid of Fire. He was intimidating and getting stronger all the time. He had barely a scratch or mark from the first two rounds. He was powerful. No one was sure what power he possessed.

26
ROUND THREE

Round three was set to start. Goliath was rested and ready to go. Phil was as rested as he could be. Daniel was a little worse for wear, but he would fight at a moment's notice without a second thought. He already proved that he would never back down from any challenge he faced. Phantom was waiting and deciding what to do. He didn't want to face Fire either. Phil was ready for whatever challenges came. They would get choice on the matchup they wanted for this round. They wanted to choose carefully.

Roxy, as their leader, had to make the choice. *Would Daniel fight Goliath or would Phil?* They both had injuries. Daniel was in worse shape, and Phil had more powerful abilities. Phil was healing but still in pain. Daniel was recovering but would need more time. Daniel might be the better matchup, and his speed would work well against Goliath. Phil could match Goliath power for power, but he didn't have a clear advantage. That's what Roxy was looking for. Goliath was probably stronger and quicker than Phil. Goliath, being a morphasis user, could be difficult to fight, depending on what his other form was. That was where Daniel would match well against him. Daniel was the fastest in this entire tournament, which gave him a special advantage. *Would the other face Phantom?* Roxy and Tina wanted to keep Phil away from Phantom after the altercation earlier. Speed would be the best weapon against Phantom since he wasn't fast. Phil wanted to fight Phantom and be done with him.

Roxy was facing her own battle, trying to decide the matchups. Goliath was extremely strong, and Spirit may be able to counteract his strength with speed. Spirit had also defeated Alligator who was a powerful morphasis user. Phil was stronger than Spirit and more powerful in terms of ability. Phil would be a good match against Goliath because there was a possibility Phil could overpower him, but there was no guarantee that tactic would work.

Goliath was a tricky opponent to match against because, as a human, he was quick. Perhaps quicker than Phil, but Daniel was much quicker than him. He was also a morphasis user, and his other form, of which they were not sure of, was extremely strong but slow. Goliath got a break when Layla exited the tournament. That's all the Circle knew of Goliath.

Damien didn't expect to have such a tough time with Daniel. He had expected to get this far and even win. He may have been looking ahead, seeing if Phil would make it to round three, and with Fire waiting, he may have given up, letting everyone else battle it out. He clearly didn't want to face Phil or Fire.

There was the question of where Goliath's allegiance lay. They wondered why Goliath wanted control of the circle. He didn't connect or interact with anyone else in the tournament from what they saw.

It seemed like the other Circles wanted Phil's circle to win and let his circle deal with Fire. He would challenge Phil's Circle for control immediately following the tournament. If Fire won, the Circle would be destroyed, but if they won, the other Circles would try to get control from them. For Goliath to win, he would have to defeat Phil. If he was defeated, Goliath would also have to defeat Spirit, or if Spirit fought him first, he would have to face Phil after, depending on what happened with Phantom. They were in a good position, but the winner of the tournament would still have to face Fire. Control of the Circle might not be enough to defeat him, but nobody wanted to think about that. The rest of the tournament might be the least of their worries as the real battle would start once the tournament was won. In the back of his mind, Phil hoped the Creator had some plan to thwart Fire in the end.

Roxy and Phil determined that they would not surrender under any conditions. They were not going to stop now because there was so much at stake. Neither of them grasped the full gravity of the situation, but they knew there was more. Tina could sense this. They all could, and they knew they had to act on this. There was no turning back.

They also knew that the Creator was giving them strength and determination. He had a plan that was being executed. He had more control, but they also had a choice. They had free will, but the Creator worked everything together for his purpose and for the good of all. There was more going on than they could understand,

and they knew there was more going on here beyond the tournament.

Roxy and Phil had to decide who would face Goliath. They got to choose because they had two members of their Circle in the final rounds. Roxy felt that Phil should face Goliath because she believed that Phil could beat him. Phil had defeated Blue and Venom. These were both enemies that were quicker than him, but Goliath was a stronger enemy and quick, depending on which form he used. Phil was stronger than his two previous opponents but not this time. He had no strength advantage. Spirit sensed that he would not be able to morph as quickly as Spirit could, and no one was sure of Goliath's other form. Goliath was also a close-range fighter, which could make Phil's abilities less effective. Phil was almost killed by Venom as well in a close quarter's battle. There were so many things to consider.

"The choice is yours, Phil," Roxy advised.

"I believe you can beat him, Phil. I believe either of you can beat him," Julie assured.

"I'm good with whatever choice you make," Daniel said.

Phil had to make a choice. Goliath was waiting to find out who he would face. Either of them would have to face him on his territory. Phil was stronger, but Daniel was quicker. Goliath could use either depending on who he would face. Phil still wanted to put Phantom in his place but decided that he needed to face Goliath. Phil was ready and willing. Goliath entered the room first to prepare. Phil did not want to take this match lightly, so he prepared himself and began to focus. Daniel would face Phantom.

ROUND THREE

Cobra vs. Goliath

"Time to become David and take down Goliath," Julie said.

"Didn't David have God on his side? Who can defeat God?" Phil asked Julie.

"God is on our side. You should know that," Julie replied.

That statement made Phil feel better. He was more determined now.

"You are unstoppable," Daniel said. "We are all with you."

"Use all your abilities," Scarlet advised. "You will need to."

"You're ready," Tina assured.

Phil entered the room, and it led to a jungle type setting. It seemed like this area had never been touched by a human presence. There were no paths, and it was beautiful and quiet. There was a clearing with healthy, green grass. The trees were taller than any Phil had ever seen. They had vines and an abundance of leaves. It would be hard to find anything or anyone here, so Phil moved slowly and cautiously.

There was a warm calmness in the air. The temperature was hot, which Phil didn't mind after the two previous matches he had. There was a peace in the air in this area, but it was a fake peace that felt synthetic. It was not true peace. He had a mission at hand and wasn't about to get distracted. The atmosphere was lulling him to relax and let his guard down. This was no doubt a strategy of Goliath to attack Phil when he got complacent. He kept his guard up.

Phil walked by a tree, watching carefully for Goliath. If he was in the trees, Phil could not see him. He was a big guy, so he shouldn't be hard to find. A large boulder came right at Phil, he moved out of the way right in time, and it hit the tree behind him, putting a huge crack in it. Phil looked ahead, and Goliath approached him. He punched Phil in the stomach, and Phil crumbled. Goliath hit hard and fast. He grabbed Phil and threw him into the tree. Phil hit the tree and landed flat on the ground in pain. Goliath was fast and strong.

He moved toward Phil and hit him in the side of his leg, and he stumbled. Phil hit him in the stomach and then in the face, knocking him back. He was startled by Phil's strength, power, and fighting skill. Phil was getting stronger and more determined. Goliath charged Phil and grabbed him by the throat and pushed him up against the cracked tree. Goliath tried to choke Phil, lifting him off the ground. Phil heated his body up so that it burned Goliaths hands. He released Phil immediately and looked at the burns on his hands. The burns made him angry. Phil took a second to catch his breath. Goliath charged at Phil. Regaining his composure, Phil stepped aside, turned, and elbowed Goliath in the side of his head. The was the same move Phil hit Venom with to win that battle. The shot took him off balance, and he hit the cracked tree, causing it even more damage. He got up slowly, visibly frustrated by his failed attacks. Phil was growing more and more confident. He had taken some of Goliath's best shots. Phil was still in a defensive mode though; he needed to get on the offensive. Phil kicked him in the stomach and hit him with a freeze ray in the chest. It stunned him, and he grabbed his chest. The water ability

ROUND THREE

was faster than fire but nowhere near as strong. Phil hit him in the face, and he fell to the ground. He picked up a broken branch and tried to stab Phil in the throat with it out of desperation. Seeing what he was trying do, Phil blocked it, they wrestled with it snapping it in half. Phil hit him in the throat, and he began to bleed. He got up and kicked Phil in the stomach, and he fell back. Phil got up quickly to strike again, but Goliath began to back up. Phil was still getting stronger while Goliath was noticeably slower ever since Phil hit him with the freeze ray. Phil gathered strength to send a heat ray towards him, but the whole area began to darken. Phil held back from striking with fire and observed what was happening. The sky got cloudy, and the wind picked up. It became cold and unpleasant. Phil couldn't even see him anymore to hit him with a heat ray. The whole atmosphere was changing.

The sky brightened up a little bit, and Phil wasn't sure what was happening. He couldn't see Goliath anymore, and he heard a growl. It was loud and all around him. A huge tree trunk came rolling at Phil, but he dodged it. Another came flying toward him. Phil dived to dodge that one. Another came flying. Phil stepped aside from that one as well. A branch hit Phil and cut him. He moved forward with more determination. Phil could see a gigantic bear in the distance: it was Goliath. His morphasis form was a huge bear with large fangs and claws. Phil had a strange feeling he had seen this bear before. He picked up a decent sized rock and whipped it as hard as he could. Phil's fire ability propelled it even faster and harder than he could throw it. It hit Goliath in the head and stunned him momentarily. Phil ran towards him as quick as he could. Goliath threw another tree towards

Phil, and he hit it with a heat ray, breaking it in half and burning it to a crisp. He tried to charge Phil as a bear, though not as quick as his human form. Phil could see the wound on his throat from the branch still bleeding, and he could also see a wound on Goliath's head from the rock he had thrown. Goliath smashed a close by tree knocking it almost on top of him. Phil dove out of the way and sprang back to his feet. He sent one of the most powerful heat rays he had ever generated at Goliath, and it hit his heart dead center, leaving a hole where the heart once was. He collapsed in a huge heap dead in his tracks. Phil had defeated Goliath. The match was over.

    Phil left the area of the match with nothing more than a few scratches. He took a lot less damage compared to the previous rounds. He was stronger than ever and still increasing. It was a huge victory and Phil had overcome. His strategy had worked.

Phantom vs. Spirit

The other match was Spirit fighting against Phantom. It would be Spirit's choice of where to fight. Daniel wanted another wide-open area to fight, but Phantom was good at all forms of combat, so it didn't matter to him. He was expecting an easy match, but with Daniel surviving Damien's attack, Phantom was concerned about this battle. Daniel proved he could fight and take an opponent's best shot. Phantom was also concerned about facing Fire if he were to win the tournament. He didn't have a solution to Fire's power. He would also have to face Phil after Daniel, and with the opponents Phil had taken down, he wasn't looking forward to that fight. He was particularly surprised that Phil defeated Blue. He had worked with

ROUND THREE

Blue and thought Phil would be defeated easily. That assumption turned out to be dead wrong.

Daniel chose the rocky desert near the cliff similar to Jump-Point Alpha to fight Phantom. It was exactly like the cliff in Phil's dream—the one he jumped off. There would be no place to hide and little room to move quickly. Daniel was faster, and although his speed would be less effective here, he wanted to fight Phantom here where it would all be a face to face battle with nowhere to hide. Phantom was not fast but was strong, and they were not sure how a fight with him at this proximity would be for Daniel. Phantom entered the battle area and smiled when he saw where they were fighting. He recognized the area. It did look like the cliff from Jump-Point Alpha. Daniel became Spirit and charged Phantom to strike and attack using his speed advantage. Phantom had trouble with his speed but came back hitting hard, and it caused Daniel to back off. Phantom had weathered the storm, at least temporarily. Daniel attempted to strike Phantom with punches and kicks, but Phantom blocked extremely well. Phantom hit harder and more accurately than his opponent did. Daniel took some of his hardest attacks and kept on fighting. Daniel's speed would overwhelm Phantom at times, and he would not be able to absorb or enter Daniel's mind with his abilities. Daniel kept those abilities at bay with his speed. Phantom used his teleportation ability to counteract Daniel's speed, and it was working, but Daniel never gave up or backed down. The fight went back and forth with no one taking a significant advantage over the other. This disheartened Phantom as he had also expected to beat Daniel easily. He was realizing that he could not do everything all himself, and he needed others in his Circle. He envied Phil because he saw the enemies Phil had defeated and thought he could do the same. Up until Daniel, Phantom had beaten all his opponents easily, but Daniel was as tough as they come. Phantom backed off the fight with Daniel and left the arena. Phantom did not have the power and strength he thought he did. This move gave Daniel the victory. It was not the way he wanted to win the match, but he would take it at this point. Daniel was victorious. Another opponent had underestimated him.

    They all rejoiced, hugged each other and were ecstatic. The tournament to gain full control of the Circle had finished, and Phil's Circle had come through. They were all overjoyed. Spirit and Phil had won all their matches. *Who would have thought that they could win this?* They used all the abilities they were given and overcame.

27
BATTLE FOR THE CIRCLE

The Creator was sitting on his throne. Phil found it odd that Ariel and Serenity were not present. Elo was not there either, but Fire was. He was ready to interfere, even while being restrained by the Creator. That restraint appeared to be weakening. They could all sense it was being released and knew that something was out of balance. This made them nervous.

The Creator gave Phil and his circle complete control of the Circle. This gave them power to create other circles, or disband them, or add, and take away from them. They became more aware and more powerful. Their senses increased as did their gifts and abilities. Other Circles that were still there pledged to follow them, but other Circles were jealous and envious. They knew that some of these circles would challenge them for full control, but they would deal with that at the proper time. The Creator was glad they won the tournament, but he was not surprised. It was as if it was his plan all along. He was all-knowing and all-powerful. They wondered if he knew all this would happen the way it did. The Creator seemed weaker after this, though. Phil noticed him appearing more human than when they had met earlier. The limitless power He displayed earlier had disappeared.

Phil gave Red permission for free reign in their Circle so he could act freely and be as connected as the other members. He was a powerful ally, and they trusted Him and treated Him as any other member. After he was given this privilege, he began to move even more freely and flowing all around them. They were connected on an even deeper level with him after everything they'd been through together. It was as deep a connection as any of them had, giving them more clarity and power. Red was overjoyed. This move made Fire upset.

After the Creator had given them control and power over the Circle, he seemed weaker than at any other time. He was sad and sorrowful. Fire was getting stronger, and they could see that something was not right. It didn't add up. This wasn't the same Creator that Phil spoke to earlier. The whole area was not as bright as it had been before. It was dull and dim compared to its former glory. There was something brewing. *Did the Creator give away all His power?* He was constantly decreasing in glory and ability while Fire was increasing without restraint to his power. This concerned everyone in the Circle. Fire stepped forward.

"I challenge for complete control of the Circle," Fire announced to Phil and the others. "You might as well just surrender; I will take the Circle for myself now. I told you this tournament was pointless. You all lose in the end. I win. I always win."

Phil didn't know what to do. Roxy was speechless, and the rest of the Circle was in shock that he could challenge so soon after the tournament had ended. They wondered what would happen if they refused to fight him. Even though they knew their abilities better, Fire was an enemy that almost killed them already, and Phil could only attack him with water. They knew this challenge would happen, but it didn't make facing it any easier.

They looked to the Creator, who was getting more and more sorrowful and weaker. He was in noticeable pain. Fire stood between them and him, and they could not get to him to try to help. They wondered what they could do but had no answer. He looked up at them.

"Do not be afraid, and do not worry. Darkness will never overtake you," the Creator reassured with a weak voice.

"But I will," Fire smirked.

Fire turned to the Creator, getting more and more powerful still. He could have been saving his energy to weaken the Creator and take over the Circle. With the Creator in such an ineffective state, Fire was posed to do as he wished.

"Do what you have come to do," the Creator said to Fire like He knew what was coming.

The Creator looked at Phil and the Circle and cracked a smile. He looked older and paler by the minute while Fire looked on, blazing and glowing. His power was growing, and his eyes were bright. Fire sent a heat ray more powerful than Phil had ever seen or generated using his ability. This ray hit the Creator flush and made a huge exploding flash of power. The Creator was disintegrated to nothing. His throne was left empty charred and damaged. Fire then went and sat on what was left of it. Nothing was left of the Creator but ash and soot.

Red shook uncontrollably for several moments but settled down on Julie's arm again. He appeared to be rattled. He was trembling and moving slow, and Julie held him close while trying to hold back her own tears. The rest of the Circle experienced the reaction.

All the other Circles fled. Only their Circle remained. Phil wondered what had happened to the Creator he had met before. They thought the Creator was all-powerful, and He had restricted Fire before. He had restrained Fire from killing them, but now He was gone. No signs of any of the angels or anyone else. *Would the Circle give them enough power to defeat Fire?* They thought about running while they still could but stood speechless and afraid.

"My challenge still stands. Do you accept?" Fire asked. "Or will you be a coward and run like everyone else? Just bow to me and give me the Circle, and I may not kill all of you."

"Is there a compromise? Can we not live in peace? Does there have to be so much fighting and death? Haven't enough people died already?" Julie replied. Her words were passionate and heartfelt, but no one wanted to make a deal with the devil. Fire was evil, and they all knew they couldn't trust him.

"Give me control of the Circle then we will discuss your surrender," Fire replied. "You are in no position to bargain."

"We will not surrender to you or give you control of the Circle," Roxy replied stepping in. Her words were strong as was her will. She had strength where all of them were weak and afraid. She was bold and not compromising in any way. They all admired her courage but still had to deal with Fire.

"Then you will die, and I will take the Circle from you," Fire shouted. "Either way I will win. I may let you live and be my slaves."

"I would rather die," Julie replied out of no where. Julie began to rise in boldness as well. She had given up on comprising. The whole circle was drawing on its strength. She rose for this situation.

"So be it," Fire announced.

Fire vs Cobra's Circle

He raised his arms, and two fireballs flew towards the top of the castle they were all in. The whole place started to crumble and shake. They dodged pieces of rubble and parts of the castle that were falling all around them. Fire struck the ground with both hands, and the ground started to crack, sending flames out of the cracks. They all began to run for it. The whole place shook with a violent earthquake, and everything around them was falling apart. No place was safe. All the exits were blocked by debris now, and there was no escape.

Tina was trying to gain her bearings and teleport them out of the castle, but it was falling apart fast. They got to a hallway where the ceiling was still intact. They all huddled, and Tina focused. The beautiful castle was falling all around them. They had no idea where Fire was once the place started to collapse. Tina used her teleport ability to move them to a safer location just in the nick of time. The room they left was nothing but a heap of rubble and rock, and they would have all been killed if she hadn't got them out of the hallway. Tina had saved them all. They were safe for the moment.

The City of fire

Overworld was in chaos and shaking, right to its foundation. They appeared in the middle of a city, but this city was in ruins. They were still in Overworld, but this place was torn to shreds. Every building was damaged from fire, and the earthquake, and some buildings were still smoking while others were on fire. Many buildings were barely standing because of the extensive damage Fire caused. The sky was dark and cloudy. There was garbage, burned cars, and pieces of buildings scattered everywhere. A huge battle had taken place here. The city was un-inhabited and un-liveable. It was a big city, yet nothing of value. There was a huge skyscraper-type building that was still in one piece, in the center of the city. It towered over all the other buildings. They headed towards that building for cover and to regroup.

These buildings and the surrounding area resembled what was found on Earth. It looked like versions of their world but damaged by Fire's actions and influence. Fire wanted to manifest this in their world from what they could tell. It would become their reality if they didn't stop Fire here and now. They were sensing this was Fire's plan since the beginning; they were sure of it. They all sensed this and Fire was making no effort to hide his intentions.

The castle they had left was in ruins, and there was nothing left of its beauty. They were sad that the Creator was dead and still did not understand what had happened. Fire was getting his power from somewhere but from where it wasn't clear. They could tell that all that power was not his own. Tina could sense Fire was closing in, but there was something different about his presence. Fire was no longer human. *Did he use the morphasis ability?*

Tina was sensing Fire, but bigger and stronger than when they had last seen him. Roxy and the rest of the Circle were sensing the same things. Phil could sense the power of Fire surging.

Fire was the strongest fire user and controlled every aspect of that ability. They could feel the heat when he approached. Phil could sense him more clearly now and knew that he was dangerously close. Whenever Fire closed in on them Phil's fire ability would increase, but Phil couldn't use it directly against him. It would have no effect. Focusing on the fire ability gave Phil no answers. They continued to move cautiously toward the building.

They were in the base of the skyscraper now. The area they were in began to increase in temperature, and red-coloured smoke surrounded them. It was hard to breathe. They needed to get to place where they could get some fresh air. They had to move. Fire was really close now, and Phil could feel his presence. They looked for a way out of this area, but Fire was coming for them.

This skyscraper was, from what they could tell, built by Fire. He created it as part of a new kingdom he wanted to establish in Overworld. The building was decrepit, in terrible condition, falling apart as they walked through it. It was as if the building was dying. It looked fine on the outside but, after a closer look, it was falling apart from the inside. Every wall and every piece of the floor was decaying right before their eyes. He wanted to make this the reality on Earth: a world damaged and corrupted by Fire.

Phil knew that they were seeing the building in its true state. In the Earth realm, it was state of the art and a pinnacle of man's creation, but the truth was far different. It was an illusion. It was falling apart from the inside out. Crumbling. It would eventually collapse. It did not lead to life but was a path to death, a wide road leading nowhere.

They also noticed this building did not have a foundation, so it was destined to fall. *Why would anyone build a building like this with no foundation?* Then, the truth was clear. Fire wanted it all gone. He was building everything on a weak non-existent foundation that would collapse and be destroyed. Fire wanted to be the destroyer of Overworld and of the Earth realm. His intention was to level everything and He had the power to do so.

Red would use his abilities to hold the building up and make it more stable than it was. If it weren't for Red, the building would have collapsed with all of them in it. Red was using his strength to keep it standing. Every motion the Circle made caused cracks and chipped away at the little support they had.

Phil saw Fire through all the smoke. His skin had turned red and He stood upright. Fire looked half-human and half-dragon but was constantly changing form. He was surrounded by flames and a glow. Everything was burning around him along with everything he touched. The heat was almost unbearable. Fire approached Phil.

"This is your last chance. You can join me right now or die," he shouted.

"We will never join you," Phil replied.

"That's too bad," Fire responded. He moved toward Phil, but Spirit came from the side, and Fire turned right into Spirit as he lunged forward. Spirit caught Fire by the throat with his teeth. Fire screamed in pain and heated his skin up, burning Spirit and causing him to release. Fire nailed Spirit with an uppercut, hurting him and burning him. Phil charged Fire and came in direct contact with him. Phil tried using his mindsonic ability to steal the fire ability from him, but it didn't work. Fire was too strong. Phil got burned in the exchange and backed off.

"You can't steal my ability," Fire screamed. "I'm too powerful. No human can possess this much power."

Phil absorbed, but it wasn't enough of Fire to do any good. He would have to take full control and be at the same level of Fire, and that didn't appear to be possible.

Fire focused on Phil and the wound he had given him before began to hurt even more than when Phil first got it. Phil stumbled back because of the pain. Fire kicked him in the stomach, scratching Phil with his claws and burning him in the process. Phil fell back and was severely injured. He had a scar on his chest burnt in by Fire who surrounded Phil with a ring of fire like before. He could not put out the fire to get free and was trapped. Julie could not get to Phil to heal him. Fire made sure of that. Julie helped Spirit recover, and she continued to try to get to Phil but was blocked at every turn. Phil was injured and trapped. She couldn't find a way to him.

Jon attacked Fire by hitting him multiple times. He knocked Fire back, but Fire was toying with him. Jon picked up and threw pieces of the building at Fire. Jon threw pieces of cars and bricks from buildings and anything he could find. Jon surprised Fire with his strength. Fire used his heat to knock Jon back and hit him with a Fire ray, but it was not fatal, but Jon was seriously wounded now too. Julie made her way over to Jon to heal him. She managed to stay out of sight to get to Jon. She was able to heal him.

Every time Julie healed someone; it would anger Fire. Julie was now his target. Fire made eye contact with her as she healed anyone who needed healing. She still could not get to Phil. Fire moved towards Julie.

Red left Julie's arm and proceeded to attack Fire. Red moved through the ground, the walls and tried to tie up Fire. Red surrounded him and enveloped him. Fire began to struggle and burned Red causing, him to release and retreat. Red was assisting and distracting more than anything else, and that technique was quite effective. He seemed to stay back and only intervene when they really needed the help. Without his intervention, they would have all died. He also continued to hold up parts of the building preventing it from caving in.

Phil was still in pain on the ground and surrounded by a circle of fire. He crawled to the edge of the ring and tried to put it out using his fire ability. Since Fire was a stronger at fire and controlled it, Phil could not put out the fire ring and was still trapped. Phil used the water ability he stole from Blue earlier in the tournament and put out the ring of fire. The water ability was strong enough to do it. Julie noticed and made her way over to Phil, so she began to heal him. Fire noticed that Julie was using her ability to heal Phil and approached them. He also wondered how Phil was able to put out the ring of fire but did not think the water ability was strong enough to put it out. Phil was still on the ground. Julie laid her hands on him. Julie touched Phil and sent a white ray from her eyes. She used as much power as she could get out of Phil to attack with another type of ability. The ray hit Fire and pushed him back. It had little effect on him except to slow him and make him angrier than ever. Julie had used some of Phil's power to attack with her own ability, but it was too weak to do any major damage. She did what she could.

Fire began to key in on Julie. He was angry at the fact that she was healing everyone he was injuring. Fire tried to strike Julie, but Spirit and Jon both tackled him, making his heat ray barely miss Julie. The ray he sent scarred her, but she healed it and completely recovered. Julie was safe for now.

"Now I'm really mad!" Julie exclaimed.

Fire knocked off Spirit, and Jon and got back up. Fire turned toward Phil to attack. Phil sent a heat ray around him, cutting into the floor. This caused the floor to collapse all around Fire, and he fell into it. The rays Phil sent into the ground went deep, and he fell a long way. Fire was down but was coming back up even more enraged. He wanted to end this now. His anger made him stronger, which was a trait of users of the fire ability. Phil had noticed the same thing in himself.

Fire came out of the floor and started sending fire that flowed like water all over the floor. Parts of the floor would burn away or collapse, and they ran as fast as they could to dodge it. They moved up the stairs of the skyscraper. They couldn't get out. Fire pursued them. Phil hit him with a freeze ray, and it partially froze him, causing him great pain. He let out a loud and surprised scream. Using fire and water together, Phil was able stop the flowing flames Fire had started. He was surprised at the power of the water ability, and he retreated slightly to reconsider the strategy he was using. He was not taking Phil lightly or playing games anymore. The freeze ray hurt and startled him.

They rushed as quickly as they could up the stairs away from Fire. He had blocked the walls and windows so that they had nowhere to go but up. Every step they took seemed to cause the building to crack or break. The building was falling apart, and they were heading up and up the burnt and broken stairs. Fire was forcing them to the top. The foundation was cracking, and it seemed unstable all around, not only under the building. This was not the best way to go, but it was the only way they could proceed. *Was Fire setting them up for a big fall?* This building would not survive this battle, and they had little time to ponder this as Fire was coming on much stronger. Fire was trying to trap them at the top of the building.

They continued up the stairs, and parts of it kept breaking. Julie stumbled on a broken step, but Phil caught her.

"I got you," Phil said to Julie, holding her close for a second.

Her reaction was fear and concern. Phil could see it in her face.

Red used his abilities to hold them steady and help them climb the steps. They made their way up at a steady pace, and they kept going up. They were too high to exit the building through the windows.

Fire began to pursue and destroyed some of the steps behind them. He was moving up at a frantic pace. Spirit, Jon, and Phil fell back while Roxy, Julie, Scarlet, and Tina continued up the stairs. Julie fell back from them a bit in case any of them needed healing. Red was free floating close by them as they prepared to face Fire again. Red was moving quickly and more aggressively than ever. He was preventing any of them from falling and holding as much of the structure as he could in place.

They could feel smashes and sounds of pieces of the building being destroyed below them. The building shook. It felt as if he was going to bring the whole building down on them. The ground quaked all around them, and the already fragile building was cracking and breaking even more. They picked up the pace and continued going up.

Phil had a funny feeling. He realized that Fire had the power to destroy the entire building with all of them in it. Fire was stronger than this, and he could come straight at them and incinerate them up in one gigantic swoop. All of them began to have these thoughts. He had killed the Creator, and he was at the most powerful they had ever seen him. There was more to this than at first sight. He was either playing games with them, or he was being held back by another powerful force. The Creator was powerful enough to hold Fire's power in check, but He was dead. Red could have been restricting his power, and Fire seemed to be afraid of Red. Still, Fire held back, but why.

Fire lit the lower levels on fire so that they were unable to go back down. The rest of the building was already falling to pieces. They did not know how the building was able to stand. So far, Red had done a great job making sure the building didn't cave in. He was doing his best to keep the building standing. He would reinforce where he could and re-create burnt beams and walls to keep the building upright. Red was constantly working in the background to keep the Circle alive.

Phil continued up the stairs, climbing up any ledge he could find. They had slowed down a bit to catch their breath. Fire seemed to be farther back than before. Tina was getting stronger. Once she was ready, their hope was that she could teleport them out from there to a safer spot. The whole area's foundation was unstable, and it looked like the skyscraper was standing on a pool of lava. It was moving and shaking constantly. There were earthquakes every so often, and nothing was stable. It was a matter of time before this building would fall and take them all down with it.

Phil was at the back of the Circle, checking behind him for Fire and trying to keep up with the rest of the Circle. It became hot around Phil, and they all detected the sudden burst of heat. The floor under Phil gave way, but he held on to the ledge, nearly losing his grip.

"Run," Phil shouted to Julie and the others.

"Not without you," Julie replied.

Red tried to grab Phil but was unable to. He barely lost grip of Phil's hand because Fire had pulled him down. The Circle could no longer see Phil anymore.

"Phil!" Julie screamed in a panic. She tried to run back to get Phil but was held back by Jon and Spirit. More of the floor gave way, and they had to keep going up.

"Keep going up till we get to a more secure location," Roxy shouted. "Otherwise, we'll all fall."

"We can't just leave him," Julie screamed back. There were tears in her eyes. She was mad at Roxy for not wanting to do something. Julie refused to keep going without Phil.

"Can you tell where he is and if he is ok?" Julie asked Tina.

"I can't tell, but I'm pretty sure he is still alive," Tina responded.

"Pretty sure?" Julie replied in shock.

Tina wasn't sure at all. Julie obeyed Roxy's instruction to keep going up. Spirit stood as close to the edge as he could, but Phil was nowhere in sight. Scarlet wasn't sure either. They were all having a hard time detecting him with all the confusion.

"Let me send Red after him. Red can bring Phil back to us. Red can protect him," Julie said to Roxy.

"Okay. Send him," Roxy replied.

"Go find Phil. Please bring him back safely. Please, Red," Julie pleaded to Red.

Red, who had wrapped himself around Julie's arm, released his grip and went down the seemingly bottomless hole where Phil had fallen. There was nothing but flames and darkness. None of them could stand the powerful heat emanating from the hole.

Phil fell further than he could have imagined. It seemed like an eternity of falling. Phil was surrounded by darkness and was trapped in a tight space. There was debris around him and on him, but he was in one piece. Phil had a few scratches and was disoriented. Red had softened and slowed the fall. He was that quick. Red went to make sure the rest of the Circle was safe because he knew Fire was close. Phil tried to regain his bearings. He was in a deep pit under the building, and he didn't know what to do.

Phil heard a voice. It felt like it was all around him, yet it was coming from the inside. It was a still, small voice, and it felt like it came from his heart.

"Do not be afraid. You will overcome. Rise above this," the voice said. "Stand. Get up."

Phil recognized the voice as that of the Creator. He seemed to know that it was his voice. It seemed impossible because He was killed by Fire right before Phil's eyes, yet the voice comforted Phil and gave him strength. It was as if the Creator were right there with him. Phil's strength was renewed, and he was recovering.

He used his fire ability to break out of the debris and burn away the things around him, freeing himself in the process. He was in some type of pit or cavern. There was a little light shining from above, but it was faint and seemed like it was fading. Yet in this, he was not afraid. Phil would rise above as the voice had told him. Red was drifting in the background again. He came close to reassure Phil and comfort him. Phil created little fireballs to float around him and give him light so he could see.

Phil felt that sudden heat again. He felt Fire's presence closing in on him, sapping Phil of his already depleted strength, weakening him. His fire ability, however, was increasing as Fire approached. Phil could feel the burn on his chest throbbing again. Fire was moving around him and limiting his fire ability so that he could not use it to see. Phil could tell he was near, but Phil could not light up the room. He was caught in darkness, and he could barely see anything but knew Fire was close. He tried to light up the area where he was, but Fire kept putting his lights out and left him in darkness.

"Do you surrender to me?" Fire asked. "have you had enough".

Thoughts filled Phil's mind of surrendering, but he could not. He would not. It was so tempting though.

"No. I don't give up. I guess you will have to kill me. Why don't you just kill me?" Phil asked.

Phil thought he saw Fire, but he didn't. Phil turned to the other side but could not tell where Fire was. He moved quickly, and then slowed down, and sped up again. He was deceptive in his movements and power. He kept it dark to keep Phil guessing. One-minute Phil could feel heat, next minute it was gone. Fire also played tricks, sending heat in one spot but being in another place. Fire was good at hiding. Red drifted in the distance but closed in on Phil.

"Killing you is not what I want. Join with me, and we will control Overworld. We will be unstoppable. You can have the Circle. We can exist in peace. No one else has to die. Don't make me destroy you. Keep the Circle if you even need it anymore." Fire was desperate to bring Phil to his side but could not convince him. Phil must have underestimated the abilities he had because it seemed as though Fire knew something about him that Phil hadn't learned yet.

"Why do you need me? Why don't you just take over this world yourself?" Phil inquired.

"Overworld is moving towards the world you came from. Soon they will be one. Overworld and Earth will be one and the same. It will happen. There is no stopping it," Fire explained with a laugh. "All you see here will be a reality in your world. Even now things are starting to change to align these worlds."

Phil realized that Fire only existed in Overworld. Everyone in his Circle including himself existed on Earth and in Overworld. Even though he didn't show it, Phil sensed Fire was afraid of what might happen once the worlds were joined. Fire's time was running out. He needed the Circle to survive, but he also needed them to take him to his final destination. He needed them and the Circle to take him there, and he wasn't taking no for an answer. If he was going to be destroyed, he would take them all with him.

"Why don't you go back where you came from?" Phil asked. "I think your time is almost up. I saw the chessboard. You were the red piece. Your time is up. I believe you have lost."

Fire was full of rage. He screamed with anger and malice. The whole cavern lit up as he pulled energy from all around him. The room got hot, and Phil wouldn't have been able to withstand it if he hadn't known the fire and water abilities. Fire was going to strike him with a powerful heat ray, but Red came down and got in the way. The ray hit Red directly, and he deflected much of it away from Phil, taking the brunt of it, and was badly injured. Phil had an opportunity to take cover and run for it, but Red was injured on the ground, unable to move. Phil moved toward him and picked him up to protect him. Fire prepared to strike again with even more force. Phil had Red in his arms and had no way to get away from Fire's next blast. Phil felt Tina's teleportation power and disappeared right as Fire released his heat ray and appeared on the top of the building with the rest of his Circle. The last blast partially caught Phil, but he survived. Julie grabbed Red and healed him, but this healing took longer because of his injuries. Fire was on his way up to them. Tina and Red had saved Phil's life. Julie healed Phil as well. Healing them both was taking its toll on Julie. Her healing saved Phil's life.

They looked over the edge, and the ground was covered with lava and fire. The bottom of the building was being enveloped in a pool of lava. The building was moving with the flow of lava. The flow was moving toward the ruins of the castle where they had fought in the tournament. There was a dome part of the castle still in one piece, but this building was heading toward that dome along with the fire. It was windy and stormy, and the sky was on fire now. There were earthquakes and explosions everywhere. Overworld was being destroyed. Everything was chaotic and unstable. They wondered what joining a chaos filled Overworld with Earth would do. Surely Earth wouldn't survive. He must want to stop Overworld from getting closer to Earth in one piece. They could do nothing but watch.

The castle was in ruins, but there was a glow coming from the dome temple there. It was a soft white glow, and it was shining a light that was piecing the darkness around it. They all saw it and were comforted by it. It had a warmth and peace that they could not explain or understand, but it was there, taking the weight off their shoulders. They all knew it was coming from the Creator. That gave them comfort and hope. All the worry and fear disappeared, but they were not sure why or how.

Fire was coming to the top of the building. He flew with a large wingspan, constantly surrounded by flames. He looked like a dragon surrounded by the hottest fire. He was moving quick and with purpose, making his intent quite clear. He intended to destroy all of them because he knew they would not join him, so he did not want them to survive. He wanted to destroy everything.

Fire sent a ball of fire, and it hit the top of the building. Tina saw this and used their shield from the Circle to disperse the flames and debris from the fireball. Her strength was drained from this attack. Phil put out the remaining flames before they got to them. The flames would chase them like they were alive, but Phil was able to put them all out using the fire ability in combination with the water ability. Fire swooped down, and they took cover as best they could but were all wide open. He came down and fast. Fire swooped with so much speed and force that he pushed Julie, Tina, Spirit, Scarlet, and Phil over the edge using fire and wind that they could not defend against. They hung on to the edge as best they could. Spirit pulled himself back up onto the roof, and he helped Tina and Scarlet back. Red wrapped himself around Phil's arm and Julie's arm and pulled them back to safety, though he was still weak from his confrontation with Fire. Jon helped everyone get to safety, but Fire was toying with them again and getting ready to make another pass. They gained back their composure and prepared to defend against Fire's next rush. Fire was in the sky making a turn to come back again for another swoop, building up his power and strength. They could see him gathering energy for a deathblow.

Fire also struck the building several times, and Phil thought it would collapse, but Red was re-enforcing the structural integrity of the support of the building. Fire could not make it collapse with all his power. He saw Red preventing it from falling and got angry. Angels appeared and were assisting them and protecting them. They still had to gather strength to fight back. Red was assisting as well. They all helped fight and keep the Circle alive.

Roxy noticed she was getting stronger and gathering energy. Roxy came to Phil and used her ability as a divider to give him all the power of the Circle. She was routing all the power to Phil she could. There was more power available because they controlled the Circle. Julie stood back with Red on her arm while their Circle absorbed power from Red, and he was glowing, giving off a limitless power. Everyone in the Circle was getting stronger and recovering. Fire closed in to strike at full speed, but Phil hit him with a powerful freeze ray using the water ability with all the power he was given. He landed in the middle of the roof of the building, and they surrounded him. Fire was slow to get up and had trouble moving because of the freeze ray. Phil was getting ready to strike again with his newfound power while the Circle strengthened him. The Creator was also giving him strength—more strength than Phil ever thought he could possess. Scarlet used her mindsonic ability to hold Fire still, and it was working. Jon and Spirit hit Fire a few times, knocking him back to the ground again. They held him at bay. He was weakening fast and trying to recover from the freeze ray. The water ability worked extremely well against him.

The whole atmosphere was changing. Light was breaking through the dark clouds in the sky. The ground shook and cracked with an earthquake, swallowing up the lava. The castle was glowing even brighter and was safe from the lava and fire. Phil caused it to start raining, which worked to put out all the remaining fires. The rain caused some flooding that was putting out the fire as well and making the area more stable by cooling the lava. The rain weakened Fire even more. Fire was on his knees unable to even stand. Jon and Spirit prevented him from getting up in his weakened state. Phil hit him with a freeze ray so intense it froze him solid, pushed him back, and he fell over the edge unable to move. He fell off the skyscraper and towards the ground. The ground shook and opened, and he was swallowed up completely. Steam came out and a huge amount of energy, and light came from the ground. The energy flooded towards Phil, and he became even stronger. He now had control of the fire ability. He had total and complete control over every aspect of fire and heat. The power of this ability was beyond words. He felt the full power of the fire ability and took control of it.

The building they were on began to crumble and fall. Tina regained her composure and used the power she had absorbed from the Circle to teleport the Circle to solid ground between the skyscraper and the castle as far as they could. Everyone was scattered, but at least they were off the building and on somewhat firmer ground. The surface around them was unstable and cracking into pieces. They all began to run as everything around them crumbled. Another huge earthquake shook the entire area.

Julie and Phil were teleported closest to the falling building, but she was falling farther behind. They were lagging behind the others, and the ground beneath their feet gave way. Julie began to fall, and she called out to Phil.

"Don't let me fall, Phil!" Julie screamed.

Phil turned toward her and dived to grab her hand. They barely caught a hold of each other's hand and Phil was losing his grip. Julie was screaming. The hole she was falling into looked like a bottomless pit. Julie's hand was slipping out of Phil's grasp, and Phil struggled to hold on.

"I can't hold you. Grab my wrist fast," Phil shouted. He was straining to hold her. He could not hold her any longer, and her hand slipped out of his.

"Julie!" Phil called out. He lost Julie's hand completely but then felt something wrapped around his wrist. It was pulling on Phil's wrist, and then he felt the soft caress of Julie's hand again. Phil grabbed her hand tightly and would not lose her this time. It was Red. He was around her wrist and around Phil's. Red pulled their hands back together, and Phil got a better grip. He pulled with Red's help and lifted Julie up to safety. Red had saved her from falling. They joined the rest of the Circle and got to a safe distance.

28

A NEW DAWN

Phil looked over all the destruction Fire had planned to unleash on Overworld and on Earth. He sent a heat ray a thousand times more powerful than any heat ray he had ever sent into the building to destroy it once and for all. The heat ray he sent was now a golden color and extremely bright. Phil disintegrated the buildings into nothing but ash. It collapsed and fell into the cracks in the ground. There was nothing left of the city Fire had created, and the castle and dome continued to glow. They glowed even brighter now. Phil put out the remaining fires and stopped the rain with his water ability. The sky began to clear. The sun looked new and glowed brightly once again. The Overworld that once seemed like it would end was now blossoming like a brand-new world. There was no trace of evil; it had vanished from here for good and would never return.

Then they all heard that soft voice clearly. It was the voice of the Creator.

"Come to the Dome," the voice exclaimed. "I am waiting for you. Come up here. There is an open door for you."

The Dome began to rise out of the remains of the castle and float up into the sky. It shone like the sun and was beautiful to see. There were birds like doves flying around it and around them as well. The Dome made the sky brighter and glowed.

It was welcoming and warm. Phil was sure it was the Creator, but they had seen him destroyed. They saw him die. There was no way he could have survived the blast he took, at such a close range, and with the amount of power that Fire possessed. Still, they had to heed the calling. All of them did. They went towards the Dome with great expectations because they were being drawn there by the Creator. Tina teleported all of them into the Dome right in front of the entrance, and the doors opened for them automatically.

They walked through the entrance of the Dome, and they saw gold everywhere. It was the most beautiful and shining gold Phil had ever seen. There were fountains with water flowing all around as well. There were also many precious stones and jewels in the walls and ceilings that everything seemed to sparkle and shine. They were in awe at the sight of this beautiful place. There were many doors, chambers, and rooms. They walked towards the main room which appeared to be the throne room.

The halls leading to the throne room were beautiful and decorated, even more so than the first halls they walked through. They continued into the throne room where they saw The Creator sitting upon the throne. He looked younger and more vibrant. Serenity and Ariel were there with him, and Elo was seated with him at his right hand. They all approached the throne boldly and with confidence. None of them were afraid to come to His throne now. They all knew where the power came from that allowed them to be victorious. The Creator gave them a welcoming look and smile, as did everyone else who was there.

"You're alive," Roxy gasped, surprised. "But how? I saw you die. We all did."

"My power reaches above and beyond time and space. I am beyond death and beyond Overworld. Death has no power over me now. Never did. Death is defeated."

"Wow," Julie exclaimed. "Just like me. I can't be killed."

"Something like that," the Creator replied with a laugh. He smiled at Julie and the rest of the Circle.

Red was curled tightly to Julie's arm as usual, but he let go and flowed freely around the room and around the throne. He was quite at home in the Creator's presence. He was connected to the Creator in some way. Red seemed to move swifter and stronger when he was in the Creator's presence. Ariel and Serenity recognized him as well. They all seemed to be well acquainted.

"What do we do now?" Tina asked.

"You will return to Earth. Back to the lives you had there."

"Can't we stay here?" Julie asked. "Do we have to go back? I would like to stay here."

"Back to the crappy lives we were living. I don't want to go back," Phil replied. "I have so many more questions."

"You will have the answers you desire. You could go back with that attitude. My hope is that you have changed and see things in a new light. I also hope that you realize why you were created and live a purposeful life. I have reserved a place for you here when you return. I will come back for you soon. I am preparing a place for you to come forever. You must go back. You must activate other circles. You must gather the other circles together. Show them how much I love them. You must act quickly. Overworld is coming to Earth, and soon they will be one. People are dying and need to hear the truth. When that happens, all evil will be destroyed. There will be no more evil and no more hate. You have all completed your purpose here. There will be many more tasks for you to complete. Prepare the world for Overworld. Multiply the circles and set people free from a purposeless life. There are forces that oppose this, but together we will defeat them."

"How do we do that? What do we do?" Roxy asked.

"Use your abilities to heal, to break the power and grasp of the evil. To set the captives free. It's for freedom. I will be there guiding you as well. I am always with you. I will be watching. Red must remain here in Overworld. He cannot go to Earth with you. Overworld's influence on the Earth will become more apparent. People are never your enemies. All your enemies are rooted in Overworld, and at the right time, we will conquer them together, but until then, they will continue to present a threat, but you cannot be defeated if you stay connected with me. Now Go."

They huddled together, looked in each others' eyes, and were returned from Overworld to the Earth realm. They were back where they had entered Overworld from, and it was as if they had never left. No time had passed on Earth, not even a second. It was almost the same moment as they had left when they returned because Overworld is outside of time and is eternal. Overworld affects Earth but time had no bearing in Overworld. Phil was surprised by the difference between time in Earth and time in Overworld, but he didn't even worry about it.

"We are back," Tina advised everyone. "It was like we never left?"

They returned to Phil's apartment in Toronto. He went back to his place, and all was in order. Phil had a place, and everything was peaceful. He didn't feel as strong as he was in Overworld, but his attitude had changed, and nothing was left undone. All his worries were gone. Everyone else in the Circle claimed the same thing. It was amazing. They didn't need to worry about anything, and things seemed to work out the best for all.

Everyone had returned to where they came from while Julie stuck around for a little bit. Phil wanted to see her again, and they both knew they would even if nothing was said.

"I guess everything is back to normal. As normal as things can be. Although I'm not even sure what normal is anymore," Phil pondered.

Phil thought for a second. He tried to get everything into perspective that had happened. It was a lot to absorb, but he would never forget the experience. It was hard to find the words that described everything he had experienced. Julie had similar feelings.

"I don't think I'll ever be the same again. Ever," Julie exclaimed.

"Me neither," Phil replied in agreement. "Will I see you again?"

A NEW DAWN

"I think we will be seeing each other very soon," Julie replied emphatically. "We are never far apart." She gave Phil a big hug, kissed him on the cheek, and went on her way. He didn't want her to leave, but he knew she would be back. There was something special between them, and Phil knew she felt the same way. He hoped he would see her sooner than later.

29
A NEW PERSPECTIVE

The next day Phil went to work early, and his whole outlook had changed. He came with a new positive attitude, and things were getting better and better. The day went well, and he couldn't wait for the next day. He had a new level of excitement about everything that had happened and was happening around him. Phil had an abundance of hope and joy. He expected things to get better and would not accept anything less.

Phil came home and put down the gun he still had with him. Phil checked the barrel of the gun, and there were no bullets in the chamber. He looked at the gun for a moment and thought about how much worse the night could have gone. At one time, he had thought about using this on himself. So much had changed on the inside that he knew he could never go back to the person he was. Phil destroyed the gun with his bare hands making it unusable. He wondered if he'd always been strong enough to defeat his demons like that. He stopped and looked at the remains of the gun but thought that was a crazy idea.

A NEW PERSPECTIVE

Phil started to wonder if it was all a dream. Doubt started to work its way into his head and tried to convince him nothing had really happened. He also knew that it was all real because there was no way he could have imagined all the things that had happened. Phil turned off all his music and cleaned up the room as he had these thoughts. One thing he knew for sure—he was a changed person. Phil did not want to go back to the way he was living before he went to Overworld. Phil was a new person; the old negative person was gone. He went to sleep early, which was unusual for him, and got some rest for the next day.

The building that had come up so fast had fallen. The foundation could not support the design they wanted, and it was in ruins. It was a huge waste of materials and time. It sat there in a prime location but was worthless. The foundation was garbage and merely a pile of rubble. A new foundation was being built properly, and a much better design was taking its place.

What happened to the people who died in Overworld? Phil wondered if they were still alive on Earth, or somewhere else. They found out later that they died in the natural as well. Some in odd ways where, in some cases, it was unknown what they died of, but they knew. He recognized their faces and would never forget what was at stake in the battle.

Phil had switched jobs and began to work for a large company in the IT field. The job was more work but rewarding, and it kept him busy. It was a definite blessing for his life. The job had dropped into his lap. Phil didn't do anything to earn it or deserve any more than anyone else. It was like there was now some special favour in his life, and others from the Circle claimed similar experiences and testimonies. Phil was on a constant adventure since returning from Overworld.

The next day while Phil was at work, he was finishing up some tasks. He was informed that he had a visitor. It was Julie. She had come to meet him and take him out for dinner. Phil was supposed to take her out to dinner because she beat him in the dream. Phil also wanted a new challenge. A rematch.

"Are you free tonight?" She asked.

"I can be," Phil responded. "It is good to see you."

"Dinner is on me. Roxy and Tina said hi," Julie said emphatically.

"Ok. Tell them I said hi as well," Phil replied.

"I just did," Julie replied. She used that Circle ability to communicate with them. Phil was glad to meet up with Julie. She always kept contact with them as well as Daniel and Jon through telepathy. She was getting much better at using that ability. It was effortless for her to do that. They all stayed in contact in their unique ways.

Julie and Phil left his workplace and went to a close by restaurant. They were both more aware of their surroundings and had a whole new perspective on life. Both of them also knew that they would be reunited again soon; the Creator had many more tasks for them to accomplish. They knew that He would call on them soon, and they knew that they would be needed, so they remained ready. Always watching. Always keeping an eye on things. Always wondering what was happening in Overworld. They would get a sense at times of things going on in Overworld. The Creator would let them see into Overworld. They would stay connected to the Creator and His guidance.

A NEW PERSPECTIVE

At times, they wondered if they had lived in a dream and came back to reality, but with all the changes they could see in themselves and each other, they knew that something deeper had occurred even if they had no proof. They had all changed for the better and lived with more vitality. Life was flowing from within them. From the inside.

They made every moment count with every step they took. Everything they looked at; they saw with a new light. Even simple things like sunsets and peaceful days were now something to be cherished. There were no ordinary moments. Every moment was special in its own way. They took nothing for granted. They always kept Overworld on their mind.

Overworld was moving ever closer. They knew it and could feel it. It was one of the things they were always sure of. They continued to imagine and hope and wonder about the Creator and what would happen when Overworld was here. They waited and watched with expectancy of what the future may hold. The future looked bright and glorious.

Phil performed live as well. He had written new songs that were a totally different style. They were more positive and made people think about things and the way they could be. Phil believed that these songs could change someone's life and get them on the right track. If they didn't change someone's life, maybe they could make someone reconsider the way they were going and choose a better path. His whole outlook was different and unique. There was more, and he wanted to share what he had learnt without compromise, not holding back any of the truth he had discovered. It was the best show he had ever done because Phil had grown more confident in himself. He had found his purpose. Many people showed up, and his new music was making an impact.

Phil had a dream again: he was back in front of the chessboard, and he noticed that the game was not over. There were many other pieces, and there were evil pieces that needed to be taken down. There was much more to this game now with Phil's new perspective. Looking at the board, he realized the game was far from over. The blue piece appeared to be drawing the most attention now. The game was on.

The end—for now.

ACKNOWLEDGEMENTS

Thank God and Lord and Saviour Jesus Christ
Sharon Job-Narsingh
Family and friends
Klemmer and Associates
Authors Academy and the Tribe
Morningstar ministries
Toronto City Church and Church Without Limits
Catch the Fire Ministries

ABOUT THE AUTHOR

Philip Narsingh is an author, coach, and musician. Overworld the Revelation is the first in a series of spiritual fantasy. God has led him to share Christ's love and help people live out their God given destiny. He lives of outside Toronto, Ontario, Canada with his wife Sharon.

THE JOURNEY CONTINUES

At Cobracircle.com

Made in the USA
Middletown, DE
26 April 2021

38511775R00176